A Good Friday

A Novel by

GUBBY PAUL

Typeset in Baskerville

Editing, design, typesetting and publishing by UK Book Publishing

www.ukbookpublishing.com

ISBN: 978-1-913179-78-6

The lightning cracked and the thunder roared when two tom-cats came
knocking at my door.
I went downstairs to let them in
and they knocked me down with a rolling-pin.
The rolling-pin was made of glass, they turned me over and ...

Frank was pondering. To be or not to be. Whether to crawl back
under the quilt and put up with Arthur's horrific snoring or pull
oneself together and get moving.

He decided to get moving.

That old ditty was running through Frank's head as he
thought ...

Oh what a pity, the pubs in the city all close at half past ten.
If I had the power they'd shut for an hour then open up again.
I could get chronic on vodka and tonic till anytime I liked,
and while the policeman watches my car I'll ride home on his bike.

The small town of Graywacke lies at the mouth of a fictitious
river on England's south coast. In the days when the public houses
were obliged to close for a period during the afternoons, in one
particular pub in the High Street, those customers who were there
before the two thirty deadline and were so inclined were welcome
to remain behind, drinking behind the locked doors until the place
opened again in the evening.

But this was on Fridays only. This is the story of one such
Friday and of what followed during the night.

1

Time and tide wait for no man.

Frank watched as the old brass timepiece moved its minute hand and settled on five to six. The light afforded by the galley's small port- holes was slight and its skylight's streaked covering of guano seemed only to add more gloom to his early morning hangover.

He downed the last of his coffee then stepped out on to the glistening moist deck of Harbour Lights and gently closed the cabin door behind him. From outside he could still hear the sonorous snoring. It would be some time before the slumbering Arthur surfaced.

Frank picked up the big, long handled shrimp net from the deck and slid down the dewy wooden planks to the footpath. The narrow dirt path ran along between the ramshackle row of houseboats and the neat rear gardens of some new bungalows. He paused for a moment and farted long and loud, a high pitched note of morning reveille.

He was on his way to the beach and he was wearing an old pair of holed trainers and an old salt-stained pair of blue shorts, and T-shirt. A canvas bag hung tied from his waist. In the bag was an empty plastic bottle and the long wooden handle of the wide shrimp net was over his shoulder.

As he walked his head thumped with vague memories of the previous night's drinking. He stopped by the last of the row of houseboats and took a few deep breaths of the early morning air. Across the river the pastel colours of the old town of Graywacke were already in bright sunshine, but he felt a distinct chill around his forty-year-old bare legs.

As the receding spring tide neared low water, the river wound a narrow course between the mud banks and ran shallow through the mussel beds under the footbridge. Frank could hear popping sounds coming from the mud as water drained away down a million tiny channels. He watched a huge flock of starlings rise from their roost behind the church tower and head off towards farmland. They followed the river upstream, beyond the lovely old iron road bridge which was soon to be replaced by a horrendous concrete arc.

There was still a white mist hanging over the river up the valley, but at the foot of the Downs the college was shining like a miniature of Palma cathedral in the sun.

Frank's stomach felt reasonably sound and he waffled that he had eaten well the previous evening before homing in on the booze. Lifting his right foot, he stood motionless like a tall blue heron and farted again with unusual confidence. He grinned as a startled gull took off from the mud a few feet away and a small dog yapped from the garden behind him.

His chest rattled and he sent a heavy gob through the air to land on the mud before turning his back on the river. He rounded the end of the row of bungalows and crossed the road there to walk up the gentle slope of Downs Dyke to the sea. Beyond the ridge of beach at the end of the road he could see an anchored cargo vessel waiting for sufficient water to enter harbour. The dark ship seemed to be suspended in the air above the land.

The Downs Dyke road sign never failed to remind him of the denim clad crowd of viragoes who gathered in the riverside bar of The Lady Caroline on Saturday nights. Pissed out of their minds, they managed to continue swilling back pints of strong lager throughout the evening whilst locked in a swaying scrum around the sagging piano. Now and then, one would break out of the pack and make a bolt for the ladies' toilet to throw up the excess liquid, then return to the melee with renewed vigour, bawling through their repertoire of female rugby songs with foul breath and gargling with fresh supplies.

The pavement of Downs Dyke was made up of pink, grey and yellow slabs. In a manner peculiar to the area, most seemed to have been deliberately laid either cracked, or turned up at the edges, or both. Frank stubbed a toe on one, offering up a loud "Fuck it!" as he stumbled, which went completely unheeded by the silver-trailing group of snails he had been watching at the time.

At the end of the road he crossed over to the concrete path that ran along for over a mile behind a string of beach huts, each a different shade of white. The strengthening sun was now above the twin chimneys of the power station, but still low enough to cast his stretched shadow some forty feet before him, huge like an ancient chalk carving on the concrete.

As he turned onto the beach between two huts, his sudden tread on the pebbles sent a pair of wild rabbits fleeing down the bank to the longer grass by a lagoon. The lagoon was below the level of the path and it was separated from the sea by the pebble beach. Its water level rose and fell with the tide. It was at its lowest now and its soft black mud was giving off a sickly sweet pong on the faint movement of air as it warmed.

Frank slid down the first steep slope of the beach with the small stones feeling like grinding marbles under the worn soles of his trainers. Further down the stones were as big as fists and twisted his ankles before he reached the rippled firmness of the sand. Near the beach the sand was drying white, but it was shining wet ahead to the water's edge. The string of yellow buoys which marked the inner limit for speedboats and skiers rested serenely on the flat silver surface, most of them carrying the dark crucifix shapes of cormorants drying their wings in the sun. The tide had made its about-turn and its lines of tiny wavelets, pushing one behind the other, brought a continuous hissing sound to his ears.

The spring tide meant there were some eighty yards of wet sand to cross. When he reached the shallow water, the sudden shock of cold as it splashed above his ankles sent a sharp leaping surge like a numbing electric shock up his legs.

"Jesus!" He jumped and cavorted a strange hopping dance with the net waving madly in the air until the water was above his knees. Then he lowered the net into the water and began the first plodding push, with the flat end of the handle pressing into his belly, feeling the wooden frame bumping along over the ripples of the sand.

The coast was brilliantly clear and bright ahead. The white dots that were the huts along the top of the beach gradually became a tapering white line and the pier, more than two miles away, seemed strangely near. He could clearly make out its spidery black legs below the three white humps of superstructure while offshore the newly painted red outlet buoy began to roll slightly with the strengthening tide and flashed in the sun. The icy numbness changed to a warm glow as he pushed along, head down, watching the spurts of dark sand being kicked up by small flatfish as they fled his shadow and the advancing net.

Fifty strides and then stop and lift the net. He threw out any small fish or crabs and odd bits of weed, then picked out the big hopping and twitching shrimps and dropped them into the canvas bag. There was a tiny squid left clinging to the mesh of the net. Frank picked it up in his cupped hand and shook it a little before releasing it into the water. The tiny creature hung still there for a moment before speeding off, its defence mechanism squirting a cloud of dark ink in its wake.

Back in with the net and on with another push. Here and there ahead of him he could see that a few bait diggers were appearing on the sand. Wellie-clad and armed with forks and buckets, they roamed from one spot to another in search of the casts which betrayed the elusive lugworm. Each time they moved on they left long heaps of wet muddy sand behind them like huge toothless crocodiles basking in the sun, defenceless against the coming of the flood tide, with gulls and angle-headed crows pecking at their backs.

The English Channel had been calm for several days and the absence of heavy weed made the going easy. In an hour he had pushed along as far as the Dolphin Beach Cafe and back again and the bag contained enough for at least a couple of days' lunches, even allowing for the inevitable visitors. Frank and Arthur were rarely short of company aboard Harbour Lights. People came to lounge and talk and drink on deck when the weather permitted, and they came to lounge and talk and drink around the stove in the snug main cabin when it didn't. Although there was rarely much cash about, the galley and the drinks cabinet were rarely drier than the sand from the direction of the harbour wall. The figure quickly drew nearer and it became obvious that it was a very feminine one. About thirty yards away she stopped to rest, leaning against the green weed covered post at the end of a groyne. There was a shallow pool there and she rested there panting, hands on hips, looking down into the clear water. She looked up as he approached with his water-filled trainers making squelching, sucking noises. When he stopped there was only that hissing from the sea behind him.

"Good morning," he said. "Lovely, isn't it?"

She smiled and her teeth were very white between lilac

coloured lips. "Yes it is," she said. "Good morning."

He thought she must be about twenty five. Her jet black hair hung in ringlets like springs, wet on her forehead and around her ears end neck. She looked into the pool again and he watched her breasts rise and fall under the pink top. They were obviously unfettered and the nipples were pushing out hard against the fabric. For some time he had had the feeling that the sea water had frozen all working parts below his waist but now he was aware of a familiar throbbing starting in the wet confines of his shorts. He thought of an old saying: "The cage door is open but the beast is asleep." It was wakening now all right, but thankfully its stirrings were hidden by the canvas bag.

"What have you been catching, then?" She smiled at him again and he shifted his feet as his throbbing discomfort increased.

"Oh, just a few shrimps," he winced. "For lunch."

"Oh my," she said and her nose wrinkled. "You really eat them then?"

"Why certainly. Lovely, they are. Have a look…"

She frowned and hesitated. "Well maybe just a peep, then. Just out of curiosity. I'm a vegetarian, you see."

Frank held the erection-covering bag open and she stooped slightly to peer into its mysterious green interior. Her scent wafted up to his nostrils, considerably increasing the throb rate in his painful restriction. She jumped back a little with fingertips to her lips like a feeding squirrel.

"Oh," she gasped wide-eyed. "They're all twitching! And those long feeler things that stick out, they're sort of well, feeling!" She shuddered. "Oh, I couldn't possibly eat a living twitching thing like that. And aren't they supposed to be pink? The ones in the shops are pink, these are grey."

No, no," Frank said. "They stop twitching and turn pink

when they've been cooked. They're dead then, see?"

"Oh how awful!" she shuddered again. "How do you cook the poor little creatures, then?"

"Same as crabs and lobsters. You just drop them in boiling water. We use sea water, actually. It gives them a better flavour. That's what the bottle's for." Any chance he might have had of ingratiating himself with this lovely newcomer was well and truly down in flames now, and he knew it. Anything he said just made the situation worse.

"In boiling water!" she wailed. "Oh my God, doesn't it hurt?"

"Only if you get splashed!" Frank joked before he could stop himself. The forlorn look she gave him made his heart sink. She gave another little shudder and bit her lip as she gazed into the pool again. Frank watched her breasts heave. The nipples had all but disappeared and so had his erection.

"I'm sorry, but I think that's horrible," she said quietly. "Being a vegetarian."

"Yes, I suppose it must be." Sod it, I've done it again, he thought. I'd better change the subject, and quickly. "Look, I'm very sorry," he said. "That was very unfeeling of me. Stupid. I can see you're upset." He watched her face but she only continued looking into the pool. "I haven't seen you along here before, have I?" He went on, trying to salvage something from the situation. "I mean, I know everyone who comes to the beach this early in the morning, Bait diggers and everyone. Are you here on holiday?" He stood there sheepishly for a while, thinking perhaps it would be better if he just walked away, after all he had apologized; but then she managed a little smile and held out her hand to him. It felt very cool as he gently held it and her smile broadened.

"My name's Coral," she said. "And I'm the one who should be sorry. I'm far too sensitive about the subject. I know I am, but I always get upset. No, I'm not here on holiday, I've just moved into the town. Only yesterday, actually."

"I'm Frank." He smiled with relief and let go of her hand. "I live on the river over there, on one of the houseboats. Harbour Lights."

Her face had brightened wonderfully and her voice came filled with a serious but happy interest. "Oh, how lovely," she said. "I came along past them this morning. They're lovely old boats, aren't they? What a wonderful way of life you must have!"

It's not all rum, bum and baccy, Frank thought; but he said it wasn't all beer and skittles instead. She laughed at that one and he felt a great deal better.

"It's just that it seems as if you've managed to get away from it all. I mean the rat race and everything." She looked out to sea. "I mean, just imagine being able to pull up the anchor and buzz off somewhere. Anywhere you fancy!"

Frank smiled. "You'd be surprised how many people ask me that," he said. "But it's not always that simple, I'm afraid. Besides, half those old tubs would fall to pieces if they ever lifted off the mud. Ours included."

"Oh, I see." She seemed saddened. "How long have they been there, then?"

"It varies. Harbour Lights twenty five years, some more and some less. There's even the odd new one nearer the harbour. There's talk of a marina development, you see, and moorings are being snapped up before prices start going through the ceiling."

"So the rat race has come to the river then," she said without questioning.

"Oh, it's always been here," Frank said. "Only now you can actually see it. On the proposed plans in the Building Control office."

"Yes, I'd heard about the marina. That sort of thing's not always everybody's idea of progress though, is it?"

"Not by a long chalk. I don't know many who want it here, although it'll bring a lot of money in, of course. It has got its supporters, or it wouldn't have got this far. It's funny how you never meet them though, isn't it? One of the great mysteries of life. Like how you never meet anyone who has won a prize in a Readers' Digest competition." Frank smiled; it was the first time he had used that one since hearing it whilst watching a well-known comedian on television.

"I have," Coral said and his grin became just an open mouth. "I know a girl who won quite a big prize, actually."

"Wonderful," Frank said flatly. He swallowed and turned his head to look out to sea. The quickly pushing tide had forced the bait diggers back to the beach, where the less experienced were digging in the drier and stonier sand at its foot. "They'll only find the baby ones there," he mused glumly, "that's the nurseries."

"You know so much about the coast. I'd always wanted to live near the sea, and now I do, but I'm beginning to realize how very little I really know about it all."

"Yes, but you've only just moved in. Being interested in things, you'll soon learn a lot."

"How long have you been here, then?" she asked. "It'll be four years in September."

"Not all that time on your boat alone, surely?" Her voice had taken on an obvious teasing tone and he felt the starter motor on his lifting tackle throb again.

"Oh no," he said. "I've got a half share in the place with a friend." "A friend?" Her dark eyes narrowed; she was obviously an experienced interrogator.

"Yes, Arthur. Arturo Bennet, that is. The well-known local painter."

Those shiny jet eyes seemed to be seeing him in a new light. "Oh, I see," she said slowly.

Catching her drift was as easy as finding his prick in the dark. "It's nothing like that," he laughed feebly, wondering why he should be explaining to someone he had only just met. "We're mates, that's all."

"Yes, I see." She was smiling again but she had that tone of voice which made him feel that was all she wanted to know. He got the impression that for one so young she had had a great deal of experience in handling men. He also felt that she was about to depart.

"Look," he said quickly, "I've got a couple of hours' work to do later this morning, but I'll be back by lunchtime. We usually meet in the Oyster Smack on Fridays – perhaps you'd like to join us for a drink?"

"Oh I'm sorry, but I don't think so. I've still got a lot of unpacking to do. I want to get the cottage reasonably ship-shape and then start on some decorating over the weekend. Some other time, though. I certainly will."

"That's my game actually," Frank said, "painting and paper hanging. That and carpentry. Perhaps I could have a look at the place and maybe give you some advice?"

"Well, perhaps," she said, but she had already begun to move off. "I really must be going. I'll be in touch." She took a few steps backwards, then gave him a little wave of her hand before turning and jogging away across the remaining strip of sand. Frank watched the wonderful motion of her firm looking rump. Sod it, he thought, I didn't even find out where she's moved into exactly. Still, it shouldn't be difficult finding her. She probably thinks I'm a raving iron hoof as well. Shit, never mind. There's always next time to put that right. I'd better get going and see how the master chef's doing with the breakfast. That's if the lazy bastard has managed to climb out of his pit yet.

***

As he trudged up the steepest part of the beach and over the ridge at the high water line, a few speeding swallows went past. They were going east very low over the stones, then rising quickly to clear the timber groynes and dropping again between.

At the top of the beach Frank stopped and sat down on the wooden porch floor of one of the beach huts. The sun was much hotter now on his arms and legs, and high up he could see the vapour trail of a jet like a tiny golden needle against the brilliant blue. He closed his eyes to the sun and rested with his back against the door of the hut.

Presently he heard the sound of metal being scraped across stone. He leaned to one side and looked round through the gap between the huts. On the paved area in the front garden of the house on the corner of Downs Dyke was a sunbed that had not been there earlier. Behind it the sliding patio door was open slightly. Frank watched for a while, but irritatingly the door opened no further. Until about ten days ago there had been a 'for sale' sign on the house for months. Since the sign had been taken down there had occasionally been a new red BMW in the side garage and new curtains had been hung, but as Frank had been going to the beach very early he had seen nothing of any occupants.

He gave it another couple of minutes, but nobody appeared and he decided to go back to the boat for breakfast.

He had to pass sideways between the huts with the net before shouldering it to cross the road. As he crossed there was a movement of the long curtains behind the patio doors and as he walked along by the low garden wall to the corner the door slid back fully open. What he saw then stopped him in his tracks by the gate. A tall blonde, with a fantastic tan and wearing a large baggy white shirt, stepped out from behind the curtain onto the crazy paving.

As she bent over to unfold the sunbed, the unbuttoned shirt fell open. She was wearing nothing beneath the shirt but a tiny pair of white panties.

As if sensing him there she looked up, still stooping, and Frank thought the sun was suddenly a great deal hotter on the back of his neck. He found himself licking his lips as she stood up, but instead of buttoning the shirt front she smiled and walked towards him across the four or five yards of neat lawn. She stopped just short of the low wall and spread her feet wide apart with her hands on her hips. Her lips and her finger and toenails were the bloodiest red, and the crisp white shirt was wide open, held by the spread of her gorgeous breasts.

Frank found it difficult looking her in the face. When he did, he saw that she had the most attractive freckles over the bridge of her nose and under eyes which were a grey-green that reminded him strangely of the slates on the roof of the old Town Hall in Croydon, and were wandering all over him.

"Hallo," she said, "what have you got in your little bag?"

The accent came as no surprise to him. Perfect sing-song Scandinavian. As perfect as she looked. And deep. In fact, it was deeper than Frank's effort, when he finally got it out. "Shrimps," he said weakly, and gulped.

"Oooooh, let me see…" The shining red nails reached slowly over the wall and held the bag open. As she stooped to look inside he felt the beast stirring in its cage again. He swallowed hard and averted his gaze to the far end of the road and the clear blue sky above the town across the river.

"Can I touch, please?"

Frank could hardly believe his ears.

"Please," he said feebly as he closed his eyes, "please help yourself." "Yes I will, please. My name is Monika. What is yours?"

"It's Frank," he almost coughed as he felt her hand slip into the bag.

He opened his eyes and tried to focus on the golden hands on the blue face of the church clock as her fingers searched amongst the wet shrimps in the bottom. All the while he was conscious that her eyes were no longer on the contents of the bag but on his face as she searched.

"Aren't they big ones! And they're prickly too, aren't they?" She laughed huskily, still watching his face.

He looked down with that feeling of hopeless inevitability as she found his balls and cupped her hand to support them from the well-worn bag's interior.

"And you are a naughty one, I think! Here is an even bigger one you have!" Her tongue darted in and out between her teeth and deep in the bag he felt a finger stroke along his tool, stiff and painfully confined as it was by his wet shorts. The hand squeezed him gently and his stomach muscles fluttered.

"Why don't you come in for some coffee now," she said, "and you can show me how you cook them. I'd love to know how you do it to them."

"I'd like to. That would be nice." He knew that he'd said it but his voice sounded like someone else's.

"Come on then," she coaxed, Still with her hand in the bag, she pulled gently and he let out a sharp gasp and shuffled forward on tiptoe, almost pitching forward over the wall.

"You'll have to let go," he gasped, imagining eyes behind every net curtain in Downs Dyke. "Your grip I mean, for Chrissake!"

Supporting himself by one hand on the wall, the net still held over his shoulder by the other, he gave a great sigh of relief as she released her hold.

"Oh I'm so sorry, Frankie," she fussed, "I was hurting you, wasn't I?" She opened the small wrought iron gate and held it back. "Come on now," she sighed gently, "come in with

Monika now and she will kiss it all better for you."

She turned to walk up the stone path and after a quick look round, Frank slipped a hand inside his shorts to adjust the angle of his thumping tool. It felt as if it would never go down again.

"Come on," she smiled encouragingly over her shoulder and he followed her up the path with the coarse wet material of the shorts chafing him painfully. A light breeze from the sea lifted the tail of her shirt, and showed him dimpled pink cheeks around the little white triangle of lace that seemed to float mesmerically on their exquisite motion.

There was a step up to the porch at the side of the house and when she turned to face him again she was a couple of inches the taller.

"You can leave your net thing there," she waved a hand, "up against the wall there."

"I think I'd better slip these wet trainers off," Frank said.

"Of course. Leave them there too. They will dry there in the sun. You can hang your bag thing on that hook there."

"What about the shrimps?" Frank asked, feeling foolish.

Removal of the bag would reveal his erection, which he was sure would be showing its head over the top of his shorts like Mister Chad at any moment.

She shook her head as she laughed and that wonderful blonde hair swished on the shirt on her back. Frank untied the string from around his waist and hung up the bag. When she looked down her eyes grew wide, like a child being handed a treat. As he stood there self-consciously, she tossed her head and laughed again.

"Oh come on, Frankie," she said. "We both know what it is I want. The hot weather makes me so."

She reached out to him, the red nails slightly clawed, and he took her hand and stepped up into the house, hardly noticing the pain as he stubbed his bare toe on the tiled step.

Frank's head was spinning somewhat. Things were happening so fast this morning, and the way this incredible woman was taking the initiative was hardly giving him time to think. He knew that she must be ten years younger than himself, but he couldn't help feeling like the virgin schoolboy that he was twenty five years before, when he had gone on that fishing holiday with his best friend and the boy's parents. Then he had fallen under the spell of, and been fucked by, the manageress of the hotel on a hot afternoon in a lush grassy meadow by the river. She had led him by the hand, round behind the small electricity generating station by the weir, and they lay down together on a flattened patch in the long grass. He remembered the heat of the still air and the smell of herbs and flowers, and the sound of water rushing over the weir and down the salmon steps. He remembered his half-frightened excitement as she removed his trousers and underpants and the unfamiliar feeling of a strange hand holding and stroking him. She wore nothing under her short black skirt and she mounted him and rode him slowly, eyes closed and her mouth hanging open with a smear of toothpaste at one side and her tongue lolling, pumping to the rhythmic clonking of the old generator while he clumsily fondled her huge hanging breasts. And all the while, below the weir, the others fished quietly for dace in the long shallow runs under the elderberry trees.

Inside the house it was cool and dim. The hall floor was tiled and there were white walls with arches and the staircase and doors to rooms off the hall were dark and heavy looking. Off to the left was an expensively fitted kitchen with more use of the dark hardwood and bright tiling. Monika was already on the second tread of the staircase with one hand on the polished handrail. Frank was looking up into her eyes when he was startled by a sudden movement as a small brown animal shot out of the kitchen to snap around his vulnerable ankles.

"What the...?"

"Don't worry," Monika laughed as he grabbed the rail, "it's only my little Pogo. He's not exactly what you call a bandog. He's a good little boy, he won't hurt you."

The dachshund stopped its snapping and merely shuffled around at the foot of the stairs, sniffing at Frank's feet and sneezing.

"There you are, Frankie. He likes you. Now come along, I want you upstairs with me. I have things to show you." She squeezed his hand and he began the ascent with difficulty, trying to avoid falling over or treading on the sniffing, licking dog, which was becoming more and more excited as they climbed. Eventually they all reached the landing at the top of the stairs. The door on the left was open to an airy white room with a white leather sofa and some cane furniture. At the far end of the room, patio doors opened onto a flat roof. There were dark blue sunloungers on the roof and white rails around. Across the road the tide had covered all sand and the sea was a deep ribbon of blue between the ridge of pebbles and the sky.

"I was on the roof there, watching you with your net this morning," Monika said. "I watched you other times too from there."

"You're an early riser, then." Frank could feel the dog licking his Achilles tendon. He wondered if it was hungry.

"Always I am out of bed early in the summer. It is so wonderful to watch the dawn by the sea, don't you think?" She curled her fingers and pulled him against her breasts. "Then one morning I saw you there," she breathed in his face. "I had seen you before, in the town from my car. I also have a little surprise for you. I bet you didn't know that sometimes I can watch you from my bedroom, did you?"

"Er, no. I can't say that I did."

The dog had lost interest in his heel and was wagging its rear end, whimpering and sniffing at another door.

Monika pushed it open and Pogo scampered into the room. "Oh yes, I can watch you from here as well you see."

It was quite dark in the bedroom and she went over and pulled a cord which drew back the long, dark brown curtains on a big floor to ceiling window. The window had a fixed bottom half and a sliding top which she opened.

"Come and look," she said.

The roof of each house down to the river was a little lower, giving a clear view across to the town. It was laid out there in the bright sunlight like one of Arthur's paintings, the little different coloured buildings around the church and along the river bank. Traffic was starting to build up on the road bridge and in the High Street and on the slowly filling river the workboats and pleasure craft were lifting from their berths on the mud and tugging at their mooring ropes.

"There you see," Monika pointed, "down there I can see the black stove pipe and the roof and the deck of your boat. And I can watch you when you go over the footbridge to the town."

Frank looked down on the row of houseboats, looking like tiny scale models facing the miniature shops and houses across the water. Under that little roof Arthur should be clattering about in the galley by now. By the skylight he could make out a speck that must be the old black-backed gull that came most mornings for breakfast scraps.

"You really have been keeping an eye on me, haven't you? And you haven't been here long."

"A little more than one week."

"And now you've got me up here. That's pretty fast going!"

"Oh, I knew it would happen," she said matter-of-factly.

She moved towards the bed, letting the shirt fall to the floor behind her. There was no white strap line across her back, only the same golden tan all over. The little white panties fell, leaving a pinkish triangle and as she stepped out of them he saw the delightful shell colour of the soles of her feet.

Frank pulled his T-shirt off over his head and started on his shorts. "Careful with the zip," she smiled.

"Buttons," he explained as they dropped.

Suddenly free, his weapon swung up and swayed in front of him. On seeing it, the dog, which had been watching with quiet interest until then, put on a frightening exhibition of snarling curled lips and bared teeth. Frank, wondering how high it could jump, quickly grabbed his shorts from the floor and covered his assets.

"No no, it's all right," Monika assured him, "he just gets excited watching. Here Pogo, this is what you want."

She picked up a cushion from the bed and threw it across the room through the open doorway on to the landing.

The little dog chased after it, pathetically impeded by an erection longer than its legs which jabbed and stubbed on the polished wooden floor as it disappeared from the room.

"There, you see. Seeing us naked makes him like that. Poor little Pogo needs a bitch to mount, just like you do. But I'm afraid that for now the poor little chap must make do with the cushion."

Frank could hear the activity on the landing. This was becoming more fantastic all the time. He watched as Monika sat on the bed and took a small packet from a drawer in the bedside table and deftly removed its contents between finger and thumbnail.

"And now we must make sure you are properly dressed," she said. "Here, let me put it on for you."

As he stood before her while she carefully fitted his

protective sheath, Frank reflected on what a remarkable morning it had been so far.

"Rather like putting a new rubber grip on a cricket bat handle, isn't it?" he said.

"Is it, Frankie?" She smiled and gave its teat-like end an affectionate tweak. "I know very little about your cricket. But this game, this is the game I like."

2

As Frank walked back along the path by the houseboats he pondered the fact that so many blondes have black beards. The gold of that glorious cascade of Monika's was certainly all her own, but down below, that carefully trimmed luscious soft muff of hers was dark and shining. As if kept lightly oiled.

From across the river the church clock showed a glistering ten past ten in the sun and the breeze was just enough to bring the familiar tink-tink from the rigging of the sailing craft. Some of the houseboats would be lifted at high water to become more mobile homes, but most would remain there on the mud, surrounded eventually by water but going nowhere. There was a mailbox at the foot of each of their gangways and the names on the boxes were mostly suited to their connections with both land and water: Landing Craft, Water Shed, DUKW, Mud Skipper.

There was a brown envelope protruding from the Harbour Lights box. Frank stopped and pulled it out with heavy heart. Postmarked London SW16. Yes, he had known that it would be. It was even a couple of days late this time, which had prolonged the agony. He shoved his ex-wife's solicitor's letter into the rear pocket of his shorts. The pocket was cold and damp and suddenly that was the way he felt too.

The sunshine of what had until then been such a fantastic morning seemed suddenly to pale, and with Responsibility on his back like a sack of cement he trudged up the boards to the deck.

As he put the bag and net down he was startled by a loud bang as Mud Skipper's cabin door flew open and crashed against its stop. Travelling at incredible speed from such a short take off, their neighbour George burst into view in his weekday garb of city suit and bowler hat. Clutching his brolly and briefcase, with arms flailing he skidded on the wet deck and then cleared the gangway with a sort of hop, skip and jump.

"Morning, Frank!" he shouted back over his shoulder; "I can't stop, late for the bloody train again. See you in the pub tonight!" He managed a perfect left turn without stopping as he landed on the path, and ran off towards the footbridge.

As Frank watched him go, another voice came from the other side. The port side it was, and appropriately too. The shrill pitch was unmistakable and delivered under its usual influence of the grape, hop or juniper, depending on which was handiest at the time.

"Yooohooo, morning Frankie! Got a nice lot of shrimps then, I see?" Liz waved unsteadily from her open bathroom window, her long hair hanging wet to her shoulders. Surrounded by escaping steam, her face had been drained of its tan by a stupendous hangover.

"Morning, Liz. Yes, I did rather well this morning", Frank said, although he was thinking of Monika's noisy vocal accompaniment.

"Oh goodeeee! Does that mean you can expect me for lunch then?" Even when feeling so ill she could sound cheerful and think of food. "There's a couple of bottles of that super wine left from last night. I say, old George has got a good turn of foot, hasn't he? It's going to be a scorcher later, we could lunch al fresco under my awning. I'll rig it up."

Frank hesitated. "I don't know. I've got some work to do. I don't really know what time I'll be back. And I don't know what Arthur's got in mind for today, you know how temperamental he can be."

"Yes, silly old fart. See you later then. Bye-eee!" She pinched her nose and sank from sight, sliding back down into the scented bath-tub for a languorous soak.

Frank's belly rumbled as he caught the smell of frying bacon; after all, he had had enough exercise that morning to work up an appetite. He could hear Arthur moving around in the galley and rummaging in the cutlery drawer. Arthur glanced at the brass clock on the wall as the door opened behind him.

3

"You were gone a bloody long time, weren't you?"
He was standing at the gas cooker wearing a
Marilyn Monroe apron over his blue and white striped
pyjamas and shaking the contents of two crackling frying
pans. The galley and the saloon area were thick with the
heat from the cooker and a fug of French tobacco smoke
hanging under the low ceiling. As Arthur spoke, the ash on
the cigarette in the corner of his mouth wagged precariously
over the spitting pans.

"There's not many about, really," Frank lied. "I had to
cover a lot of ground."

"You remembered the sea water, I hope?"

"Remember it? I could hardly forget it, Arthur, could I?
It's freezing in there, it is. Bloody freezing!"

Arthur put the two pans back on the gas rings and the ash
scattered as it dropped to the floor. "It should have warmed
up a bit by now," he said.

"And you'd know, of course," Frank answered. "You
haven't got a clue, Arthur, not a clue. You ought to try getting
out of your sack and going out there at dawn. We're not on
the shores of the Med now, you know. And watch that ash,
will you? I don't know how you can smoke that shit this early
in the day. Look at it, it's like a fucking opium den in here!"
He opened the galley's portholes and the skylight in the roof.

Arthur began sawing at a French stick on the table. He

waited until Frank sat down at the table then made a display
of throwing his fag-end out of a porthole onto the mud.

"I'll tell you something, shall I …" He picked up a
spatula and started prodding at the contents of one of the
frying pans. "I got up about two minutes after you left this
morning. I flaming well had to, didn't I, with that dirty great
big feathered friend of yours hammering away at the skylight!"

"Old Gulliver? He was only asking for his breakfast!"

"Banging away with his beak like a Gatling gun he was. I
tell you, I thought the bastard was coming through the glass
that time!"

They both looked up as a loud rapid tapping noise came
from the skylight.

"I don't believe it!" Arthur screamed. "That's him back
again and I've already given him some crusts! Go on, sod
off out of it, you greedy bastard!" He grabbed a broom and
jabbed ferociously at the ceiling.

"You'll frighten him, doing that," Frank said calmly.

"He must be permanently frightened shitless, judging by
the amount of crap he leaves on deck."

"Yes I know. The poor old bird can't help it though. You
shouldn't get yourself so worked up about it."

Arthur thought of lighting another cigarette but decided
against it. "You're right," he sighed as he calmed down. "Of
course he's got to shit somewhere. It's just a pity it's always on
us. Do you think he's trying to tell us something?"

"It could be a comment on your culinary skills, I suppose."

"No, it couldn't be that," Arthur said seriously. "Did you
bring the paper in with you by the way?"

"Don't be daft, he'll be miles away by now." "Oh very
funny, I meant the newspaper."

"I didn't give it a thought, actually. You could say I had
something else on my mind."

Arthur craned his neck to look out of one of the portholes.

"It's still there," he said, "sticking out of George's mailbox. He'll be doing his nut, sitting on the train with nothing to read again. Serves the bugger right for getting up late. I'll have a quick look at it after breakfast, just to make my racing selections."

"Make sure you put it back, he was very suspicious about yesterday's going missing."

Arthur was shovelling great heaps of fried eggs and bacon, sausages, mushrooms and potatoes onto two plates on the table.

"That wasn't my fault," he said. "I told you how it blew into the water while I was pegging out some washing. The tide was running so fast I had no chance of catching it, did I?"

"Maybe not, but you could have bought another one for him, couldn't you?"

"I had every intention of getting one on my way back from the betting shop," Arthur said defensively.

"I know you did. The trouble is the sailing club's on the way back and by the time you crawled out of there it was nearly midnight!"

"Yes I do remember, thank you. Well most of it anyway." Arthur was still feeling fragile and knew he must get the steaming food down at all costs. He sat down at the table opposite Frank. There was a brief silence broken only by the last few drops being thumped out of sauce bottles.

"These spuds are bloody hot," Frank mouthed as he tried to dislodge a scorching potato from the roof of his mouth and suck in cooling air at the same time.

Arthur followed the lip movements. "Yes, they are rather," he nodded, "they came from a hot place." He pushed a carton of orange juice across the table and Frank took a long swig. He let his scalded tongue soak for a while before swallowing.

"Ah, that's better. Oh, I saw Liz on the way in. She looked ghastly, like she was rising from a watery grave. Talk about the Wreck of the Hesperus. She wanted to know what we were doing for lunch."

"I know, I heard her. She's already three parts to the wind y'know. She was out on deck earlier, tottering around with a bottle."

"Probably just picking up a few empties left from last night."

"Creating a few, more likely. Do you know, in the club yesterday she was putting the gin away so fast we got her on to pints of bitter to slow her intake and she drank them almost as quick! Where do you reckon she puts it all?"

"At least she buys her round, Arthur."

"Blimey, she can afford to, can't she? Copping a bloody great fat cheque every month off that latest ex of hers in Mallorca!"

"Or wherever he is at present. Keeps on the move a lot, doesn't he?" "Mysterious tax reasons. That boat of his is a floating palace, apparently. Jacuzzi and computers, the lot. Do you know what she told me?"

"What's that?"

Arthur leaned forward through the heat haze of his breakfast. "She reckons he's got the tallest mast in Palma harbour."

"Well, there's a novelty! He must be into something really big then. If you'll pardon the expression."

Arthur smeared some strong mustard on half a spicy sausage and forked it into his mouth. Through the open porthole behind Frank he could see Liz's bare legs on the neighbouring deck. "Oh Christ," he coughed, almost swallowing the smarting mouthful whole, "there she is now! You don't think she's inviting herself over for breakfast, do you?"

"No, I don't think so. The pubs have been open half an hour already. She'll have a couple in the Smack, then pick up her shopping for the weekend. Then she'll have a couple more and come back to sunbathe. It'll be pitching hot later."

"Well, I won't be here when she gets back." Arthur had carefully lifted a fried egg onto a slice of buttered bread and was cutting it into four pieces. Frank leaned over and speared a piece with his fork.

"What have you got planned for this morning, then?"

Arthur's early morning crapulence had given way to a far more pleasant feeling as his insides worked on the hot food. He pushed his chair back a little and stretched contentedly.

"I thought I'd do a small watercolour this morning," he mused, "set up the old easel past the footbridge there and…" His mental picture of the idyllic scene with the painter seated at his work in the sunlight, the boats anchored before him in the river with the old town spread along the far bank, was rudely shattered by Frank sending half chewed egg and soggy breadcrumbs across the table at him like shrapnel.

"Not 'view of the old church from cuckoo corner' again, Arthur, not another one!"

Arthur was stung by this attack on what had become his favourite, if somewhat mass-produced work.

"That just happens to be my best seller," he retorted. "I must get a few into Peter's gallery window now there's a few more summer visitors about."

"Let's hope it's going to be better than last year. He must have sold more umbrellas than anything else."

"You're becoming a pessimist, mate, that's your trouble. Old Ernie Rudd reckons it's going to be a wonderful, long hot summer. Reckons he can feel it in his water."

"Water! Old Ernie? You must be joking!"

"I've got a feeling about it too," Arthur said. "There'll be hordes of holidaymakers about, an unprecedented demand for my paintings..."

Frank sat chewing slowly. With knife and fork in his fists on the table he stared wide eyed at the topless girl on the wall calendar. She smiled impishly back at him, personifying the feeling of the beach days ahead. He could hear the girlish laughter as they paraded around the harbour in shorts or bikinis. He could smell the Ambre Solaire wafting in on the breeze from the sea and pictured Monika emerging from the sparkling water wearing nothing but a smile and a thong.

"It would be nice though, wouldn't it?" he said dreamily. "You know how the girls in the sailing club can get when it's really hot."

Arthur's mind was on more serious matters. After all, he had his back to the calendar and Frank's glazed expression was lost on him as he harpooned an inverted mushroom. "Oh yes, I shall be turning them out like a conveyor belt," he said, "the paintings, I mean. All watercolours of course, for speed. Maybe Peter could set up an open air gallery for me on the green."

Frank had come back to the reality of the breakfast table. "That's a good idea. I could do some of my quick portrait sketches."

Arthur was visibly shocked. Frank's lack of any success as a writer or painter had meant that he had returned to his carpentry and decorating, working on houses and boats to help make ends meet. As Arthur would never even dream of taking any kind of job, he saw any movement on his friend's part which looked like a return to the arts as a threat to his own position. He was something of a local celebrity and enjoyed being introduced to visitors as 'our local artist'. He was especially fond of the expression of awe on the faces of young ladies as he shook their soft hands, half expecting them to curtsy. It was bad enough with all those part-timers turning up every summer. He couldn't bear the thought of sharing the boat with another 'name'.

"You'd be better off sticking to your decorating jobs," he said bluntly. "Mr O'Looney said he had more than enough work for you, didn't he? Keep it up and we might save enough to get away from the cold for a while next winter. Liz said her ex could fix us up with a place over there."

Frank's instant technicolour imagination immediately had them taking off from Gatwick and flying over France. One moment they were in bright moonlight above clouds that resembled a polar landscape, the next they were over real snow, with remote villages like a black and white photograph. After losing height over the Bay of Barcelona they circled above the twinkling lights of Palma.

"I liked Puerto Andratx," Frank said, "and that restaurant at San Telmo with the paella for Sunday lunch overlooking Dragonera Island."

They had been to Mallorca together three years before, when Arthur had been commissioned to paint some views of a newly constructed villa, and Frank to paint the villa itself.

"I liked Puerto Soller in the rain," Arthur said.

"It seemed to fall in slow motion, didn't it? In great big heavy blobs. It dripped from the palm trees quicker. I could get on with the novel there, eh? Might even get it finished."

"There you go again," Arthur brought him back. "Go again?"

"About the novel. That was good, about the rain and the palm trees. You've got good observation but you never get anything down on paper. Get it finished, that's a laugh. We'd never have enough money to stay there that long! Be fair, Frank, how long has it been since you wrote anything, not counting betting slips, I mean? It must be at least a couple of months."

"Writers' block," Frank explained feebly.

"Writers' bollocks! It's the age-old problem, mate. Procrastination with a big pee. Oh, and then of course there's the little matter of Doreen over there in the pub, begging you to go over there at every opportunity while Norman's away. That bloody phone hardly ever stops ringing, what with her or Helen and her solicitors after you. I bet that letter's another one from them, isn't it? I saw you take it out of the mailbox. You don't know whether you're coming or going, do you? Whether to shit or get a haircut. Jesus Christ, talk about infernal triangles!"

"That was a long speech," Frank said, "and it's called eternal."

"Oh no, Frank. This one isn't. All the others are, but not this one." Arthur was becoming more and more theatrical. "You've got to get everything straight and get your head sorted, or you'll never write again," he added dramatically He got up from the table and put his empty plate on the draining board by the sink unit. He felt pleased with himself. He'd delivered a barbed dart there all right. A real banderilla that wouldn't come out in a hurry.

"You've got too much on your plate, mate," he threw in as he took Frank's empty one.

He squirted some washing up liquid into the sink, then poured some hot water from the kettle.

"You've just got the needle because nobody phones you and you haven't had your leg over for I don't know how long," Frank said. "You can't fool me, I know you too well."

It was Arthur who felt nettled. "Aren't you supposed to be finishing that job this morning?" he snapped, clutching for any straw that might win back a point.

"That's right," Frank said casually. "I told you, it won't take long."

Arthur put the plates and the knives and forks in the hot water and started swilling around with a small white mop. As tiny, rainbow coloured bubbles floated up on the steam before his eyes and drifted towards the open porthole, he looked out just as Liz, in a yellow bikini, blew him a kiss.

"My God, she's still out there. And she's not even dressed for going to town yet!"

Frank didn't hear him. He was thinking of what had happened at the beach that morning and the two whole hours he had spent with the lovely Monika. And they say walking a dog is a good way of meeting the ladies, he thought. Shrimping seems to beat it hands down. And you don't have to clean the shit up or risk being fined!

He watched as Arthur lit up another Gauloise and flicked the dead match out onto the rising water. He thought of telling him about it. Then he decided not to.

4

The bath water had been as hot as Liz's coaxing of her clanking old gas heater could make it. She emerged a glowing pink from the scented steam, and running with perspiration. Spending some time naked while she cooled down, she cleared up some of the debris in the main cabin of the converted barge.

She vaguely remembered it all starting as someone's birthday celebration in the pub by the railway station. Then they had visited each pub in turn, missing only the Flying Scud where she was barred from entering, and finished the legal lunchtime session in the Oyster Smack, where she had come close to being refused more than once, but wouldn't have remembered anyway. By that time they were about a dozen strong, give or take the few strangers who had tagged along, when someone had organized a whip-round and they had all descended thirstily on the supermarket. Suitably provisioned, they crossed the footbridge heaping curses upon the country's licensing hours and performing a half-hearted conga, led by Liz herself who was making a surprisingly good job of steering the supermarket trolley. After that it all became a bit confused. She could remember one of the strangers walking straight off the wrong end of the barge at some time during the evening, smiling vacantly with his glass clutched to his chest. What she couldn't remember was whether they had fished him out or not. Anyway, she could see no sign of him this morning in the surrounding mud. The carousing had gone on until well after midnight, by which time few of the revellers left there were conscious. A few had gone back to the pub during the evening and not returned, some had wandered off aimlessly into the night and others had simply fallen asleep, like the stranger who had come from Bexhill for the day to visit friends who had not been at home when he called. On the stroke of midnight, Liz was stood alone on deck. She was barefoot, wearing a long flimsy cotton thing with flowers on it, looking like the sole survivor of a sixties pop festival. Pissed out of her mind, she was crying as she sipped her gin and watched the lights of the town on the river. She thought she was back on the yacht in Palma.

And now next morning. Feeling cooler, and with the pink glow having changed back to her light tan, she put on her yellow bikini and stepped out into the new day. As she put a few empties from the wheelhouse in a black dustbin bag she thought it really had been like one of her Spanish days. The sunshine, the all-day drinking, the great black holes in her memory.

She heard a door close and looked round to see Frank out on Harbour Lights' deck. He had changed into his white decorators overalls and was putting on his crash helmet. Liz picked up the black bag and struggled with it clinking down the gangplank of her home as he descended the other.

"Off to work now then, Frank?" She reached the bottom and put the bag down on the sandy path.

"Hallo Liz. Yes, I'll be finished around lunchtime with a bit of luck."

"Don't forget it's Friday, will you, you'll have to be in the Smack before half two for last orders. If you want the afternoon session, that is. And I suppose you do!"

As she moved closer he could smell the bath salts and

shampoo and the fresh underarm deodorant coming from her. She rather overflowed the bikini top. He thought she'd kept her figure rather well, considering.

"I won't be there until this evening," she said. "I'm riding up at the farm this afternoon, but I'll be back by the time they open at six." She put her hand on his arm and turned her eyes up enquiringly to his. "You'll still be there, won't you?"

Frank forced himself to look away from those eyes. They're a bit bloodshot, he thought. Still, that's not surprising really. He pictured the scene in the pub. He would be standing at the bar with Monika and Liz while Doreen is watching him with that icy stare of hers from behind it. Liz is pissed and going on about Spain and how she'd like to get him over there. Monika, on the other hand, being a newcomer to the place, is feeling decidedly left out of things. And getting the hump. As if all that wasn't enough, he had just remembered that Norman, good old 'no-sex-Norman' was leaving that evening for one of his mysterious weekends in France. That meant Doreen would be expecting to be entertained. And he had invited Monika along for her introduction to the traditional, but outside licensing hours, Friday afternoon extension of drinking time. It was going to be a tricky afternoon and evening, one way or another.

The bar scene vanished and he was face to face with Liz again.

"Yes, I'll probably see you later. Bye." He wanted to get away and get his work done; his ancient Ariel square four with its box sidecar was waiting on the concrete public hard by the footbridge. Liz watched him walk off along the path. Inside the crash helmet he sensed they had been watched from a certain bedroom window.

Liz heard the same door close. This time it was Arthur at the top of the gangplank. He was wearing a long green artist's smock and beret, thinning corduroy trousers and greying tennis shoes. He came down to the path with some difficulty, carrying an easel, a large leather bag containing his working materials, and a folding canvas chair.

"Bonjour, Liz. A lovely morning, n'est ce pas?" He spoke from a corner of his mouth whilst adopting his Left Bank posture with another Gauloise dangling from the other side.

"Yes, wonderful, isn't it, Arthur? Oh, I'm sorry. I suppose it should be Arturo this morning, as I see you'll be working."

"I'll admit that I do prefer to be known as Arturo where my work is concerned," he replied haughtily.

"Arturo Bennet. Yes, it does sound more arty, sort of, doesn't it?"

"The signature looks good too, of course."

"Mmm, yes. On the paintings. What have you got in mind for this one, then?"

Arthur put the leather bag down and waved his arm in an expansive sweep of the low spread of the town across the half full river.

"Well," he began enthusiastically, "I thought I'd set up the old easel on this bank past the footbridge and …"

Liz interrupted. "Not another 'View of the old church from cuckoo corner', Arthur! Sorry, I mean Arturo!" She threw her head back and laughed, at the risk of starting it thumping again. "I should think you could do one of those with your eyes shut by now!"

That laugh of hers irritated him considerably. It reminded him of that sound that comes from the dense jungle treetops when the boat is creeping up the Amazon in some film. He wasn't sure if it was some kind of bird or a monkey.

They heard a loud bang followed by a healthy roar as the big old engine of Frank's bike started. They watched him engage gear and disappear on it behind the bungalow at the end of the path, then they turned to look upstream as he appeared again, roaring at speed across the roadbridge, with a red towel flying fiercely from the rear end of the ladder on the sidecar like a dragster parachute. Liz was shielding her eyes and screwing up her face to watch.

"How are the new contact lenses, by the way?" Arthur asked.

"They're terrible, Arthur. Awful. I put them in this morning and now I'm almost blind in one eye!"

"Well, they do say it can happen." "What can?"

"You know, after a lifetime of profligacy, depraved tendencies etcetera…"

Liz echoed the Amazonian tree tops again. "You rascal! No there's definitely something wrong with them. I'll have to call into the optician's this morning and see what he says. I've got some shopping to do as well and then I'm going riding."

"Anyone I know?"

"Don't be naughty, you know what I mean. Frank said he should be back for the afternoon session, but I won't be around. See you in the pub this evening though, yes?"

"Only if you get the contact lenses put right: ha-ha!"

"Very good, Arthur. Very good. You really are on form this morning."

That was a great booster for Arthur's morale. Frank's reminder about his lack of any sex life had stung him badly. Although Liz could be annoying he had always harboured a healthy carnal interest. He knew that making them laugh was half the battle, and the way she was spilling out of that bikini was making him have second thoughts about working. Getting his pipes cleaned out seemed a far more attractive proposition. Unfortunately, while he was hastily considering his next move she went off on a very different tack. With her good eye, Liz had spotted a pair of figures on the footpath

approaching from the direction of the roadbridge. The hugely
round Mick O'Looney and the slimline Coral were being
followed by a half-grown Dalmatian.

"Isn't that Mr O'Looney?" Liz screwed her face up again.

"It is." Arthur studied her shaved armpit as she shielded
her eyes.

"He's a nice chap, isn't he. I do wish he wouldn't call me
'Bruv' though."

"You're not on your own there," Arthur said, "he calls
everyone 'Bruv'. Who's that girl he's got with him?"

"Oh, that's Coral. I met her in the town. She's just moved
into that little cottage behind the museum. Didn't I tell you
last night?"

"If you did, I don't remember."

"No, neither do I. It was one of those days though, wasn't
it!"

She let go with that laugh again. Arthur winced and put
a different fly on the water.

"On her own there then, is she?"

"No, there's some chap there. Lucas I think she called
him."

As the strollers drew near, Mick's big red face split like
a pumpkin into a huge, crooked-toothed grin. Despite the
heat, he was wearing a hairy brown tweed suit and hat and
brown brogues. His thick red neck rippled over the collar
of his check shirt and a bright yellow tie was knotted tight.
Arthur estimated that the cheerful local building contractor
must be about eighty pounds overweight. He must have been
slowly cooking under that lot.

"Morning bruvs, this here is Coral. Our new neighbour.
Well almost a neighbour, anyway!" He boomed with obvious
admiration.

Coral had showered after her run and was now wearing

a cornflower blue tracksuit. "Hello." She smiled at Arthur as if at a camera.

What a gorgeous girl, he thought. I bet I know what's going through O'Looney's mind while he's playing the friendly neighbour. The same thing that's going through mine, the dirty sod!

"Coral and I have already met actually, Mr O'Looney," Liz said. "How was your first night in the cottage?"

The girl was putting Arthur and his equipment under close scrutiny. Although he didn't know it, he was feeling the same way Frank had earlier.

"Oh, I slept quite well really, Liz," she answered. "Lucas was very restless, though."

"Don't worry, he'll soon get used to it, won't, he Arthur? Oh, Coral this is Arthur. Arthur, Coral."

Silently cursing Liz for not introducing him as Arturo, he shook the proffered hand clumsily, the easel and chair pinned under his arm.

"I see you paint," she said. "You've been out to catch the sun coming up, have you?"

"Er, no. I'm just going out now, actually."

"What a pity, you missed a beautiful sunrise. I love to watch it, especially by the sea!"

"Well, I do too actually. I mean, I'm often out there at the crack, as it were. Painting or sketching." He looked at Liz apprehensively. She was staring unblinkingly at him with raised eyebrows. "And fishing or shrimping, of course. I'm often out there when the tide's right."

He knew instantly from her expression that he had put his size nine in something.

"Oh dear, not you as well," she said. "I saw another chap out there this morning, catching shrimps. I think it's horrible. I'm totally vegetarian, you see. I couldn't eat the tiniest living creature. I've got Lucas onto a totally veggie diet now too. He didn't like it at first, but he's come round."

"Oh good," Liz said insincerely.

'Oh Christ' Arthur thought sincerely. Not another one. He thought of telling her the tiny creatures aren't living when you eat them. No, she'd probably heard that one before. They're cropping up everywhere, the whining bastards. Opening up their bloody rabbit food restaurants and shops. That was good, 'Bloody rabbit', she'd like that. Try telling a bad-tempered mangy old lion that he'd be better off eating lettuce leaves. And who would take the slightest interest in the great white shark if all it ever tore to pieces was seaweed?

Mick had been trying to think of something to say next. The mention of food put him on home ground.

"Youse don't know what you're missing, bruv," he told Coral. "I just had meself a great mountain of a fry-up with a piece of steak the size of that on the top of it!" He demonstrated with hands resembling huge bunches of fat pink sausages. "A steak like that, I tell yer!"

Arthur had come across Mick's steaks. He thought it would have weighed at least a pound and a half.

Coral couldn't hold back. "Well, Mr O'Looney, I have to stick to my principles and say that I find that repulsive. Those poor defenceless animals ..." Her eyes filled. "I must be getting along. Goodbye. Please excuse me."

They watched her walk off along the path with the dog following a yard or so behind.

"Poor girl," Liz broke the silence, "she's really upset."

"It seems she's already met Frank, then," Arthur added lamely. "That's some queer sort of a girl, sure enough." Mick scratched his huge overhang of belly. "I wouldn't like to be in that fella Lucas's shoes, and that's a fact!"

By one of the mailboxes the dog stopped and sniffed at

a freshly stained clump of grass at the foot of its post. Coral half turned as she walked. "Come here, Lucas! Leave that and come here!"

Liz burst out laughing. "Now you know who Lucas is. Oh Arthur, you should see your face!"

"Do you mean you knew all along?" "Oh, yes!" She laughed again.

"A vegetarian dog, eh?" Mick marvelled. "Did you ever hear of anything like that in your life before?"

"The poor little sod," Arthur sympathized, "he doesn't even get the choice, does he?"

"Desmond would be a better name for him altogether," Mick said. "Didn't there used to be a cuddly toy dog called Dismal Desmond?"

Lucas had caught up with his owner. She had clipped a leather leash to his collar and they were on the footbridge.

"A beautiful girl though, Arthur," Liz observed. "If you were to go totally veggie, who knows?"

"Not even for that, Liz," he said solemnly. "I love my roasts and meat puddings too much. How anyone can resist the smell of a good bit of meat cooking beats me!"

"My idea of a vegetarian diet would be illegal," Mick said. "And why is that, Mr O'Looney?" Liz asked.

"Three square vegetarians a day, bruv!" he exploded as he bent double and made a noise like a diesel engined cement mixer.

It's funny isn't it, Arthur thought. How Mick calls everyone bruv, and they all call him mister. The previous summer, when they had known each other for more than three years, they were one day together in a pub in Worthing. He recalled how there had been such a fug in the place that it had been rather like sitting too close to, and down wind of, a damp bonfire. O'Looney had suddenly told him that he could call him Mick. Had begged him to, actually. He was now the only person who did so, and that included the Irishman's wife who had gone back home for last Christmas and never came back. Still, as Mick had told him in a little verse he was fond of singing to the tune of 'the Mountains of Mourne', "She's far better off digging peat round Mayo, far away from George Wimpey and Taylor Woodrow!"

"Are you all right now, Mr O'Looney?" Liz asked as he finally stopped spluttering and straightened up.

"Sure. I'm fine now. That was a great crack though, eh? Go on then, you two. It's time both of you were off to do the necessary."

She looked at Arthur and had to laugh again.

"Go on, Arthur, the 'old church' is waiting. Oh, I do wish you could have seen your face!"

The two men moved off towards the footbridge, Arthur to set up his easel on the public hard and Mick to get into his car. After going to the bank he would follow the route that Frank had taken to the foot of the Downs, where at the beginning of a chalky track the O'Looney name hung on a tree. The new farmhouse that he had built there was nearing completion.

Arthur turned and called back to Liz. "You knew all the time, eh? See you in the Smack this evening. And please make it, Arturo!"

5

Mr O'Looney drove the big silver Mercedes over the river to the town and parked outside the bank by the main gate of the old churchyard. Just inside the gate a big old tree lay across some broken gravestones. Torn up by a freak wind some months before, its huge roots had lifted clay and chalk and demolished part of the old flint graveyard wall.

An elderly American tourist, in regulation Hawaiian-type shirt and Bermuda shorts, asked him to pose for posterity by the massive bole- end. While the camera's shutter clicked away, O'Looney smiled an idiot's smile as he imagined his own image in tweeds, winging its way across the big pond to be shown to sticky fingered grandchildren, or passed around in some smoky pool hall.

After this pleasant interlude in his schedule he went into the bank to withdraw the necessary funds for his merry band of workers. He also wanted an extra amount for his own expenses, the reason being that for the past two years he had been in the habit on the second weekend of each month of enjoying the company of one of the young ladies employed by a certain escort agency in Brighton, which was run by a strange old woman named Miss Steine.

Since his wife's departure before Christmas, instead of using a particular discreet hotel, he had taken boldly to having his escort stay overnight Friday on his floating home. Miss Steine and her girls had come to know the wants and the needs of this generous regular customer. For Mick himself, one of the delights of the arrangement was that Miss S chose which one was to be his each time, and he had never been disappointed.

Inside the bank it smelled of lavender polish and was as hushed as any library. He stood there at the counter watching the young girl's nimble fingers speeding through the notes. His mind was half a mile away in the teak-clad master bedroom aboard his luxurious sea-going Dutch barge. He liked to invent new themes for his special evenings and he had something wonderful in mind for this one. The young money dispenser smiled sweetly as she pushed the notes under the glass. If she could have read his thoughts she would have found them far more interesting than the trashy soap opera she had watched the night before.

The next step after leaving the bank was to pay the men he had working on the conversion of a big old ivy-covered house on a site upstream from the roadbridge. The old place had once been the headquarters of the local sailing and angling club, whose fun-loving members had now moved to a more modern building nearer the harbour, also built and owned by himself. The older property was soon to be opened as a casino and restaurant, despite some placard waving and petition signing by a number of locals. The idea of having gambling and good food and drink under one roof appealed to Mick O'Looney. The fact that he was sole owner of the place only added to the warm glow that he felt as he left the site and drove out of the town onto the bypass. His voracious innards had already digested that enormous breakfast and he began to think about lunch. He felt a delightful gastric gurgle as a possible menu ran down the windscreen before his eyes, pulled down in jerks like a roller towel on a lavatory wall.

Window down and elbow out, he drove happily through

the warm countryside, tugging out an expired Dubliners tape
and pressing in a Brendan Shine. Just before the turn off that
he would take was a filling station. The little needle on the
Merc's petrol gauge was near low and he turned onto the
concrete forecourt and stopped at the row of pumps.

At the side of the garage workshop a bright red hard top
sports car emerged from the spray of the vivid green boas of
a car wash. The car moved slowly in little rabbit hops, as if
being driven by a learner who had yet to gain mastery over
the clutch pedal. O'Looney watched as it stopped outside the
workshop and the driver's door opened.

A girl with hair dyed a red that matched the car, swung
out very long legs and red shoes to make a practised exit. She
was wearing a tight white T-shirt and a short red pleated skirt
which just about covered what it should.

Red shoes no drawers, Mick thought as he sat there
with Brendan warbling pleasantly on. He would watch the
proceedings with some interest, all thoughts of lunch or petrol
temporarily abandoned.

On high heels the girl walked over to the workshop and
returned with a leering mechanic in oily blue overalls who
lifted the bonnet of her car and inspected the contents.

As he pointed knowledgeably to some defect, the front of
her little red skirt hung over the radiator cap. Two more grease
monkeys had come out to watch, grinning and wiping oily
hands on even oilier rags. As she bent over more, O'Looney
could see a tiny white triangle of panties and a roundness
of firm young cheeks. He eased his foot off the brake pedal
and let the car roll on to the end pump to get a closer look.
Under the PAY HERE sign, the little man behind the glass
was stabbing a finger at him and trying to tell him something
with exaggerated silent mouthings. Mick looked in his rear
view mirror.

What's he on about he thought. There's nothing behind me. Oh well, I'd better fill up.

He switched off the engine and got out of the car and went round to the pump, took off the filler cap, inserted the nozzle and pulled the trigger. The knight in shining overalls was smiling triumphantly – obviously the damsel in distress was out of danger. From her car anyway.

"Just some water got in from the car wash, miss," O'Looney heard. Down went the bonnet and the girl got into the car and drove off, smiling and waving to the cheering workmen, one of whom gestured with a rigid forearm and clenched fist.

O'Looney released the trigger and replaced the nozzle on the pump. He put the filler cap back on and strolled over to the PAY kiosk. The gnome behind the glass watched him approach.

O'Looney pushed money under the glass and said, "Give us a bill, would youse?"

Silly fat bastard, the little man smiled. Pumping diesel into a petrol engine because he couldn't keep his piggy eyes off that bit of crumpet. He took a tiny receipt from the till and pushed it under.

"No. I want a written one." O'Looney pushed it back.

For fuck's sake, the sprite thought. He wants a written one. I'm fucked if I'm going to tell him now. It's too late anyway. He's going to find out soon enough when he gets up the road a bit. The big cunt.

O'Looney stuffed the bill into a jacket pocket and returned to his car. Brendan was still lilting away as he drove off and turned into the lane which eventually passed the dusty chalk track leading up to the new house. With his mind still on the firm looking cheeks beneath the little red skirt, he hadn't yet noticed the thickening blue haze behind the car.

6

The new farmhouse was built in traditional local style, with a stone exterior featuring a good deal of knapped flint work and heavy oak posts and beams inside. The roof covering of old peg tiles had come complete with a covering of lichen, from a priory which in its time had withstood a bombardment from Cromwell and a stray doodlebug from Hitler, only to collapse without warning one night from old age. The original house had been burned to the ground twelve months before in what had been viewed by some as suspicious circumstances. Never one to allow himself to be influenced by local opinion, Mick O'Looney had bought the remains and the adjoining acres from the incredibly aged and strangely uninsured owner. Farmer Toms had lived alone for many years and for the past ten had not even known who he was. Mick had arranged for him to be installed in the comparative luxury of a Duncaring-type Home for Retired Gentlefolk, Goring-by-sea. And nobody could be more gentle than Farmer Toms, he couldn't do so much as lift a finger to prevent it.

The new building was much larger than the old one. Four bedrooms, the master with en-suite bathroom, two separate bathrooms, a very large lounge with inglenook fireplace, a large country kitchen and laundry room, and an outside toilet off the rear porch for anyone caught short whilst in muddy boots. There was also a room off the lounge which O'Looney

referred to as his 'den', and which since the completion of
decorating had been kept mysteriously locked. There were
views over lovely country to the sea and there were stables
and a swimming pool building with a sliding roof. The main
building work and decorating had been finished but the place
was devoid as yet of furniture. All but one room.

Frank's motorcycle and sidecar combination was parked
in front of the house behind a carpet layer's van. Frank, in
his white overalls, was sitting on a gallon paint tin happily
putting the finishing touches to the gloss coat on the front
door. The voice of a babbling idiot disc jockey was coming
from a transistor radio upstairs where the carpet layer, who
was called Archie, was working. The heavy front door was
held open by a brass hook on the wall behind.

Frank left it open to dry and went back to the laundry
room to clean his brushes. He was surprised to find himself
humming along to the infantile chanting of some current
top ten hit coming from above. He stopped and smiled as he
farted a comment and watched the last traces of white paint
mixed with blue brush cleaner rinse away down the plug-hole
of the big stone sink. His work there was now finished. Soon
Mr O'Looney would be along with the wages, and then he
could go back to town for the after hours session in the pub
which always marked the start of the weekend. Despite the
blaring pop music and the inane chattering from the radio he
thought he would go up and pass some time with the carpet
layer. The din drowned his tread on the wide, expensively
spindled staircase.

Archie was sitting on the ledge inside the bay window
of the master bedroom, rolling a cigarette. He had finished
laying the pale grey carpet and a few curled, off-cut strips lay
here and there on it. The disc jockey was squawking from the
radio on the ledge, Archie looked up as Frank entered the

room and considerately turned the volume down.

"Allo mate," he said, "lovely view from up 'ere innit?"

"Certainly is." Frank moved over to the open window.

Archie tossed the cigarette into the air and caught it between his lips as it dropped.

"Yeah, it'd be nice to 'ave a gaff like this, eh?" The cigarette wagged as he went on, "Just get a whiff of that air, will yer!"

Frank pushed the window open further and took a deep breath of the southern breeze, the summer smell coming up from the warm earth through the trees with a hint of the sea. Over the tree tops the Channel shone silver bright and he could see a tiny cargo ship entering the miniature harbour. It must be nearing high water.

Archie lit his cigarette from an old Tommy lighter and puffed out a blue cloud that drifted back into the room on the zephyr.

"Yeah, it's all right for some. O'course you don't get that sort of money by working," he philosophized, "yer crooks and bookmakers, that's all that gets to live in places like this!"

"Mmmmm," Frank half agreed and farted again. It produced a long, high-pitched note, a stretched out beep borne by considerable pressure.

"Nice one," Archie nodded appreciatively. "'Ere, I've been watching that big Paddy down there. What d'yer reckon he's doing of?"

Down below, a giant Irishman named Hughie, who stood nearly seven feet tall even without his socks, was setting out a large twelve-sided figure on the earth using pins and lines.

He was wearing a string vest and a pair of shorts which had once been white, but which were now a filthy brown, and a pair of boots which in size resembled the stone ones sometimes seen in ornamental gardens. The odd shape that

he was working on was to be a flowerbed in the new front
lawn. There was a huge stack of turf beside the track down
to the lane.

"He's setting out a dodecagon," Frank said.

"Oh yeah," Archie said as if remembering, "he's a big
bastard, isn't he!"

Big seemed hardly adequate when describing Hughie.
Back home in the remote bog country he had been known
as Hugh the Tree, as indeed he still was in the pubs of
Camden Town and 'county' Kilburn. Even in that world
of scrubbed red faces and huge-knuckled teeth-smashing
draught Guinness connoisseurs, his sheer size had usually
been a sufficient deterrent. A few dedicated lovers of hospital
food had ignored the warning signs and attempted to break
their hands on him, only to discover that they had until then
never met a truly angry man, and very soon they would be
sampling once more the delights of National Health catering.

Back in Ireland it was sometimes whispered over smoky
peat fires on haunted nights, that Hughie had been cursed
at birth by some evil little demon of the bogs. Doomed to go
through life with the burden of a high-pitched squeaky voice,
so absurd that very few people could talk with him and look
him in the face. Indeed, many who had spoken with him once
would afterwards avoid him altogether, and some who could
not avoid speaking to him adopted a strange form of language
that eliminated the need for him to answer.

And so it was that the giant with a heart to match led a
rather sad and lonely life. And on this particular bright and
beautiful morning it was even more sad than usual.

Having moved from London to the coast to work for
O'Looney, he had befriended another employee, a fellow
Irishman named Danny. But Danny had not turned up on
the job for the past two days, hadn't phoned and hadn't been

seen in the pub.

Danny had been his only real friend, and now it seemed he was gone.

Frank and Archie, watching from the upstairs window, had no knowledge of this upheaval in the giant's tiny closed world. As they watched him working slowly and methodically around the odd shape in the earth, a battered yellow truck with a blue front wing and driver's door was coming up the track from the road in a cloud of white dust, and with a loud growl coming from its damaged exhaust silencer.

"Who's this then?" Archie asked.

"That's Danny. I hope that dust doesn't blow onto that door I've just glossed!"

The truck stopped by the earthworks and the dust settled without spreading too far. Danny waited for it to clear before getting out of the cab. He had spent the past two days laid up with a painfully seized larynx that had developed from a sore throat, brought on by some over-enthusiastic singing following an uncustomary win at a darts match. He was scrubbed and shining and wearing his best weekend suit, and feeling somewhat better, he had come to take his pal for a lunch-time drink.

The kneeling Hughie looked round as Danny slammed the truck's door and walked towards him with a broad smile on his bright pink face.

All the pent-up emotion in the giant's great frame exploded as he rose to his towering height. "Where the fock have youse been, yer little cont!" he trilled. The two spectators at the bedroom window were somewhat shocked by the outburst. So was Danny, to say the least, being considerably nearer. "Oi've been here on me jack for two days, and not a word from you, yer little wanker!"

Now Danny himself was a big man by any normal

standards, but standing there before The Tree he did indeed feel little. He decided to ignore the suggestion that he found his own right hand more attractive than his lady friend and struggling to maintain his smile, he held out his hand.

Hughie was having none of it. "Oi'm sorry, Dan," he said as solemnly as his trilling allowed," but oi'm going ter have ter marmalize yer."

Danny's outstretched hand dropped and he clasped his sore throat with the other. His eyes wide with terror stricken panic, he blurted out a last ditch explanation.

"Hughie, oi've been in me bed with the laryngitis ..." The cruelly cracked falsetto came from his poor raw throat as a near perfect mimic, an unintended, but final insult.

Frank and Archie looked on in amazement as Danny's mouth seemed to open to the size of a football to accommodate the huge fist. Like a train going into a tunnel at incredible speed, with Hughie's twenty four stones behind it, the force lifted him through the air in an arc before landing, where he performed two perfect backward rolls before coming to rest against a front wheel of the truck in the sitting position. A mash of blood and teeth foamed from his mangled lips.

Hughie shook his massive head of black curls as he looked down and rubbed his grazed knuckles on his shorts. "Well dat's dat den," he squeaked.

7

"What the fuck …?"

Shortly after turning into the narrow lane, Mr O'Looney felt a sudden loss of power under his right foot. An unusual roaring noise came from the engine, followed by a long howl and three loud bangs. All ahead was bright cloudless sunshine, whilst looking in the mirror showed all behind as a blue-grey fog. He coaxed the stricken Merc along, cursing with increasing volume as each new expensive sounding clangour drowned Brendan's happy warbling.

An impatient sounding horn blasted from somewhere behind in the smoke. O'Looney waved angrily out of the window, making a perfect but invisible 'you may pass' hand signal. The horn blared again.

"For fuck's sake!" Mick bawled. "Can't yer see I'm having a spot of bother?"

The horn sound changed to a Baa-da-baa-da then a Woo woo-woo-woo. O'Looney couldn't believe it. "I don't believe it," he said. "I get a bit of engine trouble in a poxy lane so narrow that you couldn't get a decent erection and leading nowhere, and suddenly all the world and his fucking uncle wants to get there!"

His shiny brogued foot flapped away at the pedal but the car lurched to a stop. Pummelling the steering wheel with his fists caused his tweedy hat to slip over his face as he screamed at the roof's interior. "You dirty rotten, filthy stinkin', no good useless son of a Pomeranian bastard!"

The car had stopped where the lane was a little wider to allow two- way traffic to pass. The blue fog overtook it first, followed by a small white hatch-back with the word VET on its rear window, then the blue flashing lights and orange stripes of an ambulance and a police Rover. Suddenly it was very quiet. A deflated O'Looney looked in the mirror.

The lane behind was clear and bright again and he opened the car door and got out. He slammed the door and started walking up the lane. It was about a quarter of a mile to the entrance to the track. In the fields on either side there were sheep scattered like sandbags on the grassy slopes, and as he passed a gate in the hedgerow on his left, one of them poked its head through and called to him. Its timing was all wrong.

"Fuck off!" he snapped.

***

In the meantime, Frank and Archie were sure they had become witnesses to a killing. They crept gingerly from the house as the giant strode off, a numbing awareness of the horror of the situation preventing Frank from making a crack about going to find a beanstalk to climb. Danny was still sitting propped in the same position against the wheel of the truck. If it's true what they say, Frank thought, about your life flashing before you at the final instant, then Danny boy must have had a hell of a time of it. His eyes were fixed wide open in horror and his spiked greying hair gave him the look of having received a considerable electric shock. His shirt front and tie were splotched with a lumpy red gore resembling bolognese sauce. Frank put out a tentative hand and touched an arm of the victim's blue suit. "Do you reckon he really is? You know, dead I mean."

"Looks like it." Archie stooped to look into the bulging

eyeballs. Just as he was thinking what a wonderful blue they were, they blinked and sent him flying backwards to clutch at the legs of Frank's overalls. "Aaaaagh, I nearly shit meself then!"

Danny made a gurgling noise and rolled his head from side to side. Through shredded lips he was trying to say something.

"Stone me, he's alive, he's alive!" Frank burst out. "Quick, the phone's on in the kitchen. Get an ambulance up here, I don't think we ought to move the poor bugger ourselves."

As Archie ran back to the house Frank sat down on the warm earth and held Danny's hand. "Hang on, mate," he said, "they'll soon be here."

Danny couldn't hear the words, but he could feel the hand on his. In his concussion he was back home in the Golden Vale and the gentle hand was his mother's. He was back on his little bed in the tiny cottage, with his head bandaged after the accident, when the boys had been diving into the river.

8

By the time O'Looney had laboured up the track from the lane, Danny had been put aboard the ambulance and it was about to leave. A young policeman was sitting in the Rover with one leg out, while he asked for reinforcements on the radio. O'Looney was blowing like an old bull from the exertion of the walk and stopped to lean against the police car. On his way up the track he had been relieved to see that the house was still standing. "What," he gasped as he loosened his tie, "is going on?" "You're the builder, are you? They said you'd be along." The young copper had a pale spotty face.

O'Looney felt as though he were on fire. As he wiped around his neck with a big yellow handkerchief, he watched the blue light on the car's roof become a pint glass of lager. He closed his eyes and imagined the first cold bite of the liquid in his throat. The young copper watched mystified as the gross figure smiled and smacked his lips. "Yes, I own the place," Mick said as he opened his eyes again, "can you tell me what's happened?"

The young man consulted his notebook. There was an incredible amount of dandruff on his uniformed shoulders, considering how short his hair was.

"You are the owner of the property then, sir." "Yes, I know that."

"Well, sir. There's a bloke on board that ambulance, we believe he is one of your employees actually, who is in a rather sorry state." He looked at his notebook again. "Danny his name is. He has become the victim in an act of extreme violence, carried out we have been told, by another of your employees, a 'gentleman' by the name of Big Hughie."

"Danny! And The Tree! Oh my God, where is he now?"

"As I said sir, Danny's on the ambulance…"

"No, The Tree, man! I mean Big Hughie!"

"He's in that little shed thing over there, sir," the youth pointed across the field; "he won't come out. Bolted the door, he has. We've been told he's a bit on the big side, isn't he? And obviously violent. Still, I've called for assistance," he added confidently.

Vivid memories of scenes of total destruction flitted before O'Looney's eyes. "Listen," he said, "if Hughie doesn't want to go, it's the army you'll have to call out!"

The youngster tried to sound unimpressed. "Perhaps you might like to have a word with him, sir. He might listen to you." He liked that line, he'd heard it on the telly somewhere.

"All right then," O'Looney said, "but I can't see him coming out with a white flag!"

The two of them set off across the newly turned earth.

For some reason they were both bent double, as if they expected Hughie to open fire from the little red pill-box. It was in fact a glass-fibre portaloo that O'Looney had had put there for the benefit of the workers. It leaned at a precarious angle, with the name Tardis painted crudely on the door.

Sergeant Chopin, who had been driving the police car, was lying in a slight hollow about thirty feet from the time machine. O'Looney fell heavily alongside him while the young cop rolled in just like he'd seen it done in the war films.

"This is Mr O'Looney, Sarge."

O'Looney and the Sarge shook hands awkwardly. The Sarge sported a superb handlebar moustache with waxed ends.

"Come to talk chummy out of it then, eh, Mr O'Looney?"

"If I can. What do you want me to do?"

"To tell you the truth, this siege business is all a bit new to me too. We don't get many in these parts. I'll just have another little try myself, like, then if that doesn't do any good I'll hand over to you."

He makes it sound like we're together in the commentary box at a football match, O'Looney thought. The youngster was thinking they should have one of those megaphone things. He'd seen those in the films too.

The Sarge raised himself on his elbows and cupped his hands around his mouth. Improvisation, that was the way. He cleared his throat. "Hallo the Tardis," he called, "it's only me again, Hughie. Sergeant Chopin. Why don't you come out like a good boy now? Nobody's going to hurt you."

You can say that again, O'Looney thought. I've seen it tried.

It was hot inside the portaloo. By necessity, Hughie was standing with his neck bent and with one huge boot either side of the pan. The sweat was dripping from his nose into it. It was impossible for him to sit down with the door closed. When he had used the toilet in the past he had left the door open with his legs sticking out into the field.

He had fallen asleep there more than once, so peaceful it was. The roof of the loo was semi-transparent and his eyes had become used to the half-light. He was reading an amusing little ditty that someone had scribbled on the door. It concerned a certain young lady from Steyning and he hadn't heard the Sergeant properly. There was a phone number too, but he couldn't quite make it out. From outside, the voice came again. "We've got a friend of yours hare, Hughie. It's Mr O'Looney. He'd like to say a few words. Over to you then, Mr O'Looney." The Sarge rolled on to his back and looked at the sky, as if keeping out of the line of fire while negotiations continued. The young officer copied him. "'Ere Sarge, I just thought of something," he said.

"Oh yes, and what's that then?"

"Well, that Tardis on the telly was a police call box. Quite a coincidence, eh?"

"Oh do shut up, son!"

Getting psyched up for the task ahead, O'Looney removed his hat and screwed it up in his fists. Then he kicked himself mentally and put it back on again. He raised himself on his elbows in true Chopin fashion, and formed an O with his hands.

"Hallo the ... Oh shit!"

"That's all right, Mr O'Looney, just try again," the Sarge said patiently. He had closed his eyes and crossed his arms on his chest like some old stone knight on the lid of a tomb. O'Looney tried again.

"Hallo there, Hughie. It's me here, Mr O'Looney. There's a couple of nice policemen here and they'd like you to go back to the town with them. Er, why don't you come out now, Hughie, before there's any more damage done, eh?"

In his bent and cramped position, Hughie found it difficult to shout. O'Looney thought the alto screech that came from the echo chamber sounded ominously like a banshee.

"You can tell them to go and fuck spiders!"

O'Looney turned to the Sarge. "He says you can go and fu..." "I heard what he said!"

From behind them came the sound of more vehicles coming up the track and then the slamming of doors. O'Looney now feared the worst. There had been a chance of getting Hughie to go quietly before, but now with all these extra uniforms and cars he knew the giant would panic and see red. Or blue. They'd even thrown in a couple of rnotorcyclists!

The Sarge made some arm waving signals, telling the Peelers to wait by the cars. "At least they didn't turn up like the seventh bloody cavalry with the sirens blaring," he said, "we don't want to make chummy nervous." He thought for a while, then spoke to the younger copper, who was watching some ants running around and over his fingers. "All right, Hardy, get back there and tell that lot to stay where they are. I'm going up there to have a quiet little chat with our man. He wouldn't be armed would he, Mr O'Looney?"

"No. At least, not in the way you mean."

"Good. Tell them he's not armed, but to be prepared in case he makes a run for it down the slope. Well, get going!"

Young Hardy set off in a silly Groucho Marx run with his hands over his ears as if expecting mortar fire or mines. The Sarge outlined his plan.

"Right, Mr O'Looney. I'm going to go up there and have a chat with him, friendly like. I'll ask him if he'd like you to come up and have a chat. I think we'll be able to get him to come out peacefully. Then we'll take him for a ride in one of the cars back to the station. I made a point of telling them not to bring the meat wagon. They panic when they see it, some of 'em. We don't want any further complications, do we? Right then, I'll be off!"

"Good luck," O'Looney said. Rather you than me, he thought.

The Sarge started up the slight incline, calling to Hughie as he went and gradually lowering his voice as he got nearer to the Tardis. He stopped about three feet short of it and Hughie could see the upper half of his face through the gap over the door. The Sarge looked down at the door handle, the little square sign above it said ENGAGED. He had already decided to use the gentle approach. He spoke very softly.

"Now then, Hughie old chap, it's Sergeant Chopin here.

Why don't you come out and we'll take a little walk down to my car and go for a nice ride to the station, eh?"

There was a long pause while Hughie figured out which sort of station he meant. "Piss off," he squeaked.

"Come on now, Hughie, there's a good chap."

"There's some terrible disgusting pictures and things some perverted bastard's written on the door in here. Why aren't you out catching the likes of that now then, eh?"

"Now you're getting off the subject there, Hughie."

"The filthy dirty bastards are everywhere, pervertin' decent people. Sure didn't me best mate Danny just tell me himself that he'd been in his bed for days with that Larry whatsisname!"

"That was laryngitis, Hughie!"

"That's the fella! And another thing, didn't I read in the paper the other day about some lady traffic warden who went into a ladies toilet, and while she was sitting there didn't she hear a whirring noise and this metal drill thing comes through the wall there at the side of her and …"

"Now Hughie …"

"And didn't she hoist up her old drawers and run around and into the Gents, and wasn't there this little fella in black there on his knees and drillin' a hole through for the spyin'? And when she shouts at him and your man turns around, who do you think it is? Only the sodding vicar, that's who! Now why aren't you out rounding up the likes o'him now, eh?"

"Where was that, then?" the Sarge asked with genuine professional interest. "It wasn't anywhere near here, was it?"

"No, it was up there in London somewhere. The dirty filthy fornicating hole that it is. It came out in your man's previous record when he got himself nicked for something or other that he'd been up to in some boys' school. In Lowestoft, that was. It was in one of them Sunday papers."

"London then Lowestoft, eh?" the Sarge said thoughtfully. "Gets around a bit, doesn't he! You're dead right though, Hughie. There's a hell of a lot of them about these days. It's catching the bastards though, that's the problem. Very often the victims don't like to talk. Too embarrassing for them, see?"

Hughie was enjoying himself, he couldn't remember when he'd held such a long conversation with anyone. "Yes, I can see that," he said, then through the gap above the door he saw the thin blue line mustered in the lower field and the assortment of police vehicles. "I'm coming out now," he added softly, "thanks for the chat."

With great relief the Sarge heard the bolt slide back inside as he watched the sign change to VACANT. With the smile of a man satisfied with a job well done, he reached for the door handle.

Unfortunately for Chopin, when Hughie had said that he was coming out he had failed to add that he didn't intend to stop. With both hands and his three hundredweight against the door, he pushed off with both feet as the handle turned. In times past, the Sarge had been made aware that he had been blessed with the gift of E.S.P. Several times in the course of his duty, it had saved him from injury by keeping him safely hidden out of harm's way when others had bravely or foolishly gone in. On this occasion, however, it was a little late in whispering in his ear. It was only in that instant as he turned the handle that he knew he shouldn't have done it.

Later on, when thinking it over in hospital, he calculated that the impact must have been something like that which would be experienced by someone foolish enough to be standing immediately in front of one of the starting stalls, as it opened at the start of a five furlong sprint at Epsom. The horse in this case being the proverbial shit-house door, which unlike the rest of the Tardis was of metal and accelerating like a Sidewinder missile, impelled by a jockey with the weight of three. A human meteorite, Hugh the Tree.

Sergeant Chopin, with a sort of 'I knew it!' expression on his face, was thrown back several feet. As he landed on his back, he felt the cracking of ribs beneath Hughie's boots as the giant used him as a silver buttoned springboard.

O'Looney had risen open mouthed from the hollow with an outstretched hand of warning as the Sarge had reached for the handle. Now, as Hughie gathered speed towards him on the downhill run, he fell flat on his face again. Hughie cleared the hollow in one great stride, and O'Looney, with tight-gripped hands pulling down the rim of his hat, saw him go over from the point of view of a fallen rider in the Grand National.

By the time he sat up, Hughie was well away down the slope of the field, running with head erect, his long arms swinging at his sides. Because of his great height he appeared to be moving in the exaggerated motions of a slowed film, but in fact he was travelling at an incredible ever increasing speed, his huge weight gathering momentum as he bore down on the thin blue line of uniforms.

Frank and Archie were watching the proceedings with some interest, leaning on the safe side of Danny's truck with elbows on the bonnet. Until then it had seemed like an old Keystone Kops film, but played slowly. Sergeant Chopin approaching the red portaloo, the silent conversation, then the noiseless explosion of the door opening and the Sarge flying through the air to be trampled under Hughie's human cannonball exit. But now, as he cleared O'Looney's refuge and the action speeded up, they could hear the thud, thud, thud of the gargantuan boots in the soil and their excitement rose as his speed increased frighteningly.

The boys in blue discarded cigarettes and newspapers,

spreading themselves out with feet placed wide apart and heads down, with big clawing hands at the ready. O'Looney was on his feet again, but motionless, wide eyed and open mouthed in wonder.

Hughie's course did not alter. At the crucial moment the burly policemen closed on him, flinging themselves in regulation rugby type tackles at the massive charging figure. It was terrible to watch. One foolhardy officer came in higher than the others and there was a sickening snapping sound as the heel of Hughie's outstretched palm caught him under the chin. Four more were thrown off like the sparks from a spinning Catherine wheel as he twisted his hips as he passed through them as easily as running through smoke. The last poor soul was dragged screaming for twenty yards, clinging to the Titan's shorts before Hughie noticed the excess weight and dealt him a crushing back hander across the bridge of his nose.

Those that were able watched in horror as the monster, who was by now going flat out, reached the bottom of the field where the track from the house joined the lane. Due to the trees and high hedgerows no one, and that included Hughie, had seen the approaching single-decker green country bus making its way along the lane. It reached the entrance to the track just as Hughie was leaving it. Travelling at full speed he ran straight into its dirty side, much to the surprise of a passenger sitting at the precise point of impact and who had just happened to look out the window at that very moment. The alert driver hit the brakes as he heard the bang. The onlookers in the field half expected to see the bus roll over onto its side and Hughie to run on over it. But no, almost disappointedly they watched as he slid slowly down the side of the bus, leaving a pale green strip in its muddy coat.

It turned out that the veterinary surgeon was present

because he had taken a wrong turning and had been forced to continue along the narrow lane by the speeding ambulance and Sergeant Chopin's police car. He had been on his way back to base when he had been caught up in this interesting diversion, and as he could be reached on his car radio if needed he decided to stay and see what developed.

Now that the excitement was over he was examining Hughie's prostrate form in the manner of an anthropologist poring over some unique find. He was used to dealing with creatures of this size of course, but until now they had all had four legs. The Tree was stretched out on his back on the grass verge with a simpleton's smile on his face, breathing slowly and evenly.

"Well, I can't see that there's any injury," the Vet said as he stood up. "He seems to be sleeping, that's all."

"I've never seen anything like it," Sergeant Chopin wheezed. "He must be made of iron." The Sarge was being supported by the two least damaged of the other officers while another ambulance was on its way. O'Looney came over from inspecting the bus.

"Have you seen the dent in the side of that thing?" he said incredulously. "You'd think it had been hit by a rocket from the military!"

One of the Sarge's props was concerned that there might be a renewal of the hostilities. "Shall we put the bracelets on 'im, Sarge?" he asked nervously. "I mean, what if he comes round and goes ber-zerk!"

As if knowing he was being talked about, Hughie grunted and turned onto his side, drawing gasps of fear from two of the passengers who had got off to have a look at the monster. "I think it's waking up," the little old man said to his wife, "we'd better get back on the bus."

"Yes, I think so too, Maurice." She hooked her arm in his.

"I'm a bit disappointed though, I thought it would have had bolts through its neck. Are you sure they're making a film?"

With a sudden loud groan that made everyone jump, Hughie sat up. He yawned and scratched at his armpits. "Is it that time already?" he said. "Bejayzus, it feels like I only just got into me bed!"

He opened his eyes and blinked at all the different pairs of shoes and trousers standing around him. He looked up and saw Sergeant Chopin being held by the two constables as if he were a shield.

"Look, you'll have to come along with us," the Sarge winced. "You've done quite a bit of damage here today, Hughie."

The giant smiled hugely. Things seemed to be coming back to him. "Oh that," he beamed, "sure that was just a bit o'sport!"

They could hear the ambulance signalling its approach as it turned off the bypass. O'Looney noted that Hughie's high pitch was for once going unnoticed.

"That's as maybe, to you anyway. But you've still got to come along to the station with us, Hughie." The Sarge was wondering how they were going to get him there if he didn't fancy going. Only two of his men were in a reasonably fit state, and any involvement by the Vet and the other civilians was out of the question. Like mass suicide. While Chopin was contemplating asking the Vet if he had any of those tranquillizer darts with him, Hughie solved the problem himself. When he got to his feet on the grass verge he stood over eight feet tall above the road. The others looked up at him as though he were a speaker on a box at Hyde Park Corner.

"I'd be happy to go back with Mr O'Looney," he said.

"Me car's broken down in the lane," Mick explained. "I'll

have to phone to get it towed in. I suppose we could take poor old Danny's truck, though."

"Sure that's a great idea," Hughie said happily; he'd never addressed a group before. "The Sergeant could ride in the front wid'you, and I could stretch me legs on the back!"

"Well, I suppose that would be all right," Chopin said thoughtfully. "Have I got your word that you won't make a run for it, Hughie?"

"You have that. How is old Dan by the way?"

"We don't know for sure yet," O'Looney said. "I'll go in and see him later."

"Good, good. Give him my best, would you?" Hughie asked sincerely.

"I will, I will."

"Well then," said The Tree, who felt he was getting better and better at organizing things, "we'll get going then."

And so, when O'Looney had phoned the garage and the wounded had been loaded, they moved off in convoy. The ambulance went off first followed by the Vet, then the truck driven by O'Looney with the Sarge sitting next to him and Hughie counting sheep from the back. With the three worst casualties in the ambulance there was one bruised Bobby to each of the other police cars and the motorcycles.

Penultimate in the chain was Archie in his van followed at last by Frank on the big old Ariel combination. As the queue waited to turn onto the bypass, Frank looked at his watch. Plenty of time before 'last orders.' It may have been only one thirty, but they all felt like it had been a very long day. All except Hughie, that is.

9

It was due to an antiquated law governing the port and its environs that the pubs of the town were able to open at ten in the morning, giving local tipplers an earlier start than those in outlying areas.

As the clock over the fireplace struck ten that morning, Norman opened the street door of the Oyster Smack's only bar and sunlight brightened the low-ceilinged room. The publican stuck his head out and sniffed the High Street air, a whiff of the sea only slightly tainted by the passing traffic. His wife Doreen was already outside, balancing precariously atop a pair of step ladders with a large green watering can, spraying the hanging baskets of colourful flowers that hung dripping along the front of the pub.

"How's it going?" he asked without caring.

"Nearly done," she answered. It was the shortest answer she could think of that quickly. After fifteen years of what was by mutual consent a childless marriage, they now spoke to each other only when necessary, staying together on a strictly business basis and enjoying separate private lives.

Doreen was still a very attractive woman, although it did take a bit more effort these days. She was dyed blonde, and blousy in that pub's landlady sort of way and heavier now of course, but it was all in the right places and she'd never had any complaints. She had no difficulty in finding what she needed elsewhere and Norman took whatever lust he still possessed on his day trips and weekends in France. Sometimes he stayed away a day or two longer. He liked to keep the trips cloaked in mystery and encouraged the bawdy comments and jiggy-jig jokes in the bar, thinking they could only add fuel to his randy reputation. In fact though, he was known as 'No-Sex Norman' to the regulars, which was encouraged by Doreen, whose disparaging remark whenever the opportunity presented itself to ridicule his past sexual prowess, or lack of it, was in turn encouraged by their customers.

Across the High Street, between the betting shop and Peter's Tea Rooms and Picture Gallery, there was a narrow cobbled alleyway leading down to a concrete quay and the filling river. Emerging from the alley was a figure familiar to just about everyone in the town, and certainly to every pub. Carrying a dirty wet canvas sack over his shoulder, Fishy Phil was dressed in his usual garb of reeking fisherman's smock over filthy dungarees, and an old pair of wellies. Below a tattered blue cap his brown face sported several days' growth of silver beard. He dodged nimbly through the traffic across the road and stopped to admire Doreen's ample bottom. She was wearing a skin-tight black creation which looked like it must have been sprayed on. Just as he was thinking that he could see no pantie-line, the stench of old fish wafted up to her nostrils and she looked down to see his expression of obvious approval. He rolled his eyes and a near toothless grin spread wide below his flattened nose.

I've been watching you from across the road, Doreen," he said cheerily, "what yer doin'?"

"She's catching rabbits, what's it look like?" The voice of an invisible Norman came from the open doorway.

"Good morning, Norman. You thought I didn't know you were there, didn't you? I could see you from across the road too, you know!"

Doreen had finished watering the last basket. She descended with a bounce of heavy bosom that was much appreciated by the cleavage-ogling Phil. "You were watching my boobs and backside. I know you, Phil, remember?" She thrust the empty watering can into his free hand and folded the stepladders.

Phil was nursing a furry tongued hangover that could only be appeased by a few hairs from the dog. "I've been out seeing to me nets most of the night. I've just grabbed a couple of hours' kip in the bottom of me boat," he looked at Doreen imploringly. "Isn't it ten yet? I'm gagging for a pint, it's the salt y'know!"

Norman stuck his head out and grinned at the fisherman's perplexed expression. "Yes, we know all right!"

"You're a cruel man, Norman. And here's me coming to give you first choice of the fish an'all!"

"Take no notice of him, Phil," Doreen said. "Come on, I'll get you one."

Norman moved back to allow his wife room to struggle through the narrow doorway with the stepladders. Phil followed her eagerly, with the sack still over his shoulder and holding the watering can with the end of its spout an inch from her shiny black cheeks.

Inside the bar it was extremely dim after the bright sun outside. It was a while before eyes became accustomed to the change. The ceiling was very low with sagging oak beams and there were old prints and photographs of the town and harbour round the walls and an oil painting of the pub hung over the fireplace under the clock. The painting showed the pub in a snowy winter setting. It was an Arturo Bennet. The clock was a small ship's one that Norman had acquired somewhere during his time in Royal Navy submarines. The room was apt to become very crowded and smoky and the big extractor fan in the window at the rear was noisily dragging out the remnants of the previous night's fug. The place had a reputation for good food and there were a few highly polished tables waiting for the lunchtime session.

Phil lowered his burden to the floor and eased himself on to one of the half dozen stools around the L-shaped bar, putting the watering can on the bar top and resting his boots on the foot-rail. The rail was in fact a pipe that was part of the central heating system, and could become extremely hot in winter. One crowded night the previous January he had fallen asleep on the self same stool, held up by the press of bodies, and ruined a brand new pair of boots. The hot pipe had gone right through the melting rubber soles and his socks before he came to with a start. A bad time of year that, for fishermen. He remembered that as about the only time last winter that his feet had been really warm.

Norman was singing loudly as he took a bucket and mop from behind the bar and disappeared into the Gents' toilet. It was one of the old navy songs that he was so fond of and included a line that went, 'While the Chiefs and the Wrens were dancing, Jack was having a feed of arse...'

Doreen had been through to the back yard to put the steps away, and she returned through the kitchen door behind the bar with Dot, the dizzy young barmaid.

"Morning, Phil." "Morning, Dot."

The girl started taking down the spirits bottles and dusting the glass ornaments on the shelves behind. Doreen took a pint glass down from the shelf above the bar.

"What's it to be then, Phil, a light and bitter?"

"Yes please. A cold light ale."

She pulled a half of bitter up with the old fashioned pump handle. It was decorated with some brightly coloured figures on horseback chasing a fox. He watched the way her fingers curled around the phallic shape of the pump handle. He always enjoyed that. That's the trouble with those modern pubs with only keg beer and no pump handles, only on and off taps. Now where's the pleasure in watching a woman fondle one of those impersonal things, eh? They took all the enjoyment out of it, they did. It was always worth specifying a cold bottled beer as well. The cold shelf was a low one and they had to bend to reach the bottles. Phil savoured the view of Doreen's extensive cleavage. Yes it was always worth ordering a cold one.

"There you are, Phil." She put the glass and bottle down on the bar top in front of him. "You'll have to pay later, old Silly Bollocks hasn't brought the tray down for the Jack and Jill yet."

Phil hid his disappointment. He had thought that she was going to treat him to the first one. In the Gents meanwhile, old Silly Bollocks had changed the song for the one about the boy standing on the burning deck with his arse against the mast, who swore he wouldn't budge an inch till Oscar Wilde had passed. The singing voice came with a strange hollow echoing as it bounced off the shiny white wall tiles.

Doreen fixed herself a gin and tonic and started slicing a lemon on a Souvenir from Polperro board with a little smiling Piskie on it. "Just listen to 'im in there," she said, "bloody navy songs! They're all queer, the lot of 'em if you ask me. You've seen that crowd of his when they come in for a reunion now and again? A few drinks and they all start singing and putting their arms around each other and that. Can you imagine what must go on on those submarines when they're all cooped up together for months on end? It fair makes my flesh creep, it does! And all that stuff about looking for the Golden Rivet and getting the young ones with their head and shoulders out of a port-hole and whose turn is it in the barrel and all that.

Disgusting, I call it. What do you think?"

Phil was downing the last mouthful of his pint with the hanging spirits bottles winking a strange confusion of colours through the bottom of his glass. "Well, I s'pose it makes a nice change from playing cards," he said as he put the empty glass down and studied it.

The door of the Gents banged as Norman came out carrying the mop and bucket. "Dirty bastards," he grumbled, "some dirty bastard laid his kit out in there last night at chucking out time. I swilled most of it away before I locked up. Now I've had to get the sticky bits off in daylight. It looked like an Indian or Chinese or something, definitely not one of our meals. Funny how it's always got bits of carrots in it though, isn't it?"

"Yes, I've noticed that," Phil agreed. "Can I have another pint please, Doreen?"

"Of course you can, Phil." She picked up his glass. "Fetch the tray down for the till, would you, Norman?"

"Right. I'll just dump these things in the back yard first. That's if it's all right with you, is it?" He opened the door and clattered through the kitchen.

"Norman's a touch bitchy this morning, isn't he?" Phil asked.

"Oh, take no notice of him," Doreen said, "I don't anymore. He's got the hump because he was supposed to be going over to France but my mother turned up late last night to stay for the weekend. She's not very well, so I'll have to look after her and that means he's got to stay here and he doesn't like it!"

Phil sympathized with the man's predicament but thought better of mentioning it. A shadow fell across the red sunlit carpet as a tall figure, silhouetted briefly against the light, came through the open doorway from the street.

Fred the Fence, local gardener and fencing contractor, part time gravedigger and full time inebriate. A strong smell of creosote accompanied him into the bar. He cocked a leg over and sat on one of the bar stools, the newly painted garden fence odour mixing with the fish smell of Phil and his sack.

"Morning, Doreen. Morning, Dot. And morning, Phil." He wiped his hands on his shiny waistcoat. It had once been an olive green colour. His hands were cracked and scarred, with black lines where the creosote had got into them and around the fingernails.

"Your usual I suppose, Fred?" Doreen was already pulling up a half into a pint glass.

"Yes please, Doreen. With a cold light ale." The two men exchanged knowing smiles as they watched her stoop to reach the cold shelf.

"There you are, gentlemen, two light and bitters. She turned as the kitchen door opened and Norman came in with the cash tray for the till. "I'm going upstairs to get changed," she said as she pushed past him.

"Of course, my pet." He grimaced as the door closed behind her. "Just leave me to it. Again."

He pushed the tray into the till then turned to his two customers. "Right then, who's paying?"

"I suppose I am, as I was first in." Phil squirmed on his stool, trying to get his hand into the pocket of his dungarees.

Norman pointed to his glass. "That's your second one, isn't it?"

"That's right," Phil answered gloomily as the chance of a free one flew out the door.

"That's three light and bitters then." Norman grinned.

Phil dumped a handful of coins on the bar. "Put the change in the lifeboat."

Fred topped up his own glass and took a long swallow

from what was left in the light ale bottle, he belched loudly and Phil felt the warm draught of beer and whiskey breath on his face. Fred always carried his hip flask of Bushmills to work in the mornings.

"That's better. First today," Fred lied. He was wearing his old chequered cap and his Brylcreemed black hair stuck out spikily from under its sides, making him resemble one of those tufted rockhopper penguins. "I see you were out last night, then," he said as he gave Phil's sack a prod with his boot. "Do any good?" He was very partial to a nice piece of fried fish. Especially cheap fried fish. "I'd bet it can still be a bit cold out there at night though, eh?"

"Oh, it's all right if you're wrapped up," Phil said.

"Or pissed up," Norman chuckled.

"I never have too much before putting to sea," Phil protested unconvincingly, "you know that, Norman. It's too bloody dangerous out there. The sea doesn't give you a second chance, you know."

"Yes, I know that. But that silly sod Mackay doesn't though, does he?" Norman pressed the small change into the slot in the plastic lifeboat on the bar. "I'll tell you what," he added as he tapped the little blue and white boat, "he'll be needing one of these before long!"

"Well there you are," Fred put in, "mixed blood you see. I ask you, Scots and Gibraltarian. It's no wonder he's a bit mixed up, is it? I mean, he doesn't know where he is half the time, does he? It beats me how he finds his way back to harbour, it does straight!"

As if he had been hovering outside waiting on this cue, Jose Mackay tripped on the doorstep in his haste and rushed in to stand at the bar between Phil and Fred as if seized by the panic caused by someone shouting 'last orders'. He was short and dark and powerfully built. He looked as though he might just have stepped off a lost Mediterranean fishing boat to ask directions.

"A pint is it, Jose?" Norman stood expectantly, his hand already on the lager tap.

"Morningsall, yessaplease." José's hot garlic breath blew in each face in turn.

Phil found some more coins in another pocket. "I'll get that," he said.

"Many sanks." Unaware of his horrendous nautical pun, the Gibraltarian took his pint and sat down at a small corner table, his steady hand and step hiding the fact that if his blood/alcohol level had been measured at that moment it would have been found that he should have been dead.

After leaving the pub the previous evening he had spent most of the night drinking Rioja on his boat, having completely forgotten that he was supposed to be going out to tend to his nets. On waking in the morning he saw to his horror that it was almost ten o'clock – he could see the church clock from where he was lying in the well of the leaning boat. Hawking and spitting, he clambered over the side and waded through the soft mud to the rear of the King's Head, where he washed his boots under the outside tap. At one minute past ten he was the first customer in the public bar of the scrumpy house, where he downed two quick pints of the rough cider for breakfast. The sour cloudy liquid, which was known locally as 'screech', had a remarkably straightening effect, and he walked an unusually straight line to the Oyster Smack where he now sat with a brilliant smile on his dark face, happy in the knowledge that it would be at least two hours before his boat would be afloat and silently vowing that he would go out to the nets that afternoon.

Next across the threshold was the punctilious, white-haired old Colonel, wearing highly polished sensible walking shoes, cavalry twill trousers and a camouflaged combat jacket. The skin of his face and the backs of his hands looked as thin as a cigarette paper and speckled like a wild brook trout. The octogenarian glanced at the clock as he marched in as if he suspected it of being late and shouted his regular order. (Gin and tonic mornings, whisky evenings!) He sat down at his regular table to which Norman would bring his regulation drink. He gave José an abrupt nod as another regular morning toper entered at high speed.

Dave Death drove a hearse for the local branch of the Co-op. In funereal attire and for some reason always in a hurry, he usually managed to get in for a drink 'between drops' as he put it. He took his pint of bitter over to the Colonel's table. "Morning, Colonel."

"Morning, Death." The old soldier said it as if he expected the real thing to appear at any time, which indeed he did. A survivor of several wars, neither the Grim Reaper nor any of his Familiars held anything to frighten the Colonel.

Dave began telling him about a mix up that had occurred the previous afternoon. Apparently it was not the first time it had happened. He had taken what he called 'an empty' to the wrong address.

"Well there we were, see. Talk about laugh! Well, you've got to really, haven't you? There we were see, and this woman's telling us we'd got the wrong house. Quite upset she was an'all, on account of how she'd got her old dad ill in bed upstairs..." He took a mouthful of bitter.

"I imagine the poor woman would be." The Colonel took his drink from Norman's tray and nodded at him. Norman bowed reverently and backed away through the opened flap in the bar.

"It was forty-three Kinaston Crescent see?" Dave went on. "We was at forty-three Kinaston Crescent when we should

have been at forty -three Kinaston Avenue, see? Get me? That
pillock in the office got it wrong again!"

"It's the old story," the Colonel said, "a breakdown in
communications to the Front. There's a Kinaston Road too,
y' know."

"I know, don't I?" Dave confirmed. "It's just as well we
didn't go round there an'all, innit? I mean, it hardly gives the
firm a good name, does it, taking empties round to the wrong
people?"

"Hardly," the Colonel agreed. He downed his drink in
one and nodded quickly in Norman's direction as if he were
bidding at an auction. Although he was inspecting a glass that
he had been polishing, Norm's expert eye caught the slight
movement.

"Coming over, Colonel," he called, and prepared another
gin and tonic.

"Did I ever tell you, Death, of when I was a boy and our
local butcher died?" the Colonel asked.

"I don't think so, Colonel." Dave smiled in anticipation.

"I thought not. The chap died you see. They'd been in
business in the village for donkey's years, the family had. Well
anyway the chap died, and following tradition they had him
stood up in the shop window in his coffin. Father got the
chauffeur to drive us all down from the Hall to have a look
at the fella. Damn fine sight it was too, seeing all the people
from the surrounding countryside filing past. Paying their last
respects as it were. The shop was damned busy as well. Doing
a roaring trade, they were. It was the busiest they'd been for
years! I'll never forget that butcher chappie. He was completely
bald and his head was flat on top. Flat as a pancake. Flat and
shiny like the marble slab in his shop."

"Was that the result of an accident, or something?"

"I never knew. Something occurred to me when I got a bit

older, though. His wife worked in the shop as well. A massive woman she was. She used to heave the great sides of meat around like a man. Her hands were always red and very cold too. If she grabbed your balls you'd hit the ceiling!"

Dave thought for a moment or two, then he said, "Sounds like a plausible explanation."

The Colonel gave another of his barely perceptible nods and the obedient stooping Norman came over with his drink on a tray. The Colonel made no move to take it, so he put the glass down on the table.

"Well done, that man. Fetch me a quartered ham sandwich of brown bread with the crust removed, would you?"

"Certainly, Colonel." Norman backed away, still stooping.

"Funny fella, that," the Colonel said gruffly, "you'd think he'd got the idea I was a raving poofter or something!"

Dave finished his drink and nervously checked his watch against the clock on the wall.

"Can I get you a refill for that, Death?" the Colonel asked him.

"I don't think I'd better," Dave deliberated. "I could murder another one, but I've got to take a customer up to the crematorium and then deliver an empty later on. Thanks for the offer though, Colonel. I'll probably see you this evening."

He left with his usual haste, as though the customer wouldn't wait for his last ride. The Colonel gave his attention to the Gibraltarian in the corner, who was apparently doing his best to outstare him. In fact José's blank looking eyes were not focused on him at all. The dark, tousled fisherman thought he was back in the Artillery Arms at the top of Castle Steps on the Rock.

Two small but sprightly ladies of about sixty came in from the street. They were carrying heavy looking shopping bags. Hettie and Lettie were sisters who shared a strange looking floating home which was basically a huge old steel barge with a railway carriage on her deck. One-time actresses of the old school, they always looked as though they had just stepped out of Ealing or Gainsborough Studios' wardrobe department, whatever the season a picture of genteel respectability. They were in fact co-authors of lusty romances and actively keen members of ornithological and naturist societies, sometimes combining the two pursuits when weather permitted. Putting the bags down, they waved coyly to the Colonel, who had stood up and saluted briskly before sinking back into the leather chair.

Hettie sat down at the table next to the one where José had dropped anchor and bade him good morning. The 'Buenos dias' she got in return was heavily laden with sour wine, cider and garlic. On the very rare occasions when he was half sober, José spoke English with a Gibraltarian type accent. After a few drinks the accent would become more pronounced, along with the volume of booze taken. By the time he was quite drunk the English became unintelligible and he reverted to Spanish, but his Spanish was one that must surely have been almost unique in that its own accent was Glasgow Scots. By that time only the very drunk could hold a conversation with him or would want to anyway, and nobody had ever stayed the pace long enough to find out what the next stage would be like.

Lettie was standing at the bar waiting to be served. Norman came back from the kitchen and hurried over to the Colonel with his sandwich. He reversed back behind the bar looking flustered.

"The usual for you girls, Lettie, is it? Sorry to keep you waiting. Doreen and Dot are both upstairs. I ask you, both of them!"

Lettie was opening her tiny black purse. She had kept

it ever since the war, when it had been given to her by a
Canadian she had met in Suffolk whilst entertaining at an
air base. Every time she touched it, she thought of him. It
was such a shiny black and he had had such wonderful black
hair. Everywhere.

"That's quite all right, Norman," she said sweetly, "but
weren't you supposed to be going over to France today?"

"I was," he said irritably, as he poured their port and
brandies. "I was going, but I had to change my plans. Her
mother decided to turn up unannounced last night. Just
turned up out of the blue she did. And of course she had to
have one of her turns as soon as she arrived. There's the two
of 'em up there now, pandering to her every whim. Oh, and
as if that's not enough, the cat's not well again." He put the
drinks down in front of her.

Lettie tut-tutted. "Oh, you poor boy. Oh well, never mind.
Worse things happen at sea, as they say."

"You can say that again, there's one of them sitting over
there." He was looking at José, who had finished his pint and
was watching her expectantly.

Lettie and her sister were very reliable. "Oh, would you
take for another pint for José, please? The poor chap looks
as though he could do with another one!" She counted the
exact money into Norman's palm and took the two port and
brandies over to the table. "I've left a pint in for you José,"
she told him and he gave her a ghastly grin of appreciation as
he got up and calculated his course to the bar. "Did you hear
that, Hettie?" she asked her sister. "Doreen's mother is here
again and the cat's not well."

Hettie sipped daintily from her glass. "I'm not surprised,"
she said.

10

It had been a toss-up between having the smoked haddock or the kippers and the kippers had won. As Duncan left the Beach Green Guest House he was wishing they hadn't. Despite several extra cups of tea to help them down he was still making noises like a sea lion with a pain in its arse an hour later. He was strolling after breakfast towards the red brick police station to call in for a chat, being off duty, sick with a bad back. It was a recurring ailment which made necessary the wearing of a bony corset, much to the amusement of his fellow officers whose cracks like, 'who are we modelling liberty bodices for today then?' or 'my girdle's killing me!' were wearing a little thin.

Young Morris was alone in the station, half asleep at the desk with only the solid clonking of the clock and a magazine devoted to the breeding of Japanese carp for company, all other hands having gone off excitedly in answer to the call for assistance at the farmhouse. He looked up with a start as Duncan released another massive kipper flavoured belch from the depths.

"All on your own, then?"

Young Morris explained the situation, then went off to make a pot of tea while Duncan hung around to see what transpired when the others returned. Due to the pain that went with sitting down, and even more so with getting up again, he stood in the porch with the warm sun on his face, watching a gang of roofers working above the florist's shop across the road. There was a sky blue painted scaffold on the front of the building with one of O'Looney's name boards displayed on it. One of the men carried a stack of roof tiles up the ladder from the pavement and over the pitch of the roof. The tiles looked heavy on his shoulder and his red T-shirt was soaked in sweat. Duncan thought of his bad back and grimaced.

"Tea up." Young Morris's call came with the tinkle of mugs and teaspoons as he put the tray down on the high countertop.

Duncan could see the truck of many colours leading the procession of police vehicles over the level crossing by the railway station. "You'd better fetch some more mugs," he said, "the Sheriff's back in town with the posse."

The barrier on the crossing came down behind them and the convoy stopped outside the police station, much to the interest of the roofing gang. As O'Looney struggled out from the truck's driver's seat, one of them even switched off their transistor radio in the hope that they might get an inkling of what he had been involved in or maybe even nicked for. There was even the possibility of his coming across with some wages, but he didn't even give them a glance as he went round to the passenger's side and opened the door. Small groups of aged shoppers and the occupants of the queue of cars waiting at the closed crossing watched as Sergeant Chopin was helped from the cab of the truck, his face contorted by pain. Duncan thought he might give them a hand, but then thought of his back and decided to administer the mugs of tea instead They were considerably lighter, after all, and he was supposed to be off duty sick.

Hughie stepped down from the back of the truck, which, relieved of his weight, rose appreciably on its springs, drawing gasps from the growing audience. He helped O'Looney get the Sarge up the steps to a gentle applause from some of the elderly pedestrians and loud cheering from the roofers. The train rattled over the crossing and the barrier lifted. The traffic started to flow again and the radio blared from the florist's roof as the shoppers began to disperse, chewing over the possible implications.

Once inside, the men stood around with mugs of tea having a chat, the others feeling something like youngsters at a children's party in the presence of Hugh the Tree, and that included Duncan who was the tallest copper there.

After a while Young Morris took down some particulars and the Sarge asked Hughie if he wouldn't mind being locked up for a while. Hughie said he wouldn't mind at all, so Young Morris signed him in as it were and showed him the way to his little cell, which looked a great deal smaller when he was in it.

O'Looney offered to take the Sarge to the hospital to get his ribs patched up. He said he was going there anyway to see how Danny was getting on, so the Sarge arranged for one of the police cars to be sent for him later.

As they went off in the truck Duncan stood on the steps in the sun, watching the roofing gang at work. He had always got a great deal of satisfaction out of witnessing the toil of others. The mug of hot tea had stirred up another pocket of wind from the breakfast kippers. He was well known locally for his feats of eructation, but just then he was wishing that the Guest House wouldn't serve him with breakfast so late in the morning. He felt the sudden upward trajectory from below his diaphragm and emitted an enormous fishy belch, just as an elderly lady who was wrapped in woolly winter clothing in the hot sun and lugging a tartan coloured shopping basket on wheels passed by on the pavement. Badly startled, she staggered to one side as if hit by an icy arctic blast, tottering in the road with the basket on one wheel before managing to right it and continuing on her way.

A brewery lorry, gaily festooned with coloured flags and bunting crossed the railway with a hollow clanking of empty metal beer barrels. Duncan smacked his lips in anticipation. He would have a couple of pints in the old Oyster Smack to qualify for the weekly after-hours session.

A glance at the church clock confirmed that there was plenty of time in hand but he avoided having to pass the open doors of the Wherry Inn by cutting through the churchyard, first reading for about the hundredth time the carving over the old lych-gate: 'All that are in the graves shall hear the voice of the son of God and shall come forth.'

Old tombs and headstones coloured with moss and lichen lay in the sun or under the trees, those in the shade having splotches of white donated by the cooing doves and wood pigeons. There were a few wooden benches around the low flint wall. One of them was occupied by two old ladies who were being watched by a sepulchral skull peering over crossed bones from beside the main church doors. One of the women was reading what looked like a modern romance novel, her frail knobby hands holding the shaking book three inches from her jam jar spectacles, while her friend tossed beak sized pieces of bread to a landlocked crippled gull that limped around her bandaged legs. On another bench a group of young French students, summer visitors dressed in bright blues and yellows, gabbled away at each other with much hand waving. There was more scaffolding here too, erected around a corner of the building where a pair of workmen, dusty like millers and watched over by the church's gargoyles, were renovating some of the twelfth century stonework.

Duncan's Peeler's eyes were, as ever, peeled. He spotted a familiar figure on the bench by the far gate. One Albert

Hoskins, of no fixed abode. Albert was lying happily supine on the bench, watching the men at work on the scaffold. There was a half consumed quart cider bottle under the bench and leaning against the wall was the sack barrow that he trundled daily in all weathers around the town in search of 'anything that might be going'. He was feeling exceptionally pleased with himself after that particular morning's work, having been given a good quality blue blazer and a pair of grey flannel trousers which he now wore. The recently bereaved lady donor lived in a big old house in Old Farm Lane, an unmade road, littered with stones which made it hard going even in dry weather with the barrow's small metal wheels. It was good to know that his labour had not been in vain and he would be calling on the widow again before long. Added to that, the roofing gang across the road from the nick had given him some lead flashings which he had exchanged for cash at Mr O'Looney's scrap yard. There was a nice twist to that, he thought. Now there was enough in his pocket to buy his daily meal and a surplus that would cover a second bottle of cider. All was well with his world. Then he spied the approaching civvies-clad Duncan. The policeman's bearing told Albert that he must be ensconced in the spiny corset and was most probably on his way to the pub. He reached expertly under the bench from the blind side and pulled the bottle out of sight.

"Hallo Albert." Duncan stopped and leaned on the gate post. "You're Clerk of the Works today then, are you?"

"Oh hallo guv'nor," Albert said as if surprised to see him there. "I'm just making sure they get it right, y'know. We don't want our dear old church fucked up, now do we? Not after all these years, eh?"

Duncan belted out another kipper flavoured blast. "Quite right, Albert." More kippers. "I'm glad to see you taking such an interest."

"Oh, you know me, guv, I could watch people working all day I could." From force of habit he lifted an arm to wipe his nose on his sleeve, but then checked himself and took a surprisingly clean handkerchief from his breast pocket and blew a long trumpet bleat into it.

Duncan caught a strong whiff of cider. "That's a nice blazer, Albert. A nice pair of trousers, too."

Albert sprung instantly into self-defence. "I got these given to me by that woman in Old Farm Lane, you can ask her," he said quickly. "You know, the one whose husband fell off his perch a while back. Jewish couple, they were. Well he was. She still is, I s'pose. 'Ere," he waved the handkerchief under Duncan's nose, "this was in one of the pockets, guv. It's a viper. A Jewish 'andkerchief, see? A viper?" A big grin split his red and blue veined face, showing irregular xanthic teeth and releasing another sour gush of fermenting apples. Duncan's chuckle almost turned to choking.

A very thin, humped backed old man with rolled up shirt sleeves went past, apparently being towed by an incredibly noisy and smoky petrol driven lawnmower. "Just look at him will yer," Albert stifled a yawn, "nearly ninety 'e is, old Dick. Bloody marvellous really, innit? Every day he's at it. Them daisies hardly have a chance to pop their little 'eads up before the silly old bugger comes along and chops 'em off. I don't know where 'e finds the energy, guv. Honest I don't!"

Duncan's thirst was nearing its zenith. "Yes. Well, I'd better be getting along, you know how it is."

"Can't stand still for too long, eh?" Albert sympathized. "The old trouble's playing you up again, is it?"

Duncan put his hands on his hips and gingerly straightened by holding his shoulders back. "Yeah, the old back again," he grimaced, "a right bastard it is!"

"Blimey, I know all about that don't I, guv, I've been on
me stick for weeks at a time, haven't I? All that heavy lifting I
had to do when I was younger, see? And when you tell people
about it they think you're having them on. They got no idea
what the pain's like. Them shooting pains down the legs is
worst, and the doctors can't do nothing for you, can they?"

"No, and they can't prove there's nothing wrong with you
either," Duncan thought. Especially if you can act a bit. He
had very fond memories of the weeks he had spent at home
the previous summer when the Olympics had been on the
telly. And getting paid for it too. "I'll be seeing you around
then, Albert," he said. "It helps if I keep on the move. You
know what I mean."

Albert lay back again, wriggling his shoulders on the
bench to get comfortable as Duncan moved off. "Yes, see you,
guv." He reached for the bottle under the bench and took a
swig from it. "I know what you mean all right," he muttered,
"you'll keep on the move as far as the boozer!"

Leaving the shade by the gate, Duncan walked towards the
High Street in bright sunlight with the chrome and paintwork
gleaming on the cars parked along the narrow side street.

There were no front gardens to the cottages along there
and it was possible to look into their dark little front rooms
from the pavement. At the corner he made a mental note to
call into the newly opened health food shop there when he
was back on duty. Such a lovely looking girl in there behind
the counter. Perhaps the uniform might impress. As he
turned right into the High Street he saw a tall, gaunt figure
wearing a flat cap and green anorak on the other side of the
road, hovering impatiently by the push-button control of the
pedestrian crossing. Duncan knew Eric's movements well. He
would have left the Lady Caroline less than ten minutes ago
and come across the footbridge over the river on his way to

the Oyster Smack, being as regular at the Friday afternoon sessions as the policeman himself. Duncan cracked a wry smile and continued on his way towards the pub.

Although he knew very well where Eric had come from and where he was going, Duncan could not have even imagined the torment he was going through as he hopped from one foot to the other, waiting for those damn lights to change at the crossing. All that morning he had been suffering from sudden searing hot bowel movements, necessitating numerous galloping visits to the outside toilet at the small beach road bungalow where he lived alone. It was a condition not unfamiliar to him, being brought on by his diet, which consisted of very little food and a great deal of draught bitter beer. After his sixth trot down the back garden, he had felt so empty that he had been confident of being able to venture more than a few yards from home, and remembering the old Boy Scouts motto he had put a half used toilet roll in a pocket of his anorak and made his way with some apprehension to the safety of the Lady Caroline.

It was the only pub on that side of the river. There were a few more old midday regulars there in the riverside bar, sitting at tables that gave them a good view of the river from the big bay window. Eric declined to sit with them, preferring to position himself on the leather bench seat on the other side of the room which gave him a clear run to the Gents. In typically masochistic fashion, he breakfasted on a cheese and very strong onion sandwich and three pints of bitter, after which he spent ten minutes sitting in the white tiled closet. During that time nothing passed but an enormous amount of wind and a desperate customer hammered on the door, only to be told in no uncertain terms to go away and use the Ladies' if necessary.

The welcome absence of anything other than wind gave

Eric the confidence to make for the Oyster Smack across the river. He went back into the bar and finished off his pint, then at the door he paused for a moment before leaving.

He considered whether or not he should play it safe and go back once more to the Gents, but lulled into the tippler's false sense of security, he decided against it and zipping up the front of his anorak he said his goodbyes and left.

Halfway across the footbridge it struck. The burning arrow of pain shot through his insides and at the same time the familiar cold sweat broke out all over his body. He grasped the iron side of the bridge and bent double, shaking and cold under the hot sun as tears came to his eyes.

Oh God, why me? He looked back to where he had come from.

The Lady C with its nice, safe little shit house. Oh why did you leave you fool, oh why, oh why? I'll bet there's nobody using it now either! It's just sitting there vacant and I'm here in such need of it! And look at all those boats on the river … I'd bet half those bastard boats have got bogs on them and there's not one fucker in use either!

It looked a very long way across the bridge, and anyway the one-time haven of the public toilets at the far end now stood closed and padlocked, with its windows boarded up by the local council. The inconsiderate bastards! He thought of going back – he might just make it to the Lady Caroline without mishap. But no, if he sat there in safety he would miss the afternoon session on the other side. The Lady C would close at two thirty and then it would be too late. Damn and blast it! These bloody decisions! Why me? Why me? Oh shit, he thought aptly. Then wished he hadn't. He released his grip on the iron rail and began to walk on, trying to straighten up without easing the pressure that was necessary to keep the cheeks of his backside firmly pressed together. He knew he must try to keep his mind on something else and focused his attention on the church clock beyond the far end of the bridge. A young woman was coming across the bridge from the direction of the town towards him. She was pushing a baby carrier. He must try to carry on as if all was well – if she thought something was wrong she might stop to help and that could be disastrous.

He could risk no further delay. The young woman was walking briskly, happily, her gurgling youngster safely strapped into the little red and white hammock on wheels. As she passed she smiled sweetly at Eric who forced a horrific grin, with the tears streaming down his face as he soldiered on, trying to concentrate on something, anything to ease his suffering and take his mind off the shiny white plastic seat and the relief that awaited him. There were liberal amounts of dogs' droppings on the decking of the bridge, some of it flattened and bearing the tread marks of bicycle tyres. Those bloody animals can do it where they like with impunity, Eric thought. Even that bloody seagull that just flew under the bridge. Think of something else. Any bloody thing else!

He was in agony. He cursed the brewers and the fortunes they made from their lousy bitter beer. He cursed the local councillors in their snug offices with their en-suite toilets who thought it fun to close down public conveniences. He cursed himself for not going while he was safe in the Lady C and for having the foresight to bring a toilet roll out with him, but not having the sense to be where he could use the thing.

At least the way was clear now. He clawed his way along the iron rail to the end. Not far now. A hundred yards along on the other side of the High Street, the colourful facade of the pub shone like a beacon next to the grey stone of the town's museum. It was beckoning to him, but at the pedestrian crossing the traffic light was green and it was busy with streams of traffic going in both directions.

Those bastard lights, there was no chance of getting across! Look at those smug bastards, comfortably seated in their cars, heedless of his desperate plight! The little figure on the pedestrians' light was red. Eric pressed the button, but it stayed on red, silently mocking him. You would, you little red bastard! As he pressed the button again he saw Duncan on the other side, heading for the pub. The lucky sod! Suddenly the lights changed and he heard the beep-beep-beep of the crossing signal.

"Oh thank you, God! Thank you, thank you!" He sobbed as he crossed the road, aware of amused drivers watching his unusual gait. When in the Navy, he had been proud of being known as 'Lofty'. Then he had walked erect and long striding, but now he was shuffling along with his hands in the pockets of his anorak, cupped around his hard swollen belly. He reached the pavement on the other side. Not far now but the pavement was busy with people going in and out of the shops and some standing in everyone else's path, gawping at window displays or chatting. In his agony, Eric had to filter through between them; the unfeeling stupid sods always moved the wrong way as he tried to pass. It was as if everyone in that High Street had come there at that very time to hinder his progress. Looking like an overdressed marathon runner nearing collapse, he staggered past the butcher's shop where a misspelt sign in the window announced that they had British Pork Lion Chops for sale. He suppressed an absurd laugh as he gathered speed in his desperation. He had one hand still clutching his stomach and the other outstretched to grasp the handle if the pub door was closed. It was open.

"Oh thank you, thank you." As he raised a foot in anticipation of the step, Pam the flower seller emerged from the gloomy interior, blocking the narrow entrance to the bar with her basket. 'She must have been sent! Oh, she must have been! Some dirty bastard down there doesn't like me!'

Pam was a round, pink, healthy looking woman who could be annoyingly cheerful sometimes. "Hallo Eric, love." She waved a colourful fragrant nosegay under his chin.

"Not now, Pam, not now…" he gasped, pushing past her and almost falling headlong into the bar. He heard a few cheerful greetings called but did not acknowledge them. There it was, before him. There. Through the smoke he could see the door leading to the toilets and an end to his torment, but as he made for the final hurdle, in a seemingly deliberate move to thwart him even now, Duncan turned from where he had been talking at the bar and cut in front of him, heading for the Gents.

"'For pity's sake, not now…" The cry caught in Eric's throat as he reached for the closing door. He pushed it open and then the next one. What met his eyes must surely have been sent as a final joke. The trough of the urinal was blocked and overflowing, so Duncan was standing in the crapper compartment with the door open, whistling in a carefree fashion as he pissed into the pan.

Eric's face was a frozen mask of horrified disbelief. To find this, after enduring so much and so far! He grabbed hold of the washbasin with both hands, his whole frame shaking with the effort of preventing the evacuation of his bowels. With a great effort he spoke like a ventriloquist through gritted teeth. "Please … could …you … hurry… Duncan … please …?"

"In a hurry then, are we?" Duncan asked cheerily. He shook his tool, then tucked it in and zipped up. "Never mind, your turn next, old chap!" He came out and slapped Eric on the back, almost the final straw.

"At last!" Eric dashed into the cubicle, dropped his strides and sank onto the plastic seat, completely disregarding the crack in it that could pinch the tender flesh of an inside thigh like a pair of steel pincers. There was a great bang followed by a whoosh of wind and then a rush of scalding hot liquid. He smiled and leaned back against the downpipe from the cistern giving thanks with great heaving sighs of relief. He noticed a crude sketch on the ceiling that he hadn't seen before. When he closed his eyes all he could hear was the faint hum of the extractor fan and the sadistic Norman shouting 'last orders'. Eric looked at his watch. There was plenty of time, it was just one of Norman's false alarms. He thought he would rest there for a while.

11

A t eight o'clock that morning Kowloon Moon was lying in bed awake after a few hours of fitful sleep in the small flat above The Moon Garden Restaurant. He had woken in a cold sweat, as he usually did after his recurring nightmare of being chased around Hove dog track by half a dozen greyhounds, each with the face of a bookmaker that he owed money to.

The Moon Garden was situated in the High Street, opposite the museum and next to a betting shop which was one of a large chain to which he fortunately had never owed a penny. Kowloon Moon owned the restaurant and a smaller one in a village some ten miles inland. Mrs Moon occupied the flat above The Little Moon Garden. In an effort to curb his insatiable desire for gambling, they had moved away from London at her nagging insistence and severed all ties with his betting cronies in Soho's Chinatown. The problem though, had not been solved. If anything, the situation had worsened and his wife had given up the struggle. Now they led almost entirely separate lives. She had the tiny flat and the income from the smaller restaurant and he stayed on at The Moon Garden cultivating an ever-growing army of hostile creditors.

One night after much drinking in celebration of a very successful afternoon at Brighton races, he had the idea of having the two restaurants completely re-decorated. He had a vision of the interiors painted in black and white Panda patterns, with new bamboo screens and huge pot plants like the bears' staple diet with luxurious fronds and green shooting sprouts and things, with discreet lighting controlled by dimmer switches.

The very next day, true to the gambler's philosophy that there's no time like the present, he instructed O'Looney to have his decorators begin the work as soon as possible.

Returning to the races that afternoon and then going on to the greyhound stadium in the evening, he dutifully returned all the previous day's winnings along with a generous bonus. But, as he had reasoned so many times before, there would be other winning days, like tomorrow for one, and the work on the two Moon Gardens must go ahead regardless.

By what he considered to be a stroke of luck, he was actually owed some money by O'Looney himself, it being the balance of the sum agreed upon when he had sold his Mercedes to the Irishman to fund a trip to the casino with Eddie the tailor. This served as a deposit and work had started on the larger restaurant a week ago. Apart from the nagging little question of how he was going to pay at the end of it, Kowloon was very pleased with the progress being made in recreating his drunken vision of loveliness.

A few minutes after eight he stirred at the hollow sound of a van's doors slamming shut in the street below. It was the decorators arriving. He lay there for a while watching the lampshade moving slightly in the draught from the half open window. The sound of the morning traffic was increasing and occasionally there was the heavy rumble of one of the big lorries coming loaded with timber from the harbour. His tongue was curled and had a taste like a rollmop, and he felt cold although he was sweating under the single sheet. It was a familiar feeling, as was the morning-after sourness in his stomach that he always had after drinking spirits. 'Fuck the spirits,' he thought, 'I'd feel better now if I'd stuck to beer.'

The light air from the window made him shiver. He wanted to close the window, but knew that as soon as he got up from the bed he would be sick and he hated the strain that came with the retching.

He lay there for perhaps another five minutes, knowing that sooner or later he was going to have to make a move, and dreading it. He swung his skinny legs out and rose slowly, standing naked and pot-bellied by the window. The decorators' van was parked below the window and on the pavement next to it, Pam was waiting for a gap in the traffic, rocking her battered old pram full of flowers back and forth, ready for the quick dash across to her pitch outside the pub. Luckily the windowsill was at the height of his navel, so if anyone did happen to look up he couldn't be accused of overexposure.

He turned and padded back towards the bathroom, dreading what he knew was certain to happen there. The bathroom was tiled a cool pale green and the floor was cold under his feet after the carpet of the bedroom. He grasped the sides of the green washbasin, hunched his shoulders and waited. It didn't take long. As he studied his even more yellow than usual physique in the pitted mirror he felt the sourness stirring and shooting up from the depths. His liver felt as if it were being wrung out like an old floor-cloth as he retched, eyes bulging, bringing up surprisingly small amounts of brilliant yellow bile. He stopped heaving and inspected his eyes in the mirror. They were like two poached eggs swimming in blood. The strain had been intense and he was shaking uncontrollably. He made his way shakily back to the bed, feeling as if he had been given a good kicking around the kidneys. After another half hour on the bed with eyes closed and breathing deeply, he felt stronger. He got up and washed and shaved in the bathroom and gargled with a very strong mouthwash. Then he dressed and went downstairs, grabbing a handful of notes and coins from the dressing table and stuffing them into a trouser pocket.

Downstairs in the kitchen the decorators were having their customary mugs of tea and fried egg and bacon rolls before starting work, all prepared for them by the cook.

Mick Tong was a cheerful old Chinaman with grey crew cut hair and a blue and white striped apron. He was chopping meat on the table with a huge cleaver and mixing the pieces by hand in a bowl of sauce.

The previous evening the place had been visited by an Elvis Presley look-alike impressionist, who had been appearing on stage somewhere along the coast and had called in for a meal with his band and his agent. While they were eating, some of the other customers remarked on his likeness to the dead super star and he produced a tape of his which one of the waiters played for them. Despite lengthy explanations, once they had heard the tape, Mick Tong and the waiters were convinced that the man was really Elvis. They simply refused to believe otherwise. In the end, when they left he let them keep the tape, which was now playing again whilst the cook tried excitedly to explain what had taken place. The decorators had been sitting around the table for half an hour, unable to make head nor tail of anything he was ranting on about. 'Painting's not a trade, it's a disease.' Someone in the building trade once coined the phrase and The Plunger was typical of that breed. The Plunger was O'Looney's foreman painter. A small dapper man with greased back hair and pencil moustache, a Capstan Full Strength cigarette almost always between his thin lips, he would arrive at his place of work (always driven by someone else) wearing a suit and tie and highly polished black shoes. During working hours he retained the tie but changed the suit and shoes for immaculately starched and pressed white overalls and spotless white plimsolls. Before leaving in the evening there was a half hour ritual of washing in his own bowl with hot water, carefully grooming the hair using his own mirror, and changing back into the suit and shoes. While the others waited in the van there would be a quick check of the fingernails and the knot of the tie, a quick wipe of the shiny black toecaps with the handkerchief, and he would be ready for the off. Haughty and aloof, he was no common or garden building worker; HE was a painter and decorator!

When Kowloon entered the kitchen, The Plunger was sitting with the others but at the head of the table, holding a lighted cigarette with one hand and a half-eaten bacon roll with the other. The Presley impersonator was singing 'Old Shep' and the cook had stopped chopping meat to listen. He was leaning against the worktop with tears welling up in his eyes, giving the others a more than welcome respite from his unintelligible jabberings.

"Morning, Mister Moon." The Plunger spoke with a mouth full of soggy bread and bacon.

"Morning." Kowloon went straight to the huge fridge and extricated a green Heineken from the frosty jumble of wine and beer bottles and flicked the top off with an opener that hung by a string from the wall. The bottle was so cold it stuck to his hand. He took a long swig from it with his head back; the foaming liquid seemed to be burning its way through the phlegm in his throat.

"Gawd blimey, I don't know how you can do that this early in the day!" The Plunger was watching open mouthed, showing the mash of food on his tongue.

With one supportive hand on the table, Moon took another long draught from the icy bottle with his eyes shut – he was appreciating the liquid's cleansing properties as it fizzed its way through his plumbing system like spirits of salts. After a few seconds, during which time it seemed that there might be a reversal of the procedure, he emitted a huge beery belch. He felt like a new man. He knew he would be all right now. A good belch without throwing up meant that he would be all right.

The prospect of the day ahead, which had seemed so loathsome as he lay on his bed upstairs, now brightened considerably. After all, the pubs would open at ten and he would be able to sit in the atmosphere that he loved so much whilst he studied the racing form and had a drink or two. Then in the afternoon there was a trip to the course to be looked forward to. Where was it today? Oh yes, Lingfield Park. Not very far away; he would be back to supervise things in the restaurant in the evening, and there was sure to be a party on somewhere later. There always was on Fridays. Yes, things certainly looked much better now. He felt so good that he was sure he could fart without any risk of a follow through. Bang! He lifted his right foot and shook it as if he thought the warm gas would defy all the laws and pass down the tunnel of his trouser leg and disperse from the bottom. He downed the last mouthful of beer and grinned broadly from one pair of white overalls to another.

"Yes, indeed. As you say, Mr Plunger, a very good morning! Mick Tong, turn that bloody awful tape off, would you? And make the gentlemen some more tea and rolls if they want some. I'm just going out for a paper."

The cook watched his boss go through the restaurant and out to the High Street. "Him bloody mad as arsehole, you know. Bloody mad," he tut-tutted. "Alla time crazy. 'E got bloody good business here and make bloody good money. 'E got pots to piss in and go pour it all down bloody drain hole. Alla time he bet and drink, bet and drink. No bloody wonder Missus Moon get right bloody arsehole and go live in

little Moon Garden all bloody time and never come out. Not
never. No bloody how," he tapped his forehead with a soy-
stained finger. "I let bloody awful tape finish before I turn off.
Bloody too right!" He went back to chopping the meat with
a renewed vigour.

The Plunger was studying the tea leaves in the bottom
of his mug. He had spent some time in Malaya in his army
days and regarded himself as an authority on anything and
everything pertaining to the East, and everything else, come
to that. "Well of course," he said, "yer Chink is known for it,
isn't he? Drinkin' and gamblin'. They love a drink they do.
Most of 'em anyway. I was out there, wasn't I? But they're
like your Red Indian see, they have to drink theirselves into a
bleedin' stupor. They can't just have a couple like you and me
do. But the gambling's the worst. They can't help theirselves,
the poor little sods. They've just got to 'ave a bet, see? It's like
a sickness with 'em, it is. A mania like. 'Ere, knock us up a few
more bacon rolls would yer, Mick Tong? Bleedin' 'andsome,
they are!"

Across the road in The Jewel Newsagents, Kowloon
purchased his daily copy of The Sporting Life from the
proprietor. Reg had as usual been up since the early hours,
preparing and addressing the stacks of newspapers that went
out for delivery on the bicycles of the youngsters in his employ.
There had been the usual run of hiccups and tantrums that
morning and he wanted to get away from it all upstairs and
have his breakfast while his wife took over in the shop. His
shiny bald pate was compensated for at the back by flowing
shoulder length white hair and facially by a huge walrus
moustache stained yellow by nicotine. He could manage no
more than a grunt from under it as he handed Moon his
change with print soiled fingers.

Moon stepped out from the shop onto the pavement. The

High Street was becoming busier and there was a blend of
various aftershaves and perfumes coming from the commuters
passing on their way to the railway station. He waited at the
pedestrian crossing for the signal. Two figures were waiting to
cross from the other side. One was the immaculately dressed,
effeminate Peter of the Tea Rooms and Picture Gallery, and
the other was the slightly hunched, world weary shape of Eddie
the Tailor. As the lights changed and the signal bleeped, Peter
quickly linked his arm through Eddie's and pranced across the
road, dragging along the startled tailor who had been on the
point of falling asleep as they waited at the kerb. In the middle
of the High Street he halted abruptly on seeing Kowloon,
causing something of a pile up of hurrying commuters. "Good
morning," the Chinaman said as he fought his way past them
through the irate jostling pack.

"Good morning," Peter trilled loud enough for all to hear.
"We've just got up!"

12

It was true in fact, that Peter, resplendent in blue and white in what he called his 'sailor boy number', had not been out of bed very long. He was on his way, a little earlier than was usual, to open his Tea Rooms and Picture Gallery which nestled snugly next to the old Toll House on the riverbank alongside the road bridge. He had spent a very fretful night, lying there alone on the big brass bed in his spotless little flat above the Off Licence. The cause of his sleepless night of worry and sudden bursts of temper, which involved a great deal of stomping around the flat with much clenching and unclenching of his soft white hands and not a little bad language, was Ted. Ted was a rather battered looking heavyweight wrestler whom Peter thought of as cuddly rather than bulky. They had been having a somewhat on-off relationship for more than a year since meeting in the bar at a grappling show in Hove, where Ted had supposedly been rendered unconscious by Mad Mick from Mitcham.

For some time Peter had been sure that Ted was seeing someone else and last night had spent about two hours getting himself ready before driving along the coast to Brighton, where the two of them had arranged to meet in the bar at the end of the Palace Pier. He intended to make the evening an 'it's me or him' occasion and took even more time and care over his preparation than he would normally have done.

After a long soak in a hot bubble bath and the use of

variously scented lotions, he sat for half an hour to cool down
in the bedroom, in the sweet air that drifted in via the open
sliding door from the flower boxes on the flat roof outside.
He had already decided to wear the outfit that he and Ted
had chosen together in Nice the previous summer. They had
driven with the roof down through wonderful country from
their rented Provence cottage to the coast, stopping at almost
every other bend for photographs against the fantastic views
of the Mediterranean. Then after a couple of drinks they
wandered away from the busiest parts of the town and found
that little boutique where they had chosen clothes for one
another.

Dressed in those memories Peter had driven the same
sky blue convertible along the coast road into Brighton. He
parked and hurried across to the pier with a certain amount
of nervous excitement. His application of the scented oils had
been far too generous, but he was so preoccupied with going
over what he had planned to say to Ted that he failed to
notice the odd looks he was attracting from the men who were
fishing from the rails along the pier, nor did he hear any of
their comments, one of which was "Cor, get a load of that,
will yer? Smells like a bombed chemist's!".

He left them chortling in his perfumed wake and pushed
open the patterned glass door of the bar. The room was about
half full, with cheerful holidaymakers and there was a small
knot of men who had obviously been fishing earlier, leaning
against the bar with their tackle bags and dismantled rods.
As Peter wafted in on the breeze they moved along, forming
an even tighter group and leaving a bar stool free. He sat on
the stool and ordered a gin and tonic from the spotty young
barman, who gave him a sickly yellow smile to go with it.

An hour later he was still waiting, during which time the
anglers left and the place became more and more crowded,

with people who were on holiday or day-trippers who were getting tanked up before catching the train home. Finally, after much impatient tapping of his polished fingernails on the bar top, he downed the remains of his third drink and left. As he stomped along on the boardwalk of the pier with the town all cream and gold in the last of the sunlight, he felt the tears welling up inside but he held them back until he reached the car. Then he sat there with white knuckles tightened round the leather covered steering wheel and had a good cry. After a few minutes he took some tissues from a box in the glove compartment, checked his eyes in the mirror and then drove very fast back home. He took the top road where he could really keep his foot on the floor, and even with the roof down he didn't think of Nice once.

And so, as the sun climbed after that sleepless night and with the sound of a gull crying from its perch on a nearby chimney pot, he pulled the cord which drew back the long curtains of the bedroom on the new day.

He had decided during the fretful night that he must forget about Ted and make a new start. Find someone else. Someone would come along. He pushed back the sliding door and stepped out onto the cool surface of the flat roof. The air was warm and sweet with the scent of the Stocks and Pinks in the flower boxes, and between the rooftops and chimney stacks he could see the shining mud of the low river which itself was sparkling in the sunlight. It was a good day to be starting over. He went back inside and switched on the radio by the bed. It's an eerie feeling, the one you get when you switch on and they are already playing the song that's in your head. The girl's voice sang "I Gonna wash that man right outta my hair..."

Peter slipped out of his dressing gown and stepped into the shower. He proposed to do precisely that.

13

When Peter left the flat and came across the semi-conscious figure waiting at the crossing, Eddie the Tailor had not seen his bed for more than twenty-four hours. He had just got off the coastway train and was on his way to open his shop after having been up all night playing at the casino in Brighton.

To begin with things had gone well at the tables and at around eleven he had sat down to a steak dinner. After that though, it had been a slippery descent until breakfast. He sipped the coffee that he had laced with brandy and sat for a while to contemplate his next move. With a nonchalant expression that belied his inner dread, he felt the trouser pocket where he kept his cash. He could feel the screwed up ball of paper that was his last ten pound note burning like a roast chestnut, but he fought off the temptation and let it grow cold. He finished the coffee and crossed the plush red carpet to the Gents for a wash and brush up before leaving.

The gentlemen's washroom was a lavishly furnished facility with expensive tiling and highly polished brass and copper fittings. There was subdued background music of classical guitar and it seemed incredibly hot after the air conditioning of the casino. Feeling a sudden movement, Eddie thought he would make use of the seating arrangements and chose the centre one of the three cubicles on his right. As he locked the door he heard someone else enter and hurried footsteps crossed the marble floor and entered the cubicle on his left. He unzipped and let his trousers and underpants fall. As he sat down and was pleasantly reminded that the seats were heated, he heard the same ritual taking place next door.

He relieved himself gently, remembering his doctor's advice against straining and giving silent thanks that there had been no need to. Despondently he reached down and fumbled for the pocket of the trousers around his ankles. He withdrew the pitifully small screwed up ball of paper and peeled it open. To his delighted surprise there was a badly torn fiver inside the little parcel. Fifteen quid, then. Well, that's an improvement on ten. He shrugged his shoulders and stuffed the money back in the pocket.

Never again, he thought. Then he thought, how many times have you said that before? Just like a hangover. 'Never again' until the next time. He shrugged again and reached up and pulled some paper from the dispenser on the wall beside him. "Shit," he said aloud as he felt the gloss of the paper between his fingertips. "That just about puts the top on it!"

"The top on what?" a deep voice asked from the next cubicle.

Eddie crushed the square of paper in the palm of his hand to soften it. "They used to have that lovely soft absorbent paper in here," he said. "Look what I've got here now; that shiny medicated stuff that slides half way up your back if you're not careful. It can cut like a razor too!"

"I know, it can be awful, can't it?" The voice softened as it sympathized. "They just don't seem to give a shit anymore, do they?"

"Well, I just have and now all I've got to mop up with is this poxy stuff!"

"Not to worry," the voice said. "I've got some nice soft tissue paper here. I always carry my own emergency supply.

Here, I'll push some through to you."

There was a gap of about three inches under the partitions. Eddie watched as a very large hand appeared, pushing a wad of carefully folded pink toilet tissue towards his left shoe.

"There," the voice said softly. "I hope that's more comfy for you." And the hand disappeared.

"Thanks very much." Eddie picked up the soft wad. He heard the owner of the voice rise from his seat and hoist his trousers, then the sound of a zip followed by a murmuring of flowing water as the expensive cistern flushed. The bolt slid back and the cubicle's door opened and closed, then the footsteps crossed the marble again and there was the sound of running water from one of the sunken hand basins. They had old fashioned brass taps and a choice of fragrant soaps.

Eddie dropped the crumpled piece of shiny paper between his legs into the toilet bowl and unfolded the soft. As it opened and hung in a strip, a white card fell from it into the crotch of his dark blue underpants. With the pink strip of tissue dangling from his right hand, he picked up the card with his left. Its message was written in ball-point capitals.

MAKE DATE FOR LUNCH?

I AM WAITING

R. S. V. P.

Can this really be happening, Eddie thought incredulously. First a right poxy day in the shop, then a disastrous night at the tables, and now this! This is like some diabolical dream, this is! Sat here on the bog, reading an invitation to lunch with a bum bandit I've never seen, who's just made me a present of some scented kazi paper! And the sod's still out there. Waiting!

Eddie was a worried man. That bastard must have been watching him in the casino and then followed him in here. He was annoyed that he should even be considered for a 'date' of that sort. He had been unhappily married to Rachel for twenty-five years and had a wonderful son and daughter. His sexual habits were perfectly normal. Well, there had been one or two deviations in his school days, but surely that was quite normal, wasn't it?

He could still hear the running water. As he could see it, there were only two courses open to him. Either sit it out until the bent bastard tires of waiting, or just walk out and ignore him. Better be prepared to give him a smack though, if he tries anything.

With a shudder he dropped the pink paper between his legs into the pan and reverted to the crisp shiny stuff. He hoisted up his trousers, making doubly sure that he zipped up the fly, then gently pressed the brass handle on the cistern to flush it. The cistern seemed to take an age to fill. When it stopped he realized that he could no longer hear the water running from the taps either. The background music had now changed. They were playing the theme from The Deerhunter. Eddie liked that one and under normal circumstances he would have taken the time to hear it through, but he had to know. Was that bastard still out there? He concentrated but could hear nothing but the music. It was becoming even hotter in the small cubicle and he felt trickles of sweat start in his hair and run down his face and the back of his neck. Why don't you just walk out, you silly sod? He asked himself. All right then, I will. Better just have a look round first.

By squeezing his somewhat stout figure down on all fours in the confined space, he could see under the partitions to his right and left and there were no shoes there, but the gap under the door was only about half an inch and it was impossible to see if anyone was standing by the washbasins. He decided to stand on the seat and take a peep over the door. He thought of the German tank periscope that he had seen in the Graywacke museum; that would have been useful just now.

With one foot on the seat, he grasped the tops of the partitions and stretched to look over the door. Bloody hell, he's a big bastard! The smartly dressed figure had his back to him, inspecting his fingernails after washing. Bollocks! Eddie swore inaudibly and let himself down to the floor again. He thought of the broad sloping shoulders under the expensive jacket. A very nice suit, that. I wonder who made it. He looks like he could handle himself as well, he must pump a bit of iron with shoulders like that. A very nice suit though, very nice indeed …

Eddie's professional interest was running away with him and taking his mind off the immediate problem. He gave himself a severe reprimand and strict marching orders. Some appropriate hackneyed sayings sprung to mind, like 'a man's gotta do what a man's gotta do' and 'take the bull by the horns' and last but not least, that old favourite 'faint heart never fucked a pig'.

I never ate one either, Eddie thought. At least, not that I know of anyway.

As he reached for the brass bolt on the door he heard a metallic clunk and then the whirring of the hand drier that he knew to be by the washbasins. He waited, still gripping the bolt until the drier finally cut out and he could hear only the music again. A few seconds and then he heard the hard tap of heels on the marble again, followed by a clamour from the casino kitchens as his big admirer opened the door leading back to the dining area. He listened as the door closed slowly on its spring with a succession of loud clicks.

"Thank fuck for that!" Eddie drew back the bolt and peered round the door. Yes, all was clear. He went over to the washbasins and washed his hands with the scented soap and splashed cold water on his face. The wall above the basins was mirrored. He leaned forward and studied his face in it. Jesus, what a mug! He supposed a Physiognomist might look upon it as interesting. Fifty years had taken their toll and a bit more besides. The face was bloated and resembled a peach, in that it was yellow with red and mauve blotches. The big brown eyes were bulbous and flecked below bushy grey brows, the nose was too broad and the lips too fat. Stiff grey hairs bristled from the nostrils and out of his ears and there was increasing flaccidity below the blue jowls.

Other than that you look a picture of health, he thought.

But that's enough of that. What are you doing this for anyway? You never worried much about the old boat race before now. Just a minute, you're not turning into one of them too, are you? No, of course not. Makes you wonder though, doesn't it? Why that geezer fancied you, I mean. So maybe he didn't have his glasses with him, who cares!

He thought briefly of the money he had lost the night before. Worse still, he thought of how much he had been up before he started losing. Then he told himself to forget it. It's only the old, old story and you've heard it more times than most. That wonderful world is still outside there, and you've still got the shop and your living. So your loss is someone else's gain. Good luck to them, the rotten lucky bastards!

He ran his comb through his crinkly grey hair and went boldly out through the reception area, giving the girl at the desk a big winner's smile as he charged at the revolving doors.

Outside in the street the morning was a dazzling blue and gold after spending so long in the casino, wherein it was perpetual night and the lights were kept on at all times. Eddie took a few deep breaths of the sea air and joined the growing crowd on its way up the hill to the station. He was reminded of how the different days of the week have atmospheres of their own. For these worker ants there were dreadful 'Monday Morning Feelings' and 'Thank God It's Friday' and unless there was some special evening event to look forward to, the three days in between were of no consequence whatsoever. This Friday morning they each carried their own little air of relief along with them. Some of them were even talking to each other.

He turned right into the top end of Trafalgar Street to look down on an area that held fond memories for him; memories that his wife would never know about. Then he went left through the arch in the wall and up the steps to the station. After an argument with the man behind the glass over the torn five pound note, which so inflamed the commuters queueing behind him that he might have been guilty of inciting a riot, he finally got his ticket and boarded the waiting coastway train. The journey was enlivened considerably by an angler who struggled onto the crowded train at one of the intermediate stops with a rod bag and a large tackle box slung from his shoulder, forcing the indignant standing regulars to press even tighter together. He then alighted at the next stop, putting a rip across both knees of the tights being worn by a seated secretary bird.

By the time he got off the train Eddie had cheered up considerably. After all, there were a few customers due in today to pick up finished articles and maybe even pay for them. Mr O'Looney for one, was due that morning to pick up that bottle green velvet jacket. If he took enough money before two fifteen he would be able to close the shop and spend the afternoon in the 'Smack'; maybe even get a couple of hours' sleep there in a corner. There was bound to be a party somewhere later in the evening, there usually was. Come to think of it, didn't Mr O'Looney mention it when he was in for his final fitting?

After passing the police station he took a circuitous route to avoid going through the churchyard. This was due neither to a fear of the dead nor out of respect for them but to the fact that his last use of the shortcut had resulted in his being waylaid by Albert Hoskins, whose pathetic tale of woe had lightened his pocket to the tune of a five pound note. Considering his own present financial position, Eddie could hardly risk walking into another one of Albert's ambuscades. The town was quiet after the bustling Brighton, and he enjoyed the walk through the narrow side streets in the sunshine but suddenly realized how very tired he was when he reached the crossing in the High Street. As he waited there he felt the strange swimming feeling of sleep overcoming him and almost keeled over; it was only the locking of Peter's arm around his own that prevented him from toppling over into the road. When the traffic stopped he was dragged forward and as they crossed he saw Kowloon Moon amongst the group of pedestrians coming towards them. Through a muzzy haze he heard Peter exchange greetings with the little Chinaman and then all at once they were on the other side and standing on the pavement outside his own shop.

"Well, here we are then, Eddie," Peter said. "If you don't mind my saying so, you don't look too wonderful, old love. Positively wan, in fact. You look as if you've been up all night. I won't ask who though, eh?" He laughed like a young girl who'd been told a dirty joke that she only half understood.

Eddie was fumbling with his key in the lock. "I have been up all night," he growled. "And now I wish I hadn't. I was in the casino."

"Oooh, horror of horrors!" Peter raised his hands. "Say no more, love, I'll leave you to it. P'raps I'll see you in the pub later?"

He was gone. Eddie shoved the door open. Yeah, see you

later. It should have been you instead of me in that toilet, he said to himself. It might have been the start of something big for you. Maybe the love of your life.

He went to the back of the shop and hung his jacket over a patina framed print of Ned Painter on the wall. He sat down at the work table with the sewing machines where there was a big window giving plenty of light and he could see across the river to the houseboats. A fishing boat with red fluorescent buoys with black flags on canes hanging out over the bow was making its way down river against the incoming tide. The flags flapped ahead of the boat like St Vincent's guiding ravens. Eddie could see its registration number in big white figures on the blue hull, but he was struggling to keep his eyes open and he couldn't read it properly. He could hear the drone of its diesel engine but it seemed strangely remote. It was very warm in the shop and bright dust particles hung in the shafts of sunlight from the window. From the open door the sounds from the increasing traffic and the people passing outside became a steady hum. As the drowsiness crept over him he rested his forearms on the table and his head bowed and lifted, then bowed again.

"All right, I know I'm late again." The newspapers made a thud as the delivery boy tossed them from the doorway onto the linoleum covered floor, but the tailor was already far away and didn't stir. The boy went in and picked up the papers and put them on the table next to the sleeping man. Of all the people on his round the boy liked Eddie best because he always joked with him and they were on first name terms which made the boy feel grown up. Eddie usually gave him a few coins on a Friday so he waited for a minute, but there was no indication that he would waken. The boy was already going to be late for school so he hurried out and picked up his bike from the pavement. As he came out there was a stout matronly figure in tweeds passing and his bag swung and thumped her leg as he picked up the bike. "I say, watch where you're going, young man!" she barked. "And weren't you taught to close doors after you, for heaven's sake? Born in a barn, were we?"

"I don't know about you," he said as he mounted," but I wasn't. Anyway, Eddie likes it open." Then he rode off, holding aloft the internationally known, fiercely erected middle finger. "Up yours, you old prat."

14

Frank rode the old combination over the road bridge then turned left off the main coast road and followed the road that doubled back along by the beach and then down to the concrete hard near the houseboats. Arthur's chair and easel were standing unattended a little above the high water mark and over by the wall outside the Lady Caroline was the green besmocked figure of the artist, talking with what looked like a holiday family.

Christ, I'll bet he's giving them some bullshit, Frank smiled. The local celebrity and all that guff. A Portrait Of The Artist As A Not So Young Has-Been, that's more like it. Still, they might buy something. Some of them do.

Leaving his crash helmet in the box sidecar with the brushes and paint kettles, Frank strolled unhurriedly across the footbridge towards the town. There was no need to check with his wristwatch, the ever faithful church clock told him that it was still only one forty five. When he came to the end of the bridge he stopped to lean on the rail and look back across the water.

High water had come and gone and the river had begun to run off again on the ebb. On the opposite bank the few houseboats that had been afloat were settling after their brief swim, the older ones nearer the roadbridge were so deeply imbedded in the mud that even the highest tides of the year couldn't move them. Some had been working craft many years before and their crews had found soundings in waters around foreign shores. This was their final port of call. Twice every day the water crept around their hulls, but they would never again respond to its call. After their brief spell of rest at high water, when the river had been a broad calm lagoon with no flow, the moored fishing boats and weekend pleasure craft were tugging ferociously at their ropes again, with the foaming current in their teeth and their mooring buoys looking like boulders in a swollen mountain stream.

Below where he stood there was a green where lunch-timers and holidaymakers were making the most of the hot sun, either stretched out on the riparian grass around the flower beds or on the benches with their backs to the sun-trap wall. Frank walked on along the High Street past another small public hard, where a cursing driver and his helpers were trying to pull a trailered day cruiser out of the mud with a Jap Jeep. Frank enjoyed the gold lettering on a ground floor office window: Tibbs and Pomeroy, Solicitors and Commissioners For Oaths. Mr Lundquist, Dental Surgeon. He wondered if they had commissioned those oaths back there, and might that have been Mr Lundquist performing the extraction?

Taking advantage of a lull in the traffic, he crossed the road. As he neared the pub he had to walk in the road to circuit a small crowd that had gathered around Pam and her perambulator full of flowers, from which she and her son were also vending T-shirts and flip-flops that were appearing as if by magic from beneath the colourful bunches. Her son was evidently a young man of many talents. With his filthy matted hair and beard, and oily leathers and boots, he could be seen on a different immaculate giant motorcycle each week. Gabriel bought and sold, but never owned.

Frank's white overalls caught Pam's eye as he skirted her audience. With professional expertise she brought him into play in her hackneyed rattle: "There you are, ladies and gentlemen! Cor blimey, talk about a coincidence! That gent just going past there—" Frank stopped and looked round— "Yes you, sir. That gentleman bought half a dozen of my T-shirts only last weekend. Isn't that right, sir?"

"Oh yes," Frank fell in with the act, "and very nice they are, too. No complaints at all."

"There you are, ladies and gentlemen. Another satisfied customer. Now come along, who's going to have three for the price of two, eh? My boy Gabe here and me have only got a few left. Come on now, who's going to be the lucky ones?" As his mother exchanged their 'last' remaining items for the ready cash, Gabriel slipped away round the corner of the museum into the side street. In the public car park there he had a van loaded with that which had fallen from the back of a lorry the night before.

You could take in the bar at a glance on entering at night or in dull weather, but the change from bright sun to the softer dark colours inside was like throwing a switch. There was the wonderful smell of roast lamb and there were a few local business people finishing their lunches at the tables. Most of the usual lunchtime characters were still there, the early starters were by now fairly well oiled and there was a good deal of chatter and laughter. Fred and Phil were still on their stools at the bar and the more than welcome American, who had snapped O'Looney earlier, was standing there between them. The colourfully dressed figure was ordering a round whilst being eyed with suspicion by the Colonel.

"And give this man a pint as well," the Yank drawled. The last word trailed off, making him sound like W. C. Fields.

"Oh, ta very much," Frank said, acknowledging the nods from various locals. Norman, who had just come up from the cellar after connecting a fresh barrel of bitter, was already pulling up his pint. The bar top was crowded with replenished glasses and a considerable backlog of empties.

"There we are, sir." Norman put the foaming pint on the bar. "Another pint of the superbous! I'll put it on your bill, shall I?" Apparently it was not the first round that the American had bought today.

"Ah guess so. Boy, am I enjoying this!"

As he lifted the glass to his lips, Norman checked him abruptly. "Just one moment, sir," he said solemnly. "I always sample the first of a new barrel." He sipped from the wine glass that he had filled before pulling Frank's pint. "Perfection, sir. Pure nectar. That's too good for the peasants, I can tell you!"

The American smiled, revelling in this eccentric British behaviour. He raised his glass again and downed half the pint. Then he held it up to what light was afforded by the bottle glass windows and studied its contents. He was closely watched by the others. The Colonel was bristling and ready to throw down the gauntlet if the Yank so much as dared to complain.

"There's nothing wrong, is there, sir?" Norman asked apprehensively.

"Hell no, I'm just savouring this experience. This is one hell of a day for me, coming back to this old place. It's been forty years since the war y'know," he said as if they didn't. The Colonel's hackles rose visibly as the Yank continued. "Yep, it's just the way I remembered it all that time. Except for one little thing. There's one little bitty thing that's bothering me."

"And what would that be, sir?"

"It's the smell. The smell, that's what it is. Smells are things I remember about a place and this one's different."

"Well, perhaps it's the cooking, sir. And then it has been a very long time sir, hasn't it? Since you were last here, I mean."

"Makes no difference," the Yank said assuredly, "you can knock a place around and paint it all you want but the atmosphere smells the same. That's what I mean, the atmosphere. And especially in bars."

Norman looked at Phil and Fred, who had raised their glasses and were sniffing at the beer. They both shook their heads reverently and put the glasses down again. "There you are, sir," Norman gushed with relief. "There's nothing wrong with that, that's good IPA, that is. India Pale Ale."

"Lupulin," Frank put in. "The bitter aromatic principle of the hop." The American looked at him blankly. The Colonel snorted.

"Yeah. Well, I guess you guys must be correct. Like I said, it has been more than forty years. Here, let me get you guys another one!" The visitor finished his drink and pushed the empty glass with a belch across the bar at Norman. "Oh, and have one yourself of course."

"Sanksaverymuch!" José Mackay called from somewhere. His accent was thickening nicely.

Feeling rather indignant at having been left out of the previous round, Lettie picked up her glass and her sister's and left their table to put them down purposefully on the bar. "We'll see you this evening then, Norman," she said sweetly.

"Aw, have one before you go, ladies?" the Yank asked.

The frail looking spinster turned to her sister who was gathering up their shopping bags. "Should we have just one more, Hettie, do you think?"

Hettie looked at her tiny wristwatch and sat down again. "Oh, one for the road, do you mean, Lettie? I think we should, don't you? It's so nice of the gentleman to offer."

Norman began the round again. The Colonel, in an unprecedented move, returned his glass to the bar, ensuring that Norman had seen it before heading unsteadily but exaggeratedly upright towards the toilets.

Frank was relishing the aftertaste of the first pint of the day, and the warm glow it creates inside, no matter how cold. He had been surprised on coming in to see Norman there behind the bar. He should have been somewhere on the other side of La Manche by now. Frank wondered where Doreen was. "Weren't you supposed to be going over to France today, Norman?" he asked innocently.

The publican was hacking another lemon to pieces. "I had to cancel everything, didn't I. Doreen's mother's here again. You know what that means," he jabbed the knife at the ceiling. "Her upstairs most of the time, and yours truly down here running the place on me Jack Jones!"

"Oh, that's charming, that is! Don't I count for anything around here then?" Dot had been dismissed from the kitchen where Doreen's mother had taken over the running of things. The barmaid was very petite and having changed her high heels for a comfortable pair of slippers she was having some difficulty replacing some glass ornaments on a top shelf. "Here, Norman," she pouted, "be a dear and put this up for me, otherwise I shall have to stand on a crate or something."

"That sounds interesting," Frank said.

"That's enough of that," no-sex Norman snapped at him. "Here, give, us it here," he added testily. "You always want me to do something when I'm busy. You can see I'm doing a round of drinks here." He reached up and put the ornament on the shelf. "They used to make a motorbike called the Dot, y'know. I had one. D.O.T. Devoid of Trouble, that's what it stood for. That hardly applies in your case, does it?"

The locals at the bar watched in eager anticipation, as Dot usually gave as good as she got. "And you had one, did you?" she asked her smirking boss.

"I most certainly did." He rose to her fly.

"Well, you're not having this one!" She burst out laughing, as did her delighted supporters.

"Oh, go and wake José up," Norman spluttered. "He's nodded off again." He dropped a chunk of lemon in the Colonel's glass. The old war horse was attempting to make as dignified an exit as possible from the toilet's door. On reaching his table, and after checking his zip in front of the spinsters before sitting down, he noticed that his glass was missing and began casting accusatory glares around the room. He finally fixed the Yank with a wide baleful eye.

Norman knew the look only too well and hurried over with the Colonel's drink. The old man took it with a grunt, muttered something about part-time soldiers, and went back to wondering where Dave Death had got to with his betting slips.

So Doreen's mother's ere again, Frank thought. At least that means she won't be expecting rumpty bumpty this afternoon. Not while Norman's on the premises. I'll bet she's got the right hump! Still, that means I can enjoy a few drinks and then go and have a shower and change this evening. O'Looney said something about throwing a party on his boat tonight. He knows how to throw one all right. Disregard the Bacchanalian amnesia and they were memorable occasions.

The voice from America brought him back to the present. "My pleasure, gentlemen. Oh, and ladies. Cheers!"

More cries of 'cheers' and 'all the best' came from around the room, followed by a belated 'Yessacheersayeah!' from José. The American downed half of his pint in one again. "The name's Weldon, by the way," he said.

Fred and Phil were impressed. Old Weldon might be getting on a bit in years, but he could put it away all right. They had already had to step up a gear from the usual steady pace that they adopted for a prolonged session, but they need not have hurried to keep pace – the volume of liquid consumed forced Weldon to leave the room for a brief interlude.

"Say, I have to use the John. Is it at the rear there?"

Norman nodded towards the back of the room. "It is indeed, sir, just through that door there."

On the way Weldon patted the Colonel on the shoulder in passing, but the gesture went unnoticed. The Colonel was deeply engrossed in the Sporting Life, wrestling in his gin haze with the pros and cons of the favourite in the three o'clock.

As the toilets' door closed, Fred chuckled frothily into his beer. "Ere, that were funny, weren't it? What he said about the smell?"

"And 'e thought it might be your beer an' all!" Phil grinned at Norman.

"What they're on about, Frank," Norman explained as if Frank didn't know, "is that putrid stench the pair of 'em bring in with 'em. You know, that subtle blend of rotten fish and lugworms mixed with creosote and shaken but not stirred."

"Well, I'm a fisherman, aren't I?" Phil said defensively.

"And I've got to paint me fences, haven't I?" Fred rolled more like a fisherman at sea on the stool. The hip flask in the greenhouse had proved a good working foundation for the beer.

Frank took a deep sniff of the pub air. "I'll tell you what, Norman. That's a good drop of stuff, that is. If you could bottle that in liquid form, you could sell it to the Frogs when you go over there on your little excursions. They appreciate a good new aftershave, you could call it 'Public Bar' in French, of course."

"Very droll, Frank. Very droll. I've got far more interesting things to do with my time when I'm over there, thanks very much." Norman thought he was sowing the seed of another rumour to develop.

"Don't leave us in suspense like that, Norm." Phil was slurring and wishing he'd eaten breakfast before he had come in. "Give us a clue, eh?"

"I'm saying nothing more," Norman said mysteriously, "for now, anyway."

The familiar bang of the gents' door heralded Weldon's return. He took his glass from the bar and went over to look at the prints and photographs on the wall. "You sure do have some fine pictures here of the old town," he said over his shoulder.

"Yes, we do indeed, sir. A very old town, ours is y'know."

Norman was hurriedly washing glasses in the old pewter sink under the bar. Weldon peered more closely at one of the prints. "Gee yeah, just look at that now. One of the old oyster smacks being built here. Must be hundreds of years ago, huh?"

Hettie and Lettie sat watching him approvingly, their eyes twinkling with port and brandy induced enthusiasm.

"In the nineteenth century they sent twenty thousand tons of oysters a year from here by train. All over the country they went," Lettie said. "You should have a look round our museum."

"And the old church," her sister added, "lovely old buildings they are. They go back to the eleven hundreds. That's Norman times." Under the influence of alcohol the ladies sounded even more delicately genteel.

"Is that so? Norman times, huh?' Weldon was impressed. All at once he saw the publican behind the bar in a new light. Norman, yes. A descendant of the invading bastard conqueror perhaps? After all, the battle was fought not far away along the coast … When Norman looked up from his glass washing, Weldon had moved back to the bar and was regarding him with a disturbing, scrutinous look in his eyes. The American was standing between Phil and Fred again and when he lifted his glass he sniffed at it with renewed suspicion. Phil started plucking at the front of his dried blood and slime encrusted smock and sniffing it as if the black looks that Norman was giving him and the earlier remarks were all new to him and that the subject of his personal hygiene, or the lack of it, had never been brought up before.

"O'course, you know what the trouble is don't you?" he said to Weldon. "It's them buggers on the council. Decided to close the public bogs by the footbridge, they did. I used to be able to have a lovely strip wash in there!"

"Yes, I know," Fred agreed. "I used to have a good old sluice down in there an'all. Then the sods went and shut them and they've never opened 'em again. I mean, where are you supposed to go for a William Pitt when the pubs are shut, eh?"

"For a what?" Weldon had lost the drift.

"That's a bloody good gents bog, that is," Phil went on.

"Six sit downs and six washbasins. Lovely hot water. There's not many public bogs where you get hot water, is there?" he asked Weldon.

"Isn't there? I really don't ..."

"When I was coming in with the boat I really looked forward to getting in there and stripping off for a wash down. Did I ever tell you about that time when I was in there? Standing there bollock naked I was, working up a bit of a lather with the old Lifebuoy soap like, and this lady schoolteacher came strolling in!"

"You don't say." Weldon's jaw fell open.

"Straight up. Looking for one of the young boys from her party, she was. They were on a day trip from somewhere or other and they'd stopped for their lunch by the river. One of 'em had gone missing and she just walked in. I was sort of up on tip-toe like, washing me wedding tackle in one of the basins."

"You never told me about that before," Fred said. He sounded something like a ventriloquist as he spoke and drank at the same time, wide eyed over the rim of his pot.

"Did she say anything?" Weldon asked excitedly.

"No, she didn't say anything at all, but she had a bloody good look though! She'd taken me by surprise really, and I turned and gave her a full frontal." Phil paused and took a long swallow from his drink; he felt sure his story would be good for another round from the Yank. "I'll never forget the look on her face," he went on, "If you ask me, she took a lot longer over it than was necessary. She even made her exit backwards. Her eyes were sort of fixed on it. Like she'd been hypnotized or something."

"Well, she did go in looking for a little boy," Fred reasoned. "I suppose she did see a bit more than she'd bargained for."

"A bit?" Phil protested. "I had a raging hard-on like a baby's arm holding out a Victoria plum!"

"As a result of all the lathering?" Weldon suggested. "That's right. The lathering. You've got to give the old chap a good clean round the gills, haven't you?"

Norman, like Fred, had heard the story before, but he also added fuel to Weldon's interest. "You're lucky she didn't have you nicked," he said.

"I suppose she couldn't very well, could she? I mean, she'd find it a bit difficult explaining what she was doing in a public gents' toilet with a naked man, and with all that soapy lather about, too!"

Lettie had floated over with empty glasses. "Yes, but did she find the little boy?" she asked seriously.

"Oh yes," Phil said, "she found him next door in the Ladies. He'd followed some of the little girls in there in the hope that he might see something they'd got that he hadn't. You know, the way they do."

"And did he?" Weldon was really hooked. "Did he what?"

"Did he see anything, for Chrissakes!"

"Oh. I don't know. It wasn't very serious, they were only small kiddies, after all."

There was a lull in the conversation accompanied by a general feeling of disappointment. Fred thought he would try and get things going again. "'Ere Phil, going back to when you were starkers in front of that lady teacher ..."

"Yes?"

Fred made a piston-like movement with his clenched fist. "You were really like that, were you? A real popcorn?"

"He means the horn," Frank told Weldon.

Norman was suddenly aware that all other talk in the room had stopped. Even the few remaining lunchers were hanging expectantly on Phil's answer as they toyed with their portions of 'Doreen's Chocolate Strawberry Bombs'. He rummaged in a drawer below the bar for a noisy tape to play as a business-like cover up.

"What on earth do you mean, Fred?" Phil asked as if his lift wasn't reaching the top floor.

Fred was alcoholically oblivious to the fact that they held an audience spellbound. "I mean, did you ..."

Eyebrows were raised and ears were cocked around the room.

Norman frantically switched on the tape and suddenly from the speakers at either end of the bar, at full volume the incredible howl of powerful motorcycles racing past the pits and the maniacal ravings of a commentator crashed around the walls like the blast from a fragmenting hand grenade.

"That's Giacomo Agostini!" Norman shrieked through the din at his shell-shocked customers. "Five hundred Isle of Man

Tee-Tee. That's Mike Hailwood right behind up his gearbox! Or is it Phil Read, I can never remember!"

"Turn it down! Oh for God's sake, turn it down!" Doreen burst in from the kitchen with both hands clamped over her ears. Hettie and Lettie were doing likewise, swaying from side to side on their chairs with their faces horribly contorted. With unintentionally perfect timing, Doreen pushed her husband aside and threw back the volume control.

"… as she backed off, my old chap lowered his head as if he knew. He just hung there in a lazy lob, really," Phil finished disappointedly.

Doreen was looking daggers. Norman pulled the plug from the sink. The gurgle from the disappearing suds seemed unusually loud. "Oh well, that's that lot done," he said cheerily, indicating the washed glasses on the drainer.

Doreen, however, was more concerned about the number of customers who had empty or near empty ones, and the office workers who were supposed to be back by two were drinking up and leaving, ten minutes late and inwardly frightened by their own bravado. In response to her rolling eye signals, Norm clapped his hands and looked from one face to the next along the bar like an eager chick awaiting its feed. "Well gentlemen, any more for any more as they say? The time's getting on, y'know!"

The Colonel and Frank synchronized watches, looking distrustfully at the pub clock. "There's twenty minutes yet," the Colonel observed aloud.

"What the hell is he talking about?" Weldon asked.

"We close at two thirty, sir," Norman told him. "I'll be calling for last orders at twenty past. We'll be open again at six o'clock."

"What? Jesus Christ, and I thought it was bad enough in London! At least they are open until three!"

"That's the way it is, I'm afraid," Frank reflected mournfully. "Mind you, if you hang on for a while you'll find that Friday afternoons can be a bit special."

"How's that?"

"Well..." Frank tapped his nose and winked as the off-duty Duncan entered the bar. "We always have what's known as 'afters' on Fridays, if you know what I mean."

Duncan took up his usual position at the bar. Being a couple of inches over six feet, to avoid having to stoop he had to stand where his head was between two of the low sagging beams.

"I'll get that one, Norman." Weldon pulled out what looked like a toilet roll made up of twenty pound notes. "And do all the others again, would you? I'm going to have just the one more and then I'll have to be getting along."

Norman presented the policeman with a pint of lager in a glass with Duncan's Pint on it in red letters. "There you are, Duncan. When are you going to start drinking real men's beer, eh? That stuff's like virgins' water!"

Duncan ignored the disparagement and emptied the glass with one long swallow, a feat he was well known for. He was also a keen practitioner of the art of 'yard of ale' drinking, which in this particular bar had to be performed in the seated position due to the low ceiling,

"Fill that up again please, Norman." He pushed the glass along and let fire with a belch that threatened to lift all the beer mats from the bar top.

Pam came in from the street with her basket full of T-shirts camouflaged by a few blooms. She saw Duncan at the bar and performed an abrupt U-turn, preventing Eric's entry in his time of desperate need. After a brief tussle in the sunlit doorway he was into the bar and at the far end of the room was the door to his deliverance. With heart in mouth

and hand outstretched, he made for his white-tiled goal, but
a tall figure in the gloom at the bar ducked his head below
the beams and made for the gents in front of him. Fuck you,
Duncan, you inconsiderate bastard! If you're going for a shit, I
hope your balls are festering and they drop off down the pan!
Oh God, let him be going only for a piss, please only a piss!

Heedless in his dreadful anguish of any greetings, Eric
grabbed the handle as the door closed in his face with a
crash like a portcullis. With relief so excruciatingly near he
summoned all for the final effort and staggered through.

"Old Eric looked like he was in a hurry, did you see the
look on his face?" Dot the barmaid was pulling the pints up.
As she put them on the bar Doreen was distributing them, all
the while discreetly making eyes at Frank. When she put his
pint in front of him she touched his hand and pushed her wet
tongue out between her lips, then drew it very slowly in again.

"Where's Arthur got to today then, Frank?" She folded her
arms and leaned forward on the bar, pushing her boobs up
and accentuating the cleavage. She glanced at the clock. "It's
nearly twenty past, he's not usually late on a Friday."

"He was going to do a watercolour this morning." Frank
smiled as she rolled her eyes at him and pulled other familiar
expressions. "He'll be here before half past all right; if he isn't
it'll be the first time ever."

"Last orders!" Norman bawled. "Your last orders, please!"

"You're staying on, aren't you, Frank?" she asked.

"Of course, I wouldn't miss it for the world."

"That's good." She looked round the room. "No sign
of anyone desperate to get out. I'll bring some sandwiches
out later. Sorry about mother being here and everything."
She went through to the kitchen where her mother was busy
washing up the lunchtime plates and cutlery. She had been
hot and aching for Frank for nearly two weeks now since

Norman's last trip to France — why did the old girl have to turn up last night like that? Her mother put the saucepan she was washing on the drainer. It was a novelty one that someone had brought back from Benidorm. Its handle was a round headed penis complete with a pair of rock-hard balls. Doreen squeezed them as hard as she could.

Before going to the Gents, Duncan had been asked by Norman if he would be staying on and with equal formality he had given his unofficial blessing to the traditional extension to drinking time. The barmaid Dot, with her mind more on getting away to the supermarket for her family's weekend shopping, was gathering up the empties and washing them while her boss was preparing yet another gin and tonic for the Colonel. As he took the glass over he paused to speak sideways from the corner of his mouth to Weldon.

"I shall be bolting the door a little after two thirty, sir. If you would like to stay on with the others, that will be quite in order." He tried to sound as conspiratorial as he possibly could, remembering the one about forbidden fruit and eager to keep so fat a fish in the net.

Weldon found the idea of being accepted very flattering. "Gee, I sure would like to, Norman. I really would. I sure as hell am developing a taste for this here IPA. The fact is, though, I arranged to meet my dear wife Ladybird and our two little bitty grand-daughters at two o'clock or thereabouts, so you see I'm already a little overdue."

"I see, sir. The ladies have been doing some shopping I suppose?" "Well, they were going to take a look around the harbour and on the other side of the river there. Mind you, if I know my little Ladybird and those little girls of ours they'll have found something they'd like to take back home with them!"

"If this is your good lady, I'd say they have done." The

dirge-like tone came from Eric, who had drifted back silently from the Gents as if on castors. He felt much better now and held himself erect, crashing his capped head against an oak beam. A sudden cachinnation turned every head to see the besmocked figure of Arthur in the doorway, doffing his beret to usher in a very tanned woman of about sixty. She was dressed casually but very expensively, and she was followed by two gorgeous teenaged girls of the long blonde hair and blue eyes and freckles mould.

"Mrs Weldon J. Largent and her lovely grand-daughters!"

"Well I'll be …, here they are!" Weldon pulled out the roll of notes again. "Ladybird! Ladybird, over here, Honey. What are you going to have to drink, darlin'?"

The Colonel had just dropped off and Weldon's shout brought him to with a start. He was in the habit of taking catnaps during the day, especially during drinking bouts. Despite his great age, his mind raced in top gear at night making sleep impossible. He woke with a gasp and a jerk and started talking to someone who wasn't there. "Do you know, one of my grandsons came to me the other day and asked me to lend him the money to buy a Transit van. Said he wanted to bugger off overland to India with some of his long-haired pals. I told him I could tell him anything he wants to know about India. And Kathmandu and all about that stuff they smoke. Bhang they called it when I was there. And I could tell him about the women. Ah yeah, the women …' He paused for a while as old memories stirred then started again as if pricked with a pin. 'They're not all as prim and proper as they make out, y'know. Not by a long chalk, they're not. I remember one little gal back there, a lovely little thing she was with hair and eyes so dark but shining at night. She used to come to my bungalow in the evenings and be gone with the first cock-crow. She was a schoolmistress too, y'know …" He broke off as Dave Death returned from the betting shop at a trot like one of his old native runners, but minus the cleft stick.

"Well Death, the Colonel demanded. "How am I doing?"

The hearse driver dug in a pocket of his dark suit and handed him a slip of yellow paper. "You've got the first one up in your patent, Colonel. Nine to two. Pissed it, he did!"

Ladybird gave her husband a puzzled look. Weldon wanted to learn more of the Indian schoolmarm. The Colonel fixed him with the look of one who was accustomed to being obeyed. "This man's done well," he said, indicating the lugubrious figure of Death. "Get him a drink, that's an order!"

15

After watching Mick O'Looney drive off that morning Arthur went through the time honoured little ritual that preceded the commencement of his work. Tomorrow the concrete hard would be busy with weekenders, launching boats from trailers and pushing noisy children off in rubber inflatables. Just for now though, it was his own. Below the high water mark the slope was green and slippery as ice. The previous summer, one day when the south west wind had made conditions too rough for swimming from the beach, a party of them had elected to use that part of the river by the footbridge for their boozy frolics. The weedy slope was safe enough for the fishermen with the cleated soles on their rubber boots, but the barefoot baigneurs had floundered like horses without their frost nails. Arthur had scars on his knees to prove it.

He set up his easel above the tide mark and adjusted the legs to suit the slope. From the depths of the old leather bag he took a tin box of paints and his brushes and screw-top jam jars of clean water. These he arranged on the chair beside the easel. Taking a sweeping look at the scene that had so often been the subject of his bread and butter work, he noted with some satisfaction that he was being observed from the footbridge by what was obviously a family holiday group. He selected a long brush and held it in the affected pose of a conductor commanding the attention of his orchestra. Then quickly checking that he was still being watched, with an exaggerated flourish he stooped to dip the brush in a water jar and began work.

As the rising tide swelled the river it became the scene of more and more activity. The water slowly crept over the mud with a yellow froth at its edge, filling and then covering the trails of giant Yeti footprints that were left anonymously in the darkness between tides. Working craft that had been resting were now afloat again and from here and there came the sound of a diesel or an outboard motor starting as men cast off and moved the different coloured boats down against the flow. Down past the timber wharves and the boat builders, past the fish market and the old stone lighthouse, to turn and face the harbour mouth, lifting on the slight swell as they met the open sea.

By one o'clock yet another 'view of the old church' stood completed on the easel. The sun had grown steadily hotter as he worked and the sudatory effect of Arthur's smock was causing him considerable discomfort, but his personal code of discipline forbid the removal of said garment. Image is everything. Well, important anyway. The punters like an artist to look like one. Worse than the prickly heat though was the fact that although a good many people had stopped on the bridge, as they always did on a fine day to take in the view of the copper spired college up the river valley, not one of the bastards had come over to look at his work in progress. Oh, he'd seen them pointing at him and shielding their eyes to look, or nudging their companions to draw their attentions to him, but not one of the buggers had had the decency to come over. Somewhat disgruntled, Arthur fingered the change in his pocket and considered going to the Lady Caroline for a pint. He might be able to drum up some trade there. There was plenty of time before he would pack up his things and go over to the Oyster Smack. He struck a match and lit another Gauloise. As he drew on the cigarette a small scruffy urchin with a yapping dog appeared from the direction of the beach. The boy stopped and screwed up his face as he studied the watercolour, while the dog yapped and chased its tail in circles around them.

"That's good, that is," the lad said. He held his head on one side, as if the picture was the wrong way up.

"Thank you very much." Arthur said. He could smell the boy but he thought it was more like the smell of a decaying old man.

"That's all right. What is it?" "Are you extracting the urine?" "Do what?"

Arthur exaggerated the words. "Are-you-taking-the-piss?" "Nah, I like the picture. Did it yourself, eh?"

"That's right."

"Are you famous then?"

Arthur hesitated; the dog had stopped circling and sat looking up at him as if awaiting his answer. "Er, I am quite well known, yes."

"What's your name then?"

By now there was a good lunchtime crowd outside the Lady C. "Arturo Bennet," Arthur said tetchily.

"What are you, some kind of a wop or something?"

"No, I'm not." Arthur was anxious to get to the pub and find a customer before taking his gear back to the Harbour Lights. 'Would you stay here and watch my things till I come back?" he asked the boy.

"You're going in that pub, aren't you? I knew you'd be going in there." "Oh yes, you can tell the future as well, can you?"

"No, nothing like that. You keep looking over there, that's all." "Very observant. You'll watch the things for me then?"

"Course I will," the boy said as Arthur moved off. "Just one thing, though …"

"And what's that?"

The boy put his head on one side again, so did the dog. "If you're so famous, then I reckon you must be holding a few bob. Put some up front."

"Up front?" Arthur dropped some coins in the outheld palm. "What do you mean, up front?"

"I mean this is only for starters. If I get you a customer, I want some commission."

"Yes, all right. What did you say your name was?"

"I didn't. My mum and dad call me Sid, but my mates call me Snakebite."

"All right then, Snakebite. I shan't be long." Arthur walked towards the Lady Caroline feeling like he was being slowly baked inside the green smock. There was a low pebbled wall around the forecourt and car park and sitting on the wall was a local character that Arthur knew well.

Ernie Rudd, part time fisherman and tourist attraction, had taken up his usual position for a fine summer's day. Dressed in the required tatty seafarer's outfit, he was sitting astride the low wall carrying out useless repairs to a hopelessly ancient fishing net. He was almost never seen in winter and where he went to then was a mystery, but by the time the mackerel returned each year he could always be found when the sun shone, in a spot where he could be sure of a pint or two in return for some wildly concocted tale of adventure on the high seas. That particular year he had turned up on the Sunday morning in early May when the vicar was performing the annual blessing of the nets on the beach. As a result of the night before, Ernie was feeling rather poorly and succeeded in throwing up noisily half way through the proceedings. Still, he was standing in the crowd below the high water mark at the time so it would soon have been washed away afterwards. He could certainly spin a yarn, could old Ernie. Conrad, Robert Louis, Melville, they all would have been proud of him. In fact, he could have wiped the floor with the lot of 'em if he had ever got around to putting pen to paper. Or so he claimed. If.

Most of the wooden benches and tables outside the pub were occupied by office staff who had driven round from the town. With ploughman's lunches and half pints under the Cinzano umbrellas, the men had boldly discarded the jackets of their sober suits and the chattering, giggling typists were exposing as much bare skin as was decently possible to the sun, laying the foundations for long dreamed of Costa hols.

The old sea dog had ignored the regular faces, of course, and had latched onto the holiday family that Arthur's equally mercenary eye had spied on the footbridge earlier. For some inexplicable reason both the parents and their two children were wearing sun hats and T-shirts that proclaimed to the world that they were all in love with Magaluf. Arthur had visited that hell-hole once with Frank when they had been working on the island. They spent a long night there, drinking into the early hours in a bar with video screens and waiters scooting around on roller skates over a floor awash with vomit and urine and broken glass. He thought the place might have been built by some Temperance society to give the bibulous a preview of what awaited them down below. And that had been in January! Just try to imagine what it must be like in summer! An ideal site for an atomic bomb test.

The parents, who were in their thirties, were sitting in the shade of an umbrella by the wall with their legs out in the sun, topping up their golden Balearic sheen. Arthur was not surprised to see they both drank lager. They probably came back from Mallorca wondering why they hadn't met any pearl divers. The children, a dark haired boy of about ten with the furtive look of an arsonist and his pretty little sister, were sucking bottled Coke through straws as they listened wide-eyed to the garrulous Ernie. He looked as if he might cast the ragged, dried weed clogged old net over them as he gesticulated wildly, adding yet more embellishments to one of his time-worn salty tapestries. As Arthur stopped to listen Ernie gave him a knowing wink.

"So there I was," he went on, "with this bloomin' great Nobby Clark, that's a shark to you, half in and half out of the boat. An uglier great brute you never saw in your life, I can tell you. His dirty great teeth were gnashing at my 'ands as I was holding on to the line with all me might and his dirty great big tail was a lashin' at the water, churning it to foam and crashing against the side of me little boat..." He cut the story in mid flight and stretched to take his glass from the table. "Ahoy Arturo!" He raised the glass in greeting and downed the inch or so of bitter that had been warming nicely in the bottom of it, then wiping the back of his hand across his lips, he put the empty vessel down with a thump in front of the parents. "This," he said reverently and waving a scarred brown hand in Arthur's direction, "is Arturo Bennet. One of our more distinguished locals. He's a painter. Arturo, allow me to introduce ..."

"Payne, Payne!" The hypothetical head of the family enthused as he jumped to his feet and pumped Arthur's hand up and down in both his own. "Ron and Yvonne. What about that then, Eve?" He spoke broad Brum. "A real live painter!"

As if they would afford her a better look at him, the wife took a pair of sunglasses from her leather shoulder bag (doubtless also souvenirs from the paraiso concreto) and gave him the once-over. When she turned her face up to look at him the lenses mirrored the sky in a chromic reflection like the windows of some hideous boutique or discotheque. She parted lips that Arthur thought were quite attractive, in a cupid's bow sort of way, to reveal a gap-toothed smile that reminded him of Salisbury Plain's cromlech. "Loveleee, loveleee" – apparently he met with her approval. The smell of pub grub that wafted across to them might have come from Magaluf itself.

Ernie, who had been only too pleased to introduce Arthur as it gave him the chance to draw Ron's attention to his empty glass, could now sense the spotlight deserting him. He picked up the glass and studied it briefly before gazing invitingly into Ron's eyes. Yvonne had also drained the last of her moiety. She shuddered. It had taken on that nauseous flavour peculiar to lager that had been left too long in the sun.

Her husband saw her grimace. "If you're going to be sick could you get it in here?" He proffered his glass and chuckled.

"Don't be so revolting, our Dad!" Yvonne spoke for the children, who didn't think their dad was being revolting at all, but very funny.

"Arturo drinks bitter the same as me," Ernie instructed as Ron went off towards the open bar door. He was holding the glasses with fingers inside, the way a milkman carries empty bottles. He was still chuckling as he went.

The small boy kicked the low wall with a white holiday espadrille and looked Arthur up and down quizzically. "What are you wearing those funny clothes for?"

The painter was aware too, that he was being closely inspected by the invisible eyes behind the chrome lenses. "These are the clothes I wear to do my work," he said self-consciously. "I'm a painter, you see."

"Painters wear white overalls," the boy said irritatingly. "I've seen them before. We had some working at our house, didn't we?" He looked to his sister for support. The little girl nodded knowledgeably without taking her eyes from Arthur's sweaty face as she sucked gurgling Coke up through the straw.

"He's not that sort of painter, silly. He paints pictures. He's an artist." Yvonne's tone of admiration was made deliberately enticing. Arthur was getting hotter and hotter inside the smock and the close scrutiny wasn't helping.

He felt a trickle of sweat run quickly down his back and another one making the slower journey through the hairs of an inside leg. With great relief he saw Ron emerge from the pub. He was carrying the drinks on a tray and as he crossed the forecourt he was fanning over the glasses with his hat.

"Oh, that is nice, Ron," Yvonne exclaimed. "Keeping then cool for us?"

"No I'm not, actually, there's a bloody wasp. Oh shit, just look at that, Eve. The bugger's got in your lager!"

"Yuk!" Yvonne tipped the glass just enough and the wasp shot the falls on a golden cataract. The little girl watched fascinated as the insect struggled for life in the frothy pool on the tarmac. Then her brother stamped his shoe down on it.

"Bottoms up, everyone!" Ernie's gnarled paw hoisted one of the pints of bitter. He gulped down a great draught from it, then wiped off the froth and continued with his story. "Well as I was saying, there we were off Porto Santo, me and this shark. The Portuguese call 'em a Tiburón, by the way. There we was, just me and 'im in the boat. The sun was beating down cruel it was and he was lashing away with his great tail fit to smash a hole in the boards and having a go at me with his great teeth, when suddenly he got hold of me leg! 'Ere, get a look at this…" Arthur looked away and the family looked on, bug-eyed in amazement as the ancient mariner stood up and tugged at the huge buckle on the leather belt that was supporting his salty old threadbare trousers.

Eyes widened yet further as the trousers fell, revealing tanned legs and a startlingly white pair of underpants.

"Just have a butcher's at that!" he shouted enthusiastically as he pointed to a crescent shaped white scar on the inside of a brown thigh, which Arthur knew to be the result of an accident on one of the local timber wharves. "There it is, that's where the blighter sank 'is gnashers in and held on!" He looked around, beaming with pride and waved politely to the lunching office girls. Unable to hear what he had been talking about, they were staring open-mouthed and wondering why he should have suddenly jumped to his feet and dropped his trousers in front of this couple and their small children.

"Bet you've never seen anything like that before, have you, Mum?" He hoisted his strides and the disappointed secretaries got on with their boring routine.

"Er, no, I haven't actually," Yvonne said. She had whipped off her sunglasses in the excitement – if she was going to see what he'd got then she wanted to see it in its true colours! What a let-down. "Thank you so very much for showing us, mister …?"

"Rudd. Capting Ernest Rudd. Us Rudds go back a long way in the town here. If you have a look round the old graveyard you'll see its full of 'em. There's even one who was Capting on the old tea clippers. The inscription on his stone tells how he sailed for some company out of Cape Town. So you could say I'm keeping the old tradition going. If you need anything while you're here, like a boat trip or some bait or something, just ask for me in the pub here or over the other side in the Oyster Smack.

"How long are you here for, anyway?"

"Only the weekend," Ron sighed. "It's back to work on Monday. We've just come back from Spain."

"Oh, really?"

Yvonne thrust her breasts forward, stretching the print on the front of her T-shirt. "Magaluf. That's Majorca." She pronounced the jay as in Marjorie. Arthur winced, but he liked the way her nipples protruded.

"Oh, I know what you mean," Ernie said though none the wiser. "You're on one of those two-centre holidays." For all he knew, Magaluf might have been a ski resort. The farthest the 'Capting' had ever been out of the country was five miles out in the English Channel, and he had only been out that far on one occasion because some dirty pirate had pulled his lobster pots and he had spent fruitless hours searching a wide area for the bastard. He stooped and picked up the net which had fallen to the ground at the same time as his trousers. "I'd better be going over to the Smack now, actually. The time's getting on." He gave Arthur another knowing wink.

"You haven't told us how you got away from the shark yet," the boy complained.

"Yes, stay and have another pint," Ron suggested.

Ernie dropped the net and sat down on the wall with surprising speed. "Well, perhaps just one more then."

"And what about you, Mr Bennet?" The silver chrome shades were back on and those lips were pouting. Arthur was sorely tempted. Well, the painting's finished, he thought. And there will be plenty of time to change into some cooler togs and still make it over to the Smack before the two thirty deadline. The heavy smock was acting like a pressure cooker and he felt as if his blood was nearing boiling point. He could see the mud above the high water line all dried and cracked in the sun. That was how his tongue felt. Must be dehydrating. It's the alcohol. I didn't drink that much last night, it must be the accumulative effect over a lengthy period. With an affirmative nod he quaffed his beer, but the last gulp caught in his throat and almost came back up into the glass as he saw them. There on the concrete hard, three female forms were examining the product of his morning's work and young

Snakebite was signalling to him like a demented tic-tac man. They were the best part of a hundred yards away but Arthur could smell money.

Lots of it. He swallowed the mouthful of bile-tainted liquid. "I'm afraid I'll have to say no," he coughed and spluttered. "Looks like I might have a customer!"

As he adopted an apologetic expression and moved off, the others smiled understandingly, none with more feeling than the Capting, who knew that if Arturo made a sale he would be good for at least a couple of drinks later on.

They watched the artist as he walked quickly away from them and then slowed to a nonchalant strolling pace as he neared the figures standing around the easel.

Drawing nearer, Arthur's eyes confirmed what his long serving nose for wealth had already told him. It must have taken a good deal of money to dress these ladies so casually. The two younger ones might well be twins. Wonderful waist length streaked blonde hair, but nothing artificial, that had been done by expensive sunshine!

They wore tops and shorts that could only have come from a top designer and tans that made Ron and Yvonne's look like diluted milky tea. He could only see their backs so far, but they were gorgeous, right down to the cute little bobbles on their top-drawer tennis shoes. The woman with them was quite a lot older. Expensively and expertly preserved though, perhaps their mother...?

"Good day, ladies, and isn't it a lovely one?" Arthur displayed his eccentric artist pose and parlance, carefully calculated to put the message over and the perfect complement to his attire. In response to Arthur's signalling, which took the form of jerking sideways head movements, young Snakebite backed off to where the painter wanted to keep him during the negotiations. That is, down-wind of these wealthy nostrils.

Arthur was impressed by the boy's quickness of mind. He caught on instantly, that lad.

At the sound of Arthur's voice the three of them turned at once. The woman he had thought might be the mother was older than he had estimated, her dark tan had that mottling taken on by older flesh. She was wearing her glasses for the scrutiny of the watercolour, they were attached to a thick gold chain and as she took them from her nose the sunlight caught in the diamonds on both hands. The specs and the chain hung over a remarkable bust that must have owed its contours to some seriously priced surgery and she noted with satisfaction that it was not going unnoticed. She held out a dazzling hand for him to hold, it hung rather limply under the weight of a gold bracelet that resembled a string of pineapple cubes.

"Well, good day to you!" It was one of those southern states accents and she was eyeing him enthusiastically.

"You must be the creator of this beautiful little picture?"

"I am, madam. I am." Arthur was having difficulty taking his eyes off the twins' front elevations. For twins they certainly were identical. Seventeen or eighteen, he estimated. Each was such a fantastic image of the other and when they smiled, the brilliant white flashes were perfectly synchronized. It was weird. Even their eye movements seemed to be as one, as if they'd been programmed or something. With that wonderful, long streaked hair and those powder blue eyes and the freckles over perfect little noses and cheekbones, they looked as if they should have been advertising something and he supposed they were really. The thing we all lose so quickly. Their all too brief, golden time of youth.

Arthur was saddened, but the girls suddenly opened up with a baffling, double barrelled rapid fire that snapped him out of it. First one would ask a question, but then before he could even think, it was followed by another from her twin.

"You really and truly painted that, sir?" "You must be so talented?"

"It must be so wonderful for you, being able to work in a place like this?"

"It must be like heaven for a painter here?" "You will sell the picture to us?"

"We'd so love to take it home with us?" "You will?"

"Oh, won't you?"

"Oh, won't you?" "Please?"

They were becoming more and more excited. Arthur got a mental picture of them as cheerleaders at an American football game. Their chestily bouncing T-shirts advertised a brand of popcorn. Popcorn. He tried not to think about the rhyming slang and got another technicolour vision of the pair of them. They were naked on silken sheets with their knees drawn up, sucking their thumbs out of boredom. There was a space waiting to be occupied between them.

"Now girls," the bejewelled doll-like elder stemmed the bombardment, giving Arthur's hand a gentle squeeze before letting go. "Do allow the poor man to get a word in edgeways, for heaven's sakes! Sir, you must think us so awfully lacking in manners, please allow me to introduce us all? I am Mrs Weldon J. Largent and these two little beauties are my darlin' grand- daughters Marylou Belle and Emmie May? We're Virginia Largents?" She looked into Arthur's face as if for some sign of recognition. Nothing doing. "We're old tobacco?"

Still not an inkling. "Well anyhow, we left Weldon over there to explore some of your wonderful little old pubs while we came over here to look around? We were told this is something of an artist's colony? So here we are, and when we saw your easel from the bridge we just couldn't believe our luck, right, girls? I mean, meeting an English painter at work like this?"

"It surely is an honour to meet you, sir. "Marylou said seriously and held out a hand.

"It surely is." So did Emmie May.

Stone me, that's the first thing they've said that didn't sound like a question, Arthur thought. He had always found that peculiarly American habit most irksome. He had noticed too, that more and more often he was hearing youngsters in the town doing it, putting question marks on the ends of what should be straightforward statements of fact. The respite was short lived, however. As he gently held each exquisite hand, the gorgeous twins let go another volley.

"You didn't sign the painting yet?" "Not yet you didn't?"

"Honeys, the poor man hasn't yet had the chance to do so much as introduce himself with you all chattering and so inquisitive?" Gran'ma was at it too.

"Oh, I'm sorry!" Arthur let slip the cool hands with regret, having fallen for the twins hook, line and sinker. "It's Bennet, Arturo Bennet. Two enns and one tee?" he mimicked.

"Why yes, of course!" Ladybird had never heard of him but she wasn't easily pooped. "Arturo Bennet, girls!" She made it sound as if they had been discussing his work just the other day.

"Oh yes, Arturo," Marylou said very slowly.

"Arturo," Emmie May echoed. Arthur felt excited yet uneasy at the same time. There was something unnerving about the way the expressions on the girls' lovely faces changed simultaneously and how he got the feeling that they even had the same thoughts at once. The way they were looking at him now made him feel as though he were standing there stark naked.

Ladybird had donned her spectacles again. "You simply must sell me this painting, Mr Bennet." She turned her eyes from the picture to look him over again. "I can just see it now, hanging in my study back home?"

Arthur's present financial circumstances meant that he couldn't have cared less if she hung it in a mountain shack. The good old pounds sterling figures rang up in his head and spun like a fruit machine. He could hear the thump-thump as it paid out. He doffed his beret and held it to his chest while he shook hands all round again.

"Please," he simpered. "Please call me Arturo."

"Of course, Arturo. You will sell it to me now, won't you?"

"Won't you?" Marylou Belle.

"Won't you?" Emmie May.

Arthur was half expecting a third echo from the grinning Snakebite, but the lad carried on with rolling a match-thin cigarette. With an exaggerated flourish for the benefit of the mercenary Ernie, who had wandered over and was watching with the affected air of one who just happened to be passing, he took a black felt tip from his breast pocket and put his Arturo Bennet on the picture.

"That's perfect. Just perfect!" Ladybird enthused.

"Perfect. Perfect!" the twins accorded.

"Now Arturo." Her tone told Ernie's experienced ear that her question of price was coming up. He shuffled closer to listen. She did not disappoint him. "How much shall I pay you for this lovely example of your talented work?"

The soggy brown remnant of a cigarette fell from Ernie's lips as he gaped in shocked disbelief. She was telling Arthur of all people to name his own price! By her tone he knew that she wanted the little watercolour very badly and he knew Arthur's ability to make the most of such a heaven sent opportunity. Ernie had once been present when one disgruntled punter had returned and demanded to be told why the same river scene that he had purchased from Arturo was only half the price in Peter's Picture Gallery. "Simply because yours was signed with the artist present" was Arturo's explanation, and incredulously the man had gone away without any further objection. Such was Arthur's power of salesmanship, but this time Ernie was not to be privy to any deal. Seeing the clock face of the painting's church tower jogged Arthur's memory and Norman's warning rang in his ears, as it would in various others at about that time in different parts of the town. "Those not here for last orders are not here for afters!"

It was two o'clock. Arthur entertained the notion of getting the twins and their Gran over to the Oyster Smack. He would have to abandon the idea of going back to the houseboat to change as time was of the essence. Might it not be possible, he wondered, that they might be game for the inevitable party later, too? It must be tried for. Nothing is beyond the realms of possibility!

"We could talk about the painting over a nice cool drink, couldn't we?" he suggested diplomatically. "It's really getting very hot and I do have a rather pressing meeting in the pub on the other side of the bridge?" He mimicked the American non-question again, basking in the adulatory vibes he felt coming from the girls. He contemplated the sign of Gemini. Those astrologers were right about one thing anyway. The twins were heavenly bodies.

"You mean that gorgeous looking little pub over there?" Ladybird pointed with a gemmy finger. "Why, we'd just love to, wouldn't we, girls?"

"We surely would?"

"It looks real quaint?"

Arthur took the watercolour, still on its board, from the easel. "Perhaps I could show you some more a little later?" he offered as he handed it to Ladybird. Her eyes sparkled and she flushed with happiness. "And now, shall we, ladies?"" He linked arms with Marylou Belle on one and Emmie May on the other. As they made for the bridge their grandmother followed them, admiring her new picture. She was somewhat surprised to find the libidinous Ernie falling into step beside her. She immediately got the impression that it wasn't the painting that he'd like to get his hands on. He looks very fit for his age, she thought. She reckoned he would be about five or six years younger than she was. She found herself growing quite excited – he put her in mind of worn driftwood, scarred by his life spent wrestling with the sea. She felt the touch of his hand on her wrist above the chunky bracelet. It felt horny and rough, just what she'd been wanting for a long time.

"Are you ladies off to the pub with Arturo, then? Perhaps you would do me the honour of allowing me to accompany you. Ernest Rudd's the name. Capting."

"Am I to take it then, that you are a friend of Mr Bennet's?"

She was all a-flutter inside. This salty, weather-worn master of the foaming billows had none of the feigned foppishness of the crowd of jerks that she was usually surrounded by, even his tarry odour was beginning to appeal. She cast a sidewise glance at him and thought he looked as if he had been stained and varnished to last for ever. Preserved like Nelson in his cask of brandy, camphor and myrrh.

"A friend, dear lady? Why bless you, me and Arturo has been mates these past good many years," Ernie gushed in what he thought was a suitably piratical sounding spiel that would appeal to the type who had read a bit. The look of pure delight on her face confirmed the accuracy of this one small facet of his professional chicanery.

Ladybird clasped the painting to her re-built bosom and sighed: "What a day we are having, Captain Rudd. What a day indeed! If you could only know what this all means to me, not only being fortunate enough to be present here in this beautiful quaint old town, but being here at just the right time? The right time to meet a local artist at work and I'm such a devotee? And then to meet such a man as yourself? A blue water seafaring Captain of the school which, to do you justice, I can only describe as square-rigged!."

"Dear lady." Ernie had both hands on her arm now. "That's the nicest thing anyone's said to me in … I don't know how long!"

They gazed into each other's eyes, still walking on slowly, and both tripped headlong over the step up on to the bridge. A step had been put at either end of the footbridge, in place of the original slopes that had enabled cyclists to leave it at break-neck speeds, causing on occasion considerable damage both to themselves and to pedestrians. The careless couple hadn't far to fall. They came down on their knees, then toppled forward to land quite gently on the piceous surface of the boards.

Snakebite came running, with the dog yapping at his heels. "I saw that," he shouted. "I saw everything. You wanna sue the council, missus!"

Ladybird got to her feet and examined her rings and bracelet. "Shoot, I must have left a tidy smear of gold on that floor there? Still, no matter."

Ernie was still writhing on the deck, clutching a shin as if he'd been felled with a pickaxe handle. He was making a noise like a small child trying on its potty. Ladybird helped him up by supporting an elbow while he gripped the railing with the other hand. He rolled up his trouser leg and inspected the shin. There wasn't a mark on it but at least he had been careful enough to examine the right one.

"There's not much wrong with that either," Ladybird assessed quickly. "A waste of time suing anybody, believe me." She shot a quick look of such malevolence at the boy that he snatched up a stone and threw it at the river as if he had been simply idling there and had seen nothing whatsoever.

Some forty yards on, Arthur was by now well into his own form of sabaism and looking forward to possibly furthering explorations. He turned the twins to see what was delaying the others. Ladybird and her limping sea Captain were on the move again and the watercolour, which was thankfully unsullied and untorn, was back in place; held to her silicone hills and valley.

"Come on, Ernest," Arthur called. "Look at the time."

"Hey, what about your bag of paints and your chair and that other thing?" Snakebite shouted as he pointed to the easel.

"Take them to the houseboat, would you? I'll see you there this evening. I'll square up with you then, okay?"

"Is he all right?" the lad asked Ernie suspiciously.

"All right? Why bless you, young 'un, right as rain he is, Arturo!" Ernie sounded even more like Robert Newton in Treasure Island. Ladybird loved it.

"He'd better be," the boy said. "He owes me a few bob. 'Ere, what's his boat called anyway, the duffer didn't say!"

"Harbour Lights." The Capting wanted to gain speed without making his anxiety obvious to the lady. With his pockets empty it was imperative that he was hard on Arthur's heels as they entered the pub. That way he would be included in the first round, giving him time to tap either the painter or some other unfortunate. He railed at her as he coaxed her into a controlled canter. "Let's catch up with those lovely girls of yours," he urged.

By the half way mark, where the bridge was fitted with a section that could be rolled back to allow the through passage of taller masted vessels, they had gained some ground on the others and at the end of the bridge they closed behind them. Arthur pressed the button when they got to the pedestrian crossing.

"What a nice name you chose for your boat, Arturo," Ladybird said as they waited.

"Do you think so? Oh, I'm so glad."

"Yes, Harbour Lights. It sounds sort of safe and welcoming, don't you think? You must have been so very pleased to see many of them in your time, Captain Rudd?"

"Eh? Oh yes," Ernie said. "Hundreds and hundreds."

16

The stream ran quickly and shallow from the chalk of the Downs, then slowed and deepened on its way across the salt marsh flats to join the river above the town. Mick O'Looney owned the stables and riding school that were situated about a mile back from the river on a bend in the stream, where it ran between banks of sedge and bulrushes. There was a field with a paddock and soundly built stables of concrete blocks with a tiled roof and beside the building stood a red and white old caravan which served as an office. Duggie looked after the place for Mr O, as well as being his driver, and crew, cook and butler aboard the builder's luxurious floating home.

The little Australian had once been a promising flyweight boxer and jockey back home, but shortly after coming to the UK a bad fall and a trampling at the old Hurst Park track had put a stop to all that and now both he and the racecourse were has-beens. He had been with O'Looney for ten years, and now that Mrs O was out of the way 'across the water' and unlikely to return, his boss had moved him from his bedsit into a smart cabin aboard the sumptuously fitted 'Pachydermatous'.

Duggie was sunning himself that afternoon in a deck chair in front of the caravan. He was minus his shirt and his boots and socks, with his trousers rolled up to the knees as he had earlier been paddling in the stream. He had been sitting there for about half an hour, almost motionless with his right hand down by his side. His eyes were fixed on the flat area before some blackthorn bushes on the opposite bank. It was not uncommon on a quiet afternoon to see a rabbit or two emerge from the bushes to bask on the short grassy bank and Duggie's powerful .22 air rifle was lying ready on the ground beneath his hand. He saw a slight movement and a change of colour where a bush camouflaged the entrance to one of the burrows. His eyes widened, then hardened and narrowed as a pair of rabbits showed and looked around cautiously before hopping out from under the overhanging shrub into the open sunlight. Duggie's hand closed around the gun. His hands were unusually large for a small man and he hooked his index finger around the trigger guard, as he lifted the weapon slowly to the support of his left hand across his knees. The bigger of the two rabbits moved further out into the open, then stopped and sat up on its haunches in a worn dusty patch in the grass. It was no more than forty yards away across the narrow bend of the stream.

"Run rabbit, run rabbit, run-run-run …" Duggie sang softly to himself as he slowly raised the gun. "Don't give the farmer his fun-fun-fun." He held the butt into his shoulder. "He'll get by; without his rabbit pie …" The creature's head looked as big as a football through the telescopic sights. "So run rabbit, run rabbit, run-run-run …" As he centred the cross-hairs on the marbled damson eye, he could see every little marking of the fur around it; even the eye's nervous twitch. He squeezed the trigger and felt the hard thud as the released air pressure jolted the end of the telescope against his eyebrow and he saw the animal start at the sound in the terrible instant before the pellet struck. Duggie lowered the rifle and got to his feet. The rabbit had rolled and was lying close to the entrance of the burrow that it had so recently left and into which its companion had bolted. He would pick it up later before leaving. He didn't need to go over to know that the shot had gone clear through the head.

His orders had been to close the stables considerably earlier than was usual in summer and to get back to the barge to prepare the buffet for the party that O'Looney had planned for that evening. Summer evenings were always popular with riders, but he had been told to take no bookings for later than three o'clock and now he had only to wait for the return of one regular client.

He returned the spent air rifle to the caravan and then released the stout line that had been tied to the deckchair. The line ran across the grass and then down into the stream where there was a deeper hole under a tree stump on the opposite bank. He hauled on the line as he walked to the water's edge and lifted the eel trap. The trap had been there on the bottom since he had swung it across into the deeper water the previous evening. Two large dark eels had been lured by the bait of rotten meat. He took a rope handled canvas bucket and filled it with water from the stream. As he unfastened the end of the trap and tipped the eels into the bucket, he heard the metallic screech of the gate. That would be the last rider coming in from the lane.

Liz had been gone for an hour on the dappled grey.

She had ridden off at three o'clock down the narrow lane with its bushes along either side all powdered white with dust like talcum, then followed the wider stony unmade road to its junction with the main coast road. It was about two miles from there along the coast to the pier, but it was possible to avoid the traffic by using the concrete path that ran along behind the beach huts for much of the way. When they reached the last hut she turned the horse and they went down the gentle slope of beach onto the sand. The horse was the one she always rode and he knew the routine as well as she did. He carried her, walking on as far as the pier and then they were under it and out of the sun. It was so very cool under there between the great iron legs of the pier.

They stopped and the air felt cool and damp like in an empty country church with the rain hammering down outside. Liz's eyesight had improved considerably since her visit to the optician. He had found that she had put both contact lenses in the same eye and they had enjoyed a good laugh together over that one.

She looked up and she could hear the footsteps of people passing overhead on the boards of the pier and the light of the gaps between the boards flickered as they passed. They moved on and she let the horse take her another hundred yards beyond the pier. Then they turned, with the horse knowing it was the start of the long gallop back and stretching out as they gathered speed. Liz sensed the people watching them from the pier and then she felt the rush of cold as they splashed through one of the shallow pools in the shade with children running across on the boards to the other side to see them burst into the sunlight again. There was a broad expanse of exposed sand here although as yet the tide was only half way out. It was a sensation like no other as she half stood, half crouched, with her hair flowing and the warm air resistance on her face, with the horse taking a strong hold as he rejoiced in his own feeling of speed and power. On their left the beach and the white and gold of the buildings passed quickly in a bright shimmer and on the right they passed shrimpers and paddlers in the shallow sea and bait diggers and shoeless strollers on the sand, who turned their heads at the passing rush of muscle and the rhythm of hooves.

Soon she could distinguish the white painted name on the red roof of the Dolphin Beach Cafe and the dark brown of the heavy clinker built fishing boats on the beach. The beach

area near the cafe was busy with holiday people and locals
and the horse and rider caused some excitement as they came
up over the ridge of shingle and passed the fishermen's boxes,
where shoppers were queueing with carrier bags for plaice
and mackerel fresh in off the boats. The sun-warmed smell
of varnish and tar and petrol from the boats mixed on the
light air with the waft of chips and hamburgers and onions
as Liz rode on at walking pace again on the path, leaving the
café and the noise from its adjoining amusements' machines
behind.

The squat white building that was the dinghy sailors' club-
house was ahead about a quarter of a mile. When they got
there she halted the horse. There was a wide bright view of
the coast in the sun on either side. To her left she could see
the tall white chimneys of the power station in the east. The
shimmering coast beyond that was lost in the haze. To her
right and way beyond the Dolphin, over the rooftops of the
beach huts she could see as far as the pier from which they had
come. It looked frail and tiny now, like a match-stick model.

This part of the beach was only busy at weekends and the
club's dinghies and competition racers were all locked safely
away in the compound. There were a few windsurfers, though,
on the shallow water. Liz sat and watched their tacking moves
for a while. They looked like hurrying worker ants carrying
brightly coloured segments of leaves. At the side of the sailing
club there was a stony road that ran back to the main coast
road. There were a dozen bungalows on one side which had
once been the site of wooden fishermen's shacks and a caravan
park on the other. At the end of the road there was a push-
button crossing to halt the traffic on the main thoroughfare
where Liz crossed on the horse and then they were back on
the pothole road leading to the bend where the lane from the
riding school joined it.

She stopped at the gate and watched Duggie pulling on the line. She had always been more than just aware of his being around. She knew of his former prowess as a jockey and a fighter, and although he was considerably shorter than her she found his wiry, hard looking frame provoked a sensual inquisitiveness in her and she had often pictured him naked in her mind's eye. She could pull back the bolt on the gate by using the handle of her crop. The gate swung open from her push and she came in on the horse and shut it. After bolting the gate, she let the horse take her over to the stables. As she swung her leg over to dismount she noticed that Duggie was looking at the soft brown leather under-crotch of her white riding breeches. She handed him the reins.

"Oh, that was wonderful, Duggie! That gallop on the sand has got a feeling all of its own, and the air along the beach was marvellous!"

"You're right there," he agreed. "Nothing quite like it, is there?"

Little Duggie had always fancied Liz in a big way. Several times in the pub he had tried to get started on chatting her up, but it was always so crowded and noisy with people butting in all the time. Once, at one of her parties, he had managed to get her alone on the torn old sofa and he was doing quite well with the old Aussie charm until she suddenly jumped to her feet and passed out. He got someone to tend a hand and they carried her through to her cabin and laid her out on the bed. She didn't surface again until the next day and had never mentioned it since. He thought the chances were she didn't remember anything of it.

She liked to have her long hair flowing when she was riding, but she had now removed her hard hat and was tying it back with a black velvet bow. There was just a touch of perspiration on her forehead and along her upper lip. Her lightweight tweed jacket was fastened tightly by a single button at the waist, emphasizing the protrusion of her breasts and the flap at the back curved voluptuously over the rounded cheeks in the tightly stretched breeches. She was aware of his admiring gaze all over her as she stood patting the horse and looking out across the fields, taking deep breaths of the warm scented air. Across the flat fields and beyond the river and the town, the humpbacked Downs looked blue and hazy.

Liz thought she would take the horse up there next time. "I was miles away then," she said. "I was riding up there, going in and out between the clumps of trees."

Duggie looked to the hills too. "They reckon witches gather up there at certain times, y'know. I've been up there early some mornings meself and there's been the remains of fires and queer shapes drawn in the soil. I bet it's real spooky up there at night."

"Oh yes, I've heard there's all sorts of goings on up there after dark," Liz smiled. "But it's wonderful in the daytime. Everything's spread out below you as if you're looking down from a plane."

"It'd be nice up there this afternoon all right." He reflected, remembering when his cousin Greig had come over from Oz with his wife for a holiday. After a few drinks in the pub one lunchtime, they took a few cans with them in their rented car and he showed them the way up the chalk track to the big clump of trees at the top. They stretched out on the grass in the sun and had some more beer while they took in the coastal views and swopped a few yarns. It wasn't long before his cousin fell asleep. His wife's name was Roz and she had been giving Duggie an obvious green light, so he wasn't at all surprised when she took hold of his hand and led him into a cluster of thorny bushes. There was a grassy clearing in there and as soon as they were in it she attacked him like a thing possessed, wrestling him to the ground and tearing at his clothes. She was wearing a white cotton dress with little blue flowers on it and after kissing him ferociously and biting his lip, she rolled off and hoisted it up above her waist. She was wearing nothing underneath, not even hair. Shaved smooth as a baby's bum, it was and she grabbed him by the ears and pulled his face down to it. When she finally let him come up for air there was a crazed look in her eyes and she was gulping in the air as if trying to hyperventilate.

"Hurry, hurry for Chrissake! I can't stand it! Get it into me, I've never done it in the open air! Oh, that's it! That's great! Great!"

Duggie smiled as he remembered the heat of the sun on his bare arse and how a skylark rose from the grass to sing over them in the blue as he pumped frantically in time with her crazed writhings, then slowing with her as her urgent gasping and clawing became long deep moans. She got her teeth into the muscle of his shoulder and held on like a terrier, shaking her head from side to side as if wanting to tear a lump of flesh from him.

She let go suddenly with a great shudder, then lay still with her eyes closed. He lay there on top of her, feeling drained like he'd just gone ten rounds. Through the bushes he could see men working below in the valley and there was a lorry tipping rubbish. There was a yellow bulldozer pushing the refuse into a great heap and being followed by a cloud of seagulls. There was blue smoke drifting across the tip from the smouldering debris. After a minute or so he felt her move under him and she opened her eyes and raised a hand against the sun. She gave him an odd look, as if she hadn't expected it to be him, then pushed him off.

"What were you doing, leaving it in soak to grow again?" She sat up and grinned at his deflated weapon. "It's not much good to either of us like that!" She laughed, but understandingly, then she gave him another shove and got up and smoothed her dress. They left the clearing and drank another beer each, sitting either side of the snoring Greig. Conversation was awkward to say the least and it was a relief when he woke and fumbled for a can of lager, saying he had a taste in his mouth "like an Abbo's armpit".

Greig and Roz stayed on for another two days then went to stay with some friends in Earl's Court before flying home. She never so much as hinted at what had happened that afternoon. Duggie didn't think that was so strange as the fact that it had been the first time for her out of doors. Especially when they'd got all that outback bush at home, just waiting for it!

Liz was intrigued by the expression on his face. "You look as if you've got some fond memories of being up there, Duggie. Nothing naughty, I hope?"

He smiled saucily. "Who me?" he said. "What can you mean?"

She returned his smile knowingly, then cast her eyes deliberately over his compact frame. He had the sloping shoulders of the fighter and his arms were muscular, with thick veins on the forearms and the hands were square and strong. There was sweat glistening in the cracks in the back of his neck and like his chest and arms, the shoulders had a light covering of blond hair. His tight trousers defined a neat firm arse and hard, muscular calves where they were rolled up. She felt the urge to unbuckle the leather belt and pull the trousers down. She wondered, is it true what they say about little men? Duggie tied the horse's rein to a post by the caravan.

He stepped up on to the first tread of the caravan's steps. Standing there he was as tall as she was. They each looked into the other's eyes, surrounded by an air of inevitability. An age seemed to pass before she could find her voice. When she did, it came with an uncontrollable tremor. "Shouldn't we see to the horse first?"

He was being painfully restricted in the tight trousers. She moved closer, her lips were less than a foot from his own. "Don' t worry," he said. "Young Sandra will be back soon. She'll tend to the horse and put him away."

Liz felt her own hot urgency overwhelming her. "The caravan door locks though, doesn't it?"

"It sure does."

"Right then...!" She gripped the cheeks of his arse and pulled him hard against her, her tongue fencing with his. In a matter of seconds they had locked the door and closed the curtains and by the time young Sandra arrived on her bicycle, the caravan was shaking and creaking, with the cups and saucers on its table rattling and crashing to the floor as if some demoniac were thrashing about inside.

Young Sandra closed the gate behind her and pushed her bicycle across the field. She was just sixteen, a pretty, athletic girl and she helped out at the stables most afternoons on her way home from school. She noticed the unattended horse tied to the post and as she drew nearer she heard the commotion coming from the closed caravan.

She had been working at the stables long enough to know a good deal about Duggie's private appetites, having discovered that he kept magazines of a certain sort under the seat cushions of the caravan and better still, a little green covered book in which he kept a fascinating catalogue of his exploits. The opuscule was well furnished with information regarding future dates too, and several times she had brought her best school friend to listen to the goings on under the cover of darkness; but this was the first time she had witnessed such an event while daylight still reigned. She had never seen any reference to Liz in Duggie's easily deciphered code, but judging by the horse that was tethered outside and the time of day, it had to be she who was with him, and they must have been in a hurry to get out of sight.

The caravan's creaking rhythm continued unbroken. Sandra leant her bicycle against its side and listened stealthily at one of the curtained windows. The window was open at the bottom with the hem of the orange curtain hanging out. The window opened outwards and with bated breath she slipped her finger-tips under the aluminium frame to ease it open further. Her girlish excitement was mounting unbearably as she raised the frame an inch and eased the curtain back just enough. The rhythm of the creaking had speeded up and was now accompanied by enraptured female moanings and Duggie grunting in tune with his exertions. Sandra had never actually seen the act being performed except in magazines, mostly Duggie's, that she had giggled over with her friend. She had quite often seen the horses at it and even dogs in the park who appeared to be gay, but never a man and a woman in the flesh. She had to raise herself on tiptoes to look through the chink at the curtain's edge. Just as her eyes rose above the sill level, the rattling increased violently and its severity caused the door of the cupboard inside by the window to spring its catch and swing open, blotting out any view she might have got of the ecstatically locked pair. Cruelly frustrated, she lowered herself as the fantastic shuddering din reached its mad crescendo then stopped abruptly. In the sudden stillness the voice from behind jolted her like an electric shock.

"They say dolphins do it face to face too, you know."

Sandra whirled round with the doomed child's feeling of being caught red handed, but it was her face that had cherried. The voice belonged to a dark haired young woman of about twenty five, but her tone held no threat of reproof. In fact she was smiling engagingly and holding a dead rabbit by its hind legs.

"Goodness, you startled me!" Sandra took her hands away from her face, which was losing its blush. "I wasn't really listening," she added lamely.

"No, of course you weren't and neither was I. But don't worry," the young woman allayed the girl's embarrassment loudly enough for the occupants of the caravan to hear, "I expect whoever is in there will be far more embarrassed about this than us!"

Sandra edged away nervously from the appropriately pregnant silence that emanated from inside the caravan, where the couple were still locked in position but whose only effort was now concentrated on listening. She allowed herself a girlish giggle. "I don't think I've seen you here before, have I?"

"No, you wouldn't have. I've only just moved in locally. I heard about the stables here and thought I'd take a walk over and have a look." She glanced back at the caravan and added quietly, "My name's Coral by the way, it rather looks like I picked the wrong time!"

The young girl felt much more at ease. "I'm Sandra," she said, "I work here, looking after the horses."

"Hallo, Sandra. Who do I see then? About the riding, I mean."

Sandra inclined her head toward the caravan. It was still standing silent as a mausoleum. "Well, um, it's a bit difficult right now..."

"Oh, I see," Coral said understandingly, "perhaps it would be better if I came back tomorrow?"

"Yes, I think so. We're closing early today anyway. You see, Duggie..." The name embarrassed her but Coral's smile coaxed her to go on. "Duggie's got to go and get things ready for the party tonight."

"That wouldn't be a certain Mr O'Looney's party, would

it, on that boat of his?"

"Why, yes. Do you know him then?"

"I met him for the first time this morning while I was walking my dog. He invited me actually, but I had to tell him I had a prior engagement. Look, if you see… Duggie… perhaps you would tell him that I'll call back in the morning?"

Sandra looked apprehensively at the caravan again.

"I'll make sure he gets the message later. I'm just going to see to the horse and then scoot off, but I will make sure he knows, really."

"I understand. Thank you very much. Well, I must get off home and get ready."

"I take it you'll be cooking that this evening, then, the rabbit?"

"Good heavens, no! I'm a vegetarian, actually. I found the poor thing in that field on the other side of the stream. I thought you might be able to get rid of the poor unfortunate creature, it looks like it's been shot."

She held the rabbit out at arm's length. "Just look at that, I can't understand why people have to do it, can you?"

She saw Sandra avert her eyes to the deck chair. There on the grass beside it she saw a small cardboard box of .22 air gun pellets. She looked from Sandra to the caravan and back again. The girl only needed to nod. Coral went over to the caravan and raised her voice by the open window. "I'll leave this poor DEAD creature on the steps here before I go, shall I? It might make a nice meal for someone. On the other hand, it might just prick a certain somebody's conscience! If you'll pardon the expression!"

17

Albert Hoskins had stayed on the churchyard bench and slept through the warm afternoon in the shade. He woke at precisely five thirty with the first chime from the church clock, just as the stonemasons, with their dusty faces and forearms were descending on a long pole ladder from the scaffolding at the end of their week's work. He watched them slapping themselves to get the dust off before getting into their van. He heard the engine start and the driver waved to him as he drove off. Albert raised a hand in reply as the van went, with only its top half showing above the flint wall. Then it was out of sight round the chemist's shop on the corner.

He moved his furry tongue around and smacked his lips. His mouth was foul and tacky from the cider and sleeping with it open. When he reached under the bench and picked up the big brown cider bottle, its weight confirmed his worst fear. He swigged back the remaining mouthful of flat tepid liquid then dropped the empty bottle into the litter basket by the bench. He winced as he reflected on days lone gone, when the bottle would have been of glass and he could have got money back on its return.

He sat up and stretched his legs out and looked at them for a while as he smacked his lips some more, then he stood and twisted his head around on his stiff neck. He thought the stiffness must be the result of lying at an awkward angle when watching the men working earlier. He made a mental

note not to do anything so physically dangerous in future. A
frown further creased his already rugous brow as he surveyed
the bare frame of his barrow leaning against the wall. There
were no 'shillings' on there. Still, although his afternoon's
sleep had kept him from his trade, it had also prevented him
from purchasing that second bottle of cider. In his pocket he
rubbed the few coins together between his fingers and smiled.
It was almost a certainty that there would be a party on later
with food available. There was no need, therefore, to waste
money on a meal. It was wonderful to know that a man could
be so happy with so little. It was Friday, it would soon be six
o'clock, and he had his entrance fee for any pub in town.

Albert couldn't have been happier if King Midas had
touched his barrow in passing whilst he slumbered. He
whistled through his teeth as he trundled the barrow along
before him, out of the churchyard and toward the High Street,
where it was becoming busy again with the homeward bound
traffic. The tune that he whistled bore no resemblance to
anything he had heard before and he was hardly aware that
he was doing it. It was just a string of happy notes that filtered
between his yellow pegs in accompaniment to his mood.
There was probably not a poorer nor a happier man in all
England.

He stopped outside the door of the Oyster Smack. Pam's
higgling perambulator was there with its brake on, empty
and unattended. He could hear subdued conversation and
laughter wafting out on tobacco smoke through a vent in one
of the windows. It could only be about a quarter to six, so he
knew it would be pointless trying the brass door handle, but
time enough to go and lock his faithful old barrow up for the
night. Ahead of him a noisy gaggle of small boys were taking
turns to press the control-button at the crossing and jeering at
the enraged drivers who were being forced to stop for the red

light. Albert took advantage of the halted traffic to cross the
road and go down to the river, with the metal wheels of the
sack barrow rattling on the cobblestones of the alley.

In summer he usually left the barrow at night, chained and
padlocked to one of the big timber mooring posts on the quay.
He himself would find a berth aboard one of the boats moored
there, or under an overturned, smaller craft on the beach. He
cast his eye over the various vessels sitting on the mud and
thought he would afford José Mackey the honour of putting
him up that night after the hoped-for party. In case the party
did not in fact materialize, or if it did but perhaps there might
be a shortage of food, Albert would have to find some stand-
by rations. Besides, he knew very well that José would have
little or nothing that was fit for consumption aboard; and so
he would procure a suitable gift for his friend. He set off along
the quay with the perfect token in mind. If they didn't need
to eat it, then they could sell it; and by tomorrow morning's
opening time they could well be in need of the money!

Along the quay the fish market was closed, with its big
metal shutters rolled down and locked; but then of course he
knew that it would be at that time and whilst passing that
morning he had taken some suitable precautions. At one side
of the market building there was a narrow passage where
empty fish boxes were stacked and in the well of the market
there was a small window. As he had done many times before,
Albert had made sure the catch of the window was unfastened
and then he stacked the boxes up high enough to hide it. Now
he lifted the top boxes off and put them down to form a step
from which he could reach the window and push it open.
Inside in the gloom were the big tanks that held live lobsters
and crabs and eels. The water in the tanks was circulated
by pumps and he could hear the constant movement above
the sound of the river. Less than five minutes later he was

climbing the corroded iron ladder back up to the quay from
José's boat, and a pair of big, indignant blue lobsters was safely
stowed in one of her lockers.

In going back up the incline of the alley, Albert passed
on his left the side window of Peter's Picture Gallery. He
noted that the proprietor of the gallery and its adjacent tea
rooms was still there inside, flicking at an old gilt frame with
a feather duster. The sound of six o clock had already come
from the church over the noise of the High Street's traffic
and Albert knew that very soon, Peter would be locking up
shop and mincing across to the pub. Here of course was a
chance too good to be missed by a self-respecting opportunist.
A chance to add some back-up to the entrance fee that was
burning a hole in his pocket. At the top of the alley, Albert
turned left into the High Street and waited by the gallery's
front door, casting a nonchalant eye over the paintings on
display in the window there.

There were the inevitable Arturo Bennets and an
assortment of other local artists well known to Albert's
practised eye. Although he could neither read nor write, once
he had seen a particular signature and learnt who its owner
was, then his incredible photographic memory for such things
would do the rest. All his years of totting around the streets on
the look-out had furbished him with an amazing inner mine
of knowledge and an infallible instinct for what was worth 'a
few bob' and what was not.

The local recent scenes didn't interest him, but his attention
was held by two much older works. Small oil paintings in good
gilt frames, they portrayed old sailing ships battling their way
through boisterous seas. They were each accompanied by a
printed white card telling their reader the names of the vessels
and off which part of the coast they were being buffeted about.
Both pictures bore the same signature, which meant nothing

to Albert either. He did recognize one of the locations, though.

The card said: 'The Excise Cutter 'Whippet' Off The Needles'. Albert knew those storm worn shapes all right. The sight of them thrusting up from the thickly oiled green billows gave the kiss of life to time locked memories. He stood transfixed, probably as near to being deep in thought as he had ever been in his life. So deep in his own past was he, that he had forgotten that he was supposed to be lying in ambush and that his intended victim was about to appear. If Peter's surprise, after locking the front door behind him, at seeing Albert smartly dressed and taking an obvious interest in the picture when the open door across the road indicated that the time had passed official 'splash-down', hadn't stopped him in his tracks then he might easily have avoided the waiting net. Instead he made a fateful mistake. During one foolish instant he thought Albert might be considering buying something that didn't contain alcohol.

"You rather like that one then, do you, Albert?" he asked as he looked him over, noting like Duncan, but for other reasons, the quality of his uncustomary attire.

Albert looked round dreamily. "Wassat?" "I said, you like that one, do you?"

"Oh, yes. That's the Needles, that is. I knows the Needles very well." "Oh, really?"

"Yes. Well, I knows all the Isle of Wight really. I lived there for years, see."

"Did you really?" Peter took a genuine interest in other people's pasts. Especially men's ones. Albert was well aware of that and he felt the bait being taken as surely as the fisherman feels the take of a fish on the line between his fingers.

"I was in Parkhurst," he said in a matter of fact way. "Were you really, Albert? I didn't know!"

"Yeah. I used to behave meself so well in there, they used

to let me out to go to the beaches and collect sand. So's the lads could watch me do the old soft shoe shuffle, when we put on a bit of a concert, like. Alum Bay was a bit special. You get all them different colours there. It adds a bit of colour to the act. I used to travel about all over the island on the old bus. All the locals knew where I came from, but they didn't care. They knew I was harmless and I'd go back, see?"

"That's really interesting, Albert. What was it you said you used the sand for?"

"The old soft shoe shuffle," he repeated, but there was no hint of recognition on Peter's dimpled face. "You know, the sand dance? Me routine, me act? Blimey, don't tell me you've never seen the bleedin' sand dance!"

"I don't recall ever having done so, no."

"Eh? Oh, yeah. Blimey guv, you don't know what you've been missing of, you don't straight! Look, first you sprinkles your sand on the floor, see? Then you dresses up in an old sheet like an A-rab and you shuffles about like, sliding your feet about and moving your 'ands and your 'ead about like you're in a sort of a trance with the A-rab music. Like them Hegyptian geezers used to do. They did a good one, they did."

"Oh, I see what you mean now. You mean like an old music hall act!"

"That's it, guv, now you've got it!" Albert said in an encouraging tone. He thought it was about time to spice the story up a bit with some insights into all-male incarceration and the personal relationships that were part of that confinement. Peter the Poofter liked that sort of thing. "That's it, 'The Old Time Music Hall', only it weren't no bleedin' music hall where we was, I can tell you! Parkhurst. They put all the nutters in there, y'know. Real hard cases. Men that would chop you up for dog meat. I could tell you stories that would make your 'air curl."

He eyed Peter's perm job and saw the spark of excitement in his eye. "I remember how one time this massive great hairy geezer got hold of this little rent boy by his …" Albert broke off at the opportune moment as a cackling laugh came from the pub doorway, Perfect timing, it was, by a master of his craft. Peter looked like a man teetering on the edge of a cliff.

They both turned to look across the road where Pam the flower seller had followed the laughter out onto the pavement. She braced herself with one hand on the wall as she stooped to check that the brake on her pram was in operation. She was rocking as if she might collapse on top of it at any moment. She finally managed to claw her way upright again and leaning with her back against the wall, seemed to inflate as she closed her eyes and took in great deep breaths of the cooling evening air. Both Albert and Peter watched, fascinated. When she did open her eyes she appeared to be weighing up the pram as if it were some creature she was about to wrestle with, and for a moment it looked as if she would lurch forward and make a grab for its handle, but she thought better of it. Taking another deep breath, she steeled herself, and after estimating the range she catapulted herself towards the open doorway. Misjudging the step, she took off with her last stride a yard short, coming down with a two-footed landing on the edge of the step and doing a passable impersonation of a windmill before staggering inside.

"It's all right for some, innit?" Albert whimpered. "I wish I could go over to the pub for a while." He withdrew a clenched fist from his blazer pocket and opened it palm up. "Just look at that, guvnor," he whined. "That's all I've made from grafting 'ard all day, that is."

Peter raised an eyebrow and looked down his nose at the pathetic collection of coins. Albert closed his fingers on them as if they might jump free. "All day it took me to get that," he continued. "Of course, I know what you're thinking, guv. You're thinking there's enough there for me entrance fee over the road, aren't you? A sufficiency for the introductory pint, like. Well, I know that too, don't I…?"

"Well, er…"

"Yeah, but what if I did go across there and got meself a drink, what then, eh? Before very long, some good soul like yourself or one of the others, would offer to get me one, wouldn't they? And what choice will yours truly have but to refuse your generous offer, eh? On account of how I wouldn't be in a position to be able to return the compliment, would I? And then you or the other party would be offended by my refusal, being gentlemen, and I would be forced by my pride to leave, wishing I had never set foot inside the place to begin with."

Peter opened his mouth and almost got a word out, but Albert would not be denied that which he was sure was about to come to him. There was just a little more of the softening up to be done, a few more body blows and then the head would surely fall. "You do see what I mean, don't you, guv? All you good, kind-hearted, generous folk would be offended and I'd be upset. And all because I didn't have the price of a few old drinks. It'd be so silly, now, wouldn't it? You do see my point?"

"Well, er …"

"Of course you do, guv. There now, I knew you'd see what I was getting at and I knew that a gent like yourself would appreciate how much it means to me!" He grabbed Peter's sleeve and looked imploringly into his eyes. "Guv," he added.

Peter had known the totter for a long time and he knew what was happening. From past experience he knew that he was being softened up and led slowly but surely to the kill. He would be going over to the pub and by now it had become a foregone conclusion that Albert would be accompanying him. The process was leading to its inevitable result, the passing of money from one to the other. And he was always the one. As he was fighting a losing battle anyway, he decided to obtain a little benefit from the prolonged agony by at least making it necessary for Albert to display his unquestionable talent for a while longer. He swallowed hard before he spoke. "What is it exactly that means so much to you?"

A strange light appeared in Albert's eyes as he tightened his grip. "Why, the way you always find a few beer tokens to spare, so's I can have a drink with you like you said, guv."

"Albert, I didn't actually say …"

"Good, good. That's the way, guv. You'll do it then, eh?"

"I'll do what?"

"Guv, oh guv!" Albert's tone was that of someone who was repeatedly having to explain the obvious to an idiot. He released his grip on Peter's sleeve and adopted his imploring stance, hunching his shoulders and holding his open palms as widespread as possible. He had to think quickly and determine if the moment was ripe for the actual mention of a fixed sum.

"What is it that you want me to do?" Peter was enjoying himself. The expression on Albert's face was a joy to behold.

Albert went for it. "Do, guv?" he explained. "Why, just let me have old Lady Godiva like you do and we'll go over and have a drink together!"

He'd done it. He kept his eyes fixed on those of his prey, half smiling as he ran his tongue over his lower lip in anticipation.

Peter could turn a thumb screw too. "A fiver," he said sadistically, "I don't remember mentioning a fiver, Albert."

"Oh guv, guv. You will have your little tease!" Albert laughed nervously. "Now come on, let's you and me go across the road and have a nice little shant, eh? It's Friday, you know and there's bound to be something going on. As a matter of fact," he looked around theatrically and lowered his voice, "as a matter of fact, I did hear something in my travels about Mr O'Looney putting on one of his do's tonight. On that boat of his." He grinned as he watched Peter's face for his reaction. It was the right one.

"Oh really!" he enthused. "Oh, that will be nice. He certainly knows how to throw a party, doesn't he? Remember the time he invited all those Norwegian sailors from that timber carrier? What a rough lot!"

"Yes, and smelly too." Albert remembered.

"One or two of them were quite nice, I thought," Peter recalled dreamily. "One of them in particular. Cash, his name was. Such lovely blond hair; and he had designer stubble before it had even been invented!"

"Yeah, I remember." Albert said. "All right if you like that sort of thing, I s'pose. I don't meself."

"I'm well aware of that, Albert. Each to his own, as they say."

"Yes of course, guv. One man's meat, eh?" The last thing he wanted to do was to hurt Peter's feelings. "Look," he said more gently, "let's you and me go over the road for a snifter, eh? Eh?"

Peter savoured this change of attitude. Albert's earlier bullshitting bravado had evaporated into thin air. This new, controlled pleading angle was much more enjoyable. He had intended to part with some 'beer tokens' as Albert called it, eventually anyway, but this time he had a little trick up his sleeve that would enable him to do it with the satisfaction of having the upper hand. He would make Albert an offer he couldn't refuse, but one that would rankle for a long time to come. One that involved doing some work.

"All right then, Albert," he said condescendingly.

"I'm prepared to let you have a little money, but you must understand that this time it's an advance and not to be thought of as a gift. Now come round the back with me and I'll show you what you have to do for it."

The glimmer of a smile had begun to develop on Albert's vexed expression, but the offer had him worried. He knew what sort of bloke this was. Brighton wasn't very far away and it was swarming with 'em. Peter had turned into the side alley and he followed but stopped at the corner.

"Just a minute," he said sheepishly. "I don't go in for that sort of thing, y'know. It don't seem natural to me. Not two men. I mean, what you get up to is your own business and I got nothing against that like, but…"

Peter's laughter bounced off the walls of the narrow wynd. Albert thought it was like a woman's laugh, but not one that he knew.

"Oh, don't be so silly!" Peter giggled. "I don't fancy you, love. Not even with your nice new clothes. Oh, you are a one. I might have split with you-know-who, but I'm certainly not desperate. Not yet anyway! Now stop being so daft and come round the back like a good boy."

The two of them went down the alleyway, with the still wary Albert a couple of yards behind. Peter opened a green door in the flint wall and they were in the cobbled yard at the rear of the tea rooms. The walls around the yard were over six feet high and there were trellises with creeping greenery and wooden tubs with bright flowers.

The yard could become a sun-trap in the afternoons; and the heavy wooden tables and benches where customers could take their teas and cream cakes were shaded by bright umbrellas. That particular afternoon had been a busy one and the big metal waste basket was full of wrappers and paper bags. One of the tables was covered with stacks of used plates and cups and saucers. Albert, who came from a long line of fairground travellers thought it looked like it was waiting for someone to start throwing wooden balls.

"Ooooh, just look at that lot!" Peter tut-tutted. "I'll have to wash them up in the morning, I can't be bothered with them now."

"I was afraid you were going to ask me to do them."

"Oh no, nothing like that, Albert dear heart. It just goes to show though, doesn't it? A girl's work's never done, is it eh? Never done!"

He went to the back end of the yard and beckoned Albert over. In a corner stood an old fashioned brick built WC. A real proverbial, it was little bigger than a sentry box with a steeply pitched slate roof; and a gap of about six inches above and below its wooden door. Albert knew the type well: marvellous ventilation in summer and a bollock freezing draught in winter.

"There now, what do you think of that, then?" Peter gestured as if showing him a priceless work of art.

"Not a lot, really."

"It's an outside toilet," Peter said as he opened the door to reveal a clean, whitewashed interior.

"I know what it is," Albert said patiently. "It's a brick built shit-house. A Karzi."

"There's not many people left with outside ones these days," Peter observed authoritatively.

"There's more than you think round 'ere. I often use them, unofficial like, in me travels. Handy for getting in out of the rain they are. I've even slept in them from time to time. O'course, you have to be out early in the morning, before some sod comes out to strain his greens or have a crap."

"Yes, well … be that as it may, Albert. However, our illustrious local council, in its wisdom, has decided that I must do away with the thing and install modern conveniences for the benefit of the tea room's patrons. At present it discharges straight into the river, you see and they don't like it. Apparently a lady councillor was recently standing on the footbridge admiring the view up-river with a friend, when someone flushed it and the two ladies found themselves watching real-life Pooh sticks floating down towards them and passing underneath. They were not over amused."

"Pooh sticks?" Albert thought for a moment. "Oh, turds you mean? Copper bolts?"

"Whatever you like to call them, old dear, the councillors don't like to see them floating down the river."

"Nor coming back in again to the town with the tide, I s'pose!" Albert chuckled.

"Exactly. Not even if they were in a perfect V-formation."

"I can remember when they used to come down-river in droves years ago," Albert mused happily. "Flow-tillas of 'em there was. Most of the boats had toilets that emptied over the side in those days, see. You should have seen the French letters at weekends! They used to go past in shoals, like mullet, they did. They were all shagging each other all the time see, the weekenders.

"Most of 'em never left their moorings; just eat, drink and shag. That's all. Eating, drinking and shagging; and mostly shagging. Things haven't changed much really, have they, not if these new marinas are anything to go by!"

"Yes, I know what you mean. But listen, getting back to this business about the toilets. Some of Mr O'Looney's men are due to start work on the project next week. On Monday morning."

Albert stepped inside the little building. "It's nice and clean, isn't it."

"Oh yes," Peter said. "The lady who cleans the tea rooms

and gallery keeps it looking nice. Do you know, in all the years I've been here, I've not used it once? I've not even been inside the thing. Amazing, isn't it!"

Albert had lifted the toilet lid and was peering into the depths of the white glazed pan. "Amazing." His voice had an odd resonance. He closed the lid and stood straight again, hitting his head on the heavy brass handle of the chain from the high cistern. "Where do I fit into this though?"

"Simple." Peter rubbed his head for him. "All I want you to do is knock it down and clear it all away before Monday morning."

Albert had already noted that the cistern was supplied with water by a heavy looking lead pipe that ran along the trellised wall from the main building. A quick glance took in the old fashioned iron scrolled cistern, the hand painted glass shade on the light bulb and the rare type of wooden toilet roll holder. The lavatory seat and its lid were made from a beautifully grained and polished dark red-brown wood and their hinges were of brass. He watched the brass handle swinging on its chain. That's good heavy brass that is, he thought.

"You want me to clear everything, do you?"

"Yes, all the lot. I want it all clear for Monday so they can start digging for the new foundations. Whatever you make on the materials is yours, and you can pay me back the ten pounds I'll let you have now. How does that grab you?"

Albert thought that it grabbed him in the nicest possible way. A nice tenner now, eh? That cock and hen would enable him to buy a round in the pub and keep enough back for his entrance fee for tomorrow. He would be bought several drinks in return during the course of the evening and if he tagged along to O'Looney's party, the booze and grub there would all be freeman's. There should also be the added bonus of being able to smuggle a bag of food away; things were looking better and better …

"That sounds all right to me, guv!" He grabbed Peter's hand and yanked it up and down. It reminded him of the feeling of squeezing warm putty.

The two of them left the yard and climbed the slope of the alley. An opportune lull in the High Street traffic saw them cross without the aid of the button; the gleeful Albert having an uncustomary spring in his step. He paused by the open pub doorway, just out of sight of the interior. Peter took a brown note from his pocket and pressed it into Albert's eager palm. The totter bowed in acceptance and said that he must insist on entering first and buying their initial drinks. Peter agreed, saying that he would be only too pleased to allow him to do so; and with the crisp brown note held tight to his chest Albert advanced on the bar.

What had cheered him so was not only the fact that the bricks of the outside loo were valuable stocks and that the slates on its roof were good; nor was it the heavy lead piping or the much sought after style of the wooden seat and other fittings. Although by his own confession Peter had never so much as stepped inside the little building, he would nevertheless have known that there was some second-hand value in all those things. What was far more important, however, was that he had absolutely no idea what Albert had seen as he lifted that polished lid. For there, staring at him fixedly from its sub-aqua lair was a beautiful blue glazed eye. And there was more to heighten his carefully concealed excitement: half-way up one side of the bowl, as if it were struggling to avoid a death by drowning, was a blue winged striped bodied insect. And the word APIS. Now Albert didn't have to be able to translate the Latin to know what a bee looks like and, like certain signatures, it rang a big bell.

18

Much to Weldon's chagrin, his darling Ladybird had insisted that they and the twins must leave the pub at the two thirty deadliner, promising to return that evening. The Colonel left about the same time, as did Hattie and Lettie, leaving a dozen tipplers behind to keep the tradition of the Friday afternoons alive; a tradition that would soon become only part and parcel with the past at the coming of officially extended opening hours.

The earlier rapid quenching of thirsts slowed to a steadier rate and Norman was able to cope with the orders on his own, which was just as well because the barmaid had gone off shopping and Doreen was perched on a stool, downing large gins. At five minutes to six Norman glanced at the clock and then at Duncan. The off-duty copper was smiling and waiting for the publican's usual jest.

"Does anybody want to order a last round before I open the pub?" His call brought no response. "No? All right then, but your next one will be a legal one," he said winking at Duncan, "and that's not half as much fun, is it!"

As the old clock rang its gloomy chime like a subdued dinner gong, Norman pulled back the bolt and opened the front door. His customers raised their voices slightly to compete with the passing traffic. He pushed the wooden wedge under the door with the toe of his shoe and went back behind the bar; when he switched on the extractor fan the thick blue fug that had been unnoticeable until the outside daylight had brightened the doorway, was slowly drawn like a change of tidal stream towards the rear window.

The sudden influx of fresh air had a heady effect on Pam, who had been clinging for the past half hour to an oak post at the bar. She had left her Gabriel to dispose of the last few items on the pram at twenty past two, and had been downing Bulldog strong ales at a steady rate all afternoon. Eric, who was feeling much better and full of false confidence now that his little bit of 'tummy trouble' had settled down, had quickly grabbed a vacated stool and dragged it along closer. Just as she was about to release her hold on the post, he lowered his backside gingerly onto the stool, pinning her against the post with his knees. More early evening drinkers were coming in, adding to the already considerable crush at the bar. From behind her big, red framed spectacles, tears streamed from her big, red rimmed eyes; it had nothing to do with her frustration at not being able to move – it always happened when the Bulldogs reached a certain level. With more and more people being crammed in below the low sagging beams, the various talks fused to become one long, rising and falling sound, like the plangent motion of the sea. Individual voices were indistinguishable from a distance of more than three or four feet and the taller drinkers were forced to stoop in order to catch the odd word and relied on lip reading for the rest. Pam knocked back what was left of a Bulldog:

"I've got to get out for some air," she gasped as she pushed against Eric's knees.

"Of course," he bawled as he went on about something she hadn't heard, "in Carlisle during the war, all beers were the same price, y'know. It was some government-cum-brewery idea, or something. It was a try- out. Only during the war of course. In Carlisle!"

"Eric … I've … got to … get some … air …"

Eric didn't budge: "I remember Dorothy Squires having a big hit at the time I was there. Now what was it called …?" As he reeked what the years of alcohol abuse had left of his memory, Pam managed to push his knees aside and make for the bright doorway. Jostling her way through the press of bodies at the bar kept her upright, but as soon as she found herself with some open space her legs buckled and she had to lean forward as if struggling against a gale force wind. She halted for a moment with one hand braced against the door jamb, took a deep breath and then launched herself through to the pavement outside.

Fishy Phil suddenly appeared like a genie out of the smoke to take her place. The grimy sack that he had brought in with him eight hours before was still there on the floor. It had gradually been pushed by various feet into the corner by the oak post and forgotten, especially by Phil himself who had come to after a brief cat-nap. Thinking that it was still around lunchtime, on leaving his seat he had found that his legs wouldn't work properly and had managed to get the support of the post in the nick of time, before what would have been a spectacular collision with a table loaded with empties.

Considerably revived by the change of atmosphere outside, and satisfied that her pram was safe and sound with its brake on, Pam returned to the fray with such an erect and steady gait that she might have come from a day of hard work, fresh air and abstinence. She gave Norman a gap-toothed grin as she pushed in between Phil and Eric at the bar, lifting the empty glass she had left there and waving it around as high as the ceiling would allow.

"The Gypsy!" Eric shouted. Seeing Pam again had jogged his memory. She recoiled and the glass flew from her hand to smash somewhere behind the bar. Her foot slipped from the rail and she trod on something soft. Whatever it was, it was not another foot. Her tread seemed to bring it to life and she felt it move with a strong, slithering sensation. She looked down and saw Phil's dirty wet sack under her shoe; it rose and fell as its squirming contents writhed.

"I've got it, Pam. The Gypsy!" Eric exclaimed again as he grabbed her arm. "A lovely song, that," he told Phil who was watching the sack's movements as if it was something new to him. "Dorothy Squires. She was a lovely girl. She was very young in those days. So were we all then, I suppose. At the time I served on a minesweeper, a converted trawler she was …"

"Never mind all that," Pam interrupted. She was trying to keep her feet on the seemingly self-propelled sack as if on a children's polished slide of ice. "What the hell is in this sack? The damn thing's got a mind of its own!"

The two men surveyed the sack, which had now taken on a gyratory movement. Amidst all the drinking and confused talk and laughter, it didn't seem out of place, somehow. Eric put the toe of his boot under it and heaved it back into the corner, where it settled down to be still.

"That's Phil's old sack," he said. "Judging by the way it was moving and the fact that it's been here for a good few hours, I'd say it contains eels. Am I right, Phil?" He grinned at Pam. "Your eel can survive for a long time out of water, y'see," he told her.

"Eels? Yeeeeeerk!" Pam was scanning the bar in vain for her missing glass. "Bloody awful great slimy things. I loathe 'em. My ex-husband used to love 'em, he did. The sod. He used to say he could eat a bucket full, jellied ones that is. When we used to go out for a day at the races, he'd eat bowl after bowl of the 'orrible slippery things. He took a wicked delight in shovelling them down his neck in front of me. He liked to watch me squirm, see. The rotten sod." Her voice caught and broke in her throat, as she fleetingly recalled good times too. She started sobbing, wiping away the tears of diluted alcohol with the back of her hand. "Eels?" she

Shuddered with loathing. "I hate them. They were just like him, really. The slippery bastard!"

"I heard that, and must protest!" Phil had somehow disentangled himself from the post and was standing with his feet wide apart and swaying to and fro as if his wellies had been nailed to the floorboards. He waved an accusatory finger in Pam's direction and addressed the assembled imbibers, who had suddenly fallen silent, not so much out of interest in what he had to say as in seeing how long he would be able to remain on his feet.

He gathered his thoughts together, all the while tilting one way and then another, like the mast of a rolling boat. After summoning up a huge belch, his voice came forth. It seemed uncannily rehearsed and queerly sober, too.

"I heard what you said about eels and I'm here to tell you that I love 'em. I love 'em, I do and I'm going to stick up for 'em. As they can't speak for themselves, like." He adopted a pose like an elephant, with an arm stretched before him like the swaying trunk. "Eels, people say, eels? Dirty, slimy creatures that creep around on the sea-bed and up the rivers like vacuum cleaners, sucking up all the shit off the bottom. Well, yes they do. They are your scavengers, but the flesh of the eel is the whitest and cleanest food you can get. Wonderful it is; and in my experience those that say they can't stand 'em and calls 'em all sorts of lousy names, are them that have never even sampled 'em." He cast a bleary look around the room.

His audience sat or stood in silence. He needed to provide them with a bigger finish, but he knew he was about to pass out. Staggering backwards, he felt for the arms of an unoccupied chair. Gripping them, he fell back heavily, tipping the chair over and sprawling in a heap. For a few moments he struggled convulsively against the overwhelming blackness, gave a last defiant shout of "up the Eel!" then lay still.

That was when Albert and Peter came in. "Is that chap going to be all right, do you think?" they heard a stranger ask of Norman across the bar.

"Old Phil? Oh, he'll be all right," he said. "He usually passes out about this time of a Friday. We'll put him in a chair and he'll wake up in about an hour and be as right as rain. It's funny how they can do that, some of 'em."

The stranger took in the scene. There was something odd about the atmosphere of the place and most of its customers who seemed to be rather over-refreshed, considering the pubs had only been open about a quarter of an hour. He watched incredulously as Frank and Arthur heaved Phil's seemingly lifeless form across the room, hoisting him up and wedging him securely between two men on a corner seat. The two men were fast asleep, Fred with his arms folded and head back with mouth agape, dreamed of sexual conquests in various greenhouses of years ago; whilst the swarthy Gibraltarian was back in the Artillery Arms, Moorish Castle again, with a box of octopuses that he had caught by hand when diving from his boat off Europa Point.

The newcomer sipped from his pint and turned to the woman who was perched on a stool next to him. Doreen had had a good many gins and was viewing what was to her a familiar scene. Her mood just then was one of booze enhanced melancholy. Norman was still in residence and although Frank was there, he had hardly spoken to her all afternoon. In fact she had just heard him agree with Arthur to go back to the houseboat and have a break before the serious business of the evening session. She suspected Frank of being up to something and was not at her most jovial.

Unaware of her seething, the weedy-looking man attempted to make neighbourly conversation.

"A nice little bar, this." "Mmmm. We like it."

"Would you be the landlady, by any chance?" "That's right."

"Do you know, I thought so!" "Really. I look like one then, do I?" "Well, er, no, it's just that, I mean …" "It's all right, I know I do."

"Ah…" He felt embarrassed and thought he ought to brighten his approach. Talking to him was the last thing she felt like doing, but he was one of those pub talkers.

"It was interesting, what that chap had to say about the eel, wasn't it?" he said. "I like eels myself. Did you know that the art of splitting an eel and broiling it is called 'pitchcocking', and that an eel thus prepared and cooked is then a 'Spitchcock'?"

Doreen watched gloomily as Frank and Arthur went out the door. Not even a wave. She downed her drink and put the glass down heavily enough to attract her husband's attention.

"Put another one in there, Norman," she said wearily. "And give this poor confused little sod something to cheer him up a bit. He's been going on about doing himself an injury. Threatening to split his John Thomas, or something."

Norman filled their glasses and the stranger watched her raise her glass and wink at him boozily. "Don't do it," she told him. "They can't give you another one!"

19

Coral's new home was a cottage that was part of a two hundred years old terrace to the west of the church. They had no front gardens and their front doors opened inwards from the pavement of the narrow street, but they had neat rear gardens which led to a stony lane that ran along between the fences at the ends of the gardens and a clear narrow stream that emptied into the main river. When she returned after walking back from the riding school, she went upstairs to take a bath. She liked to soak for about half an hour in a hot tub, maintaining the temperature by pulling the plug at about half time and topping up the water level from the hot tap. Then she liked to stand under a gradually cooling shower.

After her shower she put on a white towelling robe and went downstairs. The two downstairs rooms were jumbled with her furniture and cardboard boxes, and her suitcases were stacked on top of tea chests in the narrow passage from the front door. She went into the tiny kitchen to fix herself a drink. One of her first jobs on arriving had been to check that the bottles had survived the journey from London. Now the colourful assortment stood on an old cabinet which would have to serve as a temporary bar. Her fridge was already in position and she took ice cubes from its tray and poured gin and tonic water over them in the glass.

Through the open latticed window she could smell the flowers of the garden and she could see the weakening sun through the fork of a tree on the other side of the stream. She took the drink and went out into the garden; there was an area of big old flagstones and then a path of flags spaced as stepping stones across the lawn to the gate in the low picket fence. There was a rusty garden table and chairs on the area, and she sat there with her drink. She could feel a glow on her back from the brick rear wall of the cottage that had been heated by the sun all that afternoon. The scented air was warm and still, and the low sunlight splayed through the pink rose bushes, making different shades of lawn and patterned flags.

She closed her eyes and leaned back in the chair with the warm sun on her face, thinking of the phone call that she had received that morning. It was the first call she had received since moving into the cottage the day before. When she had first met O'Looney whilst walking her dog and he had invited her to his party, she had told him that she had a previously arranged engagement. What she didn't tell him was that it was a professional one and that she did not yet know who with. That particular private information she would later get from the daily call which came at the same time each morning, Monday to Friday. He would have been most surprised to have learnt that she was employed by the London branch of Miss Steine's agency; and the fact that she worked only in the city or thereabouts, meant that she knew nothing of O'Looney himself being one of the best clients of the Brighton end of operations. When she picked up the receiver that morning she expected to hear the old girl's exaggeratedly polished accent informing her of who her client was to be that evening and whether she was to be collected by car or be met at some rendezvous. That would have been in the West End; and that was how Coral had wanted to keep it. Moving to the coast had always been her dream and she had saved for a long time to be able to afford the place she wanted. She worked a five night week and the fact that she would be able to spend just a few hours of the afternoons there more than compensated for the travelling involved. And she would have such wonderful weekends! But now, like a pin pricking the balloon, one of the Brighton girls had decided at a minute's notice to retire; having been offered a more permanent position with some Libyan diplomat. Dear old Miss Steine was at her wits' end after failing so far to find a stand-in. And the client was Mick O'Looney. Coral's first thought was to refuse the assignment and stick to her intention of only working in London. Miss Steine was a reasonable old girl. She said she understood how Coral felt about wanting to live on the coast and keep her place of work well away from home; but then she added that not only was Mr O'Looney one of their best regulars, but he was by necessity the most discreet and he was- also most generous in his treatment of the girls that he called her 'little packages of fun'.

Coral asked for half an hour. She talked it over with herself and it was a lot easier to think clearly off the phone. She reasoned that as she was known to practically no one in the town, and O'Looney would keep it known only to the two of them, then there was no real reason why tonight's work shouldn't be done nearer home. She called Miss Steine and gave her the good news she wanted. Miss Steine told her she was a good girl for getting her out of a mess and that she wouldn't forget it. Then she said there would be a car at eight and rang off with her usual 'Tootaloo!'

Eight o'clock was still a good way off. As she sipped her drink, Coral wondered what her client had got planned for the evening and what he would say when he saw her. She knew he was throwing that party later, of course, but he had told her that it wouldn't get under way until 'after the boozers have

chucked out'. In London it was usually dinner somewhere
and then on to a club or casino before getting down to the
nitty-gritty. What would Graywacke's answer be? The pubs
wouldn't close until eleven and the car was coming for her
at eight; now that she had committed herself, she found the
intrigue was exciting.

Half an hour later the sun was gone but all the sky was still
bright. She was watching swifts in the golden air over the trees
to the west and she could hear their screeches as they hawked
flies, swooping down through the gardens and careering with
perfect control between the bushes.

"Devil birds," she murmured and smiled at recalling the
old folklore name. She got up and took the glass with her into
the cottage, leaving it in the kitchen and going through to the
front room. It had become darker inside and cooler.

From the front room window she could see the low flint
wall of the churchyard and above the trees the bright face of
the clock on the tower. It was almost six thirty and time she
was getting ready. She found the small case that she wanted
in the passage and took it upstairs with her to her bedroom.
It was the back room and it was in dire need of redecorating,
but she could picture it as being a lovely room, so very quiet
and with a wonderful view. Looking beyond the garden there
was the lane and then the stream; and then behind the trees
along the bank was the broad preen of the coarse marsh grass
to the river. The river was low but was beginning to fill again
with the in-coming tide. The stretch that she could see was
up-river from the road bridge and few boats moored there,
but she could see an old clinker built boat lying over on one
side and a man there in thigh waders. He was scrubbing with
a brush at the under parts of the hull and all around were
the green, decaying ribs of long abandoned craft protruding
from the mud.

Coral let the robe she was wearing slide to the floor. She had already decided what she was going to wear that evening and had left the clothes laid out on the bed. There was a very slight movement of air from the open window, but the room was still very warm and she sat naked while she finished making up her reflection in the mirror over the dressing table. Then she got up and took a black leather shoulder bag from the wardrobe and packed the accessories that she might need later in the evening. As the church bells rang seven she took an elegant silver wristwatch and two rings from a drawer and corrected the watch before slipping them on. After dressing she put on heavy silver earrings that swung with the bounce of her jet black ringlets as she shook her head. She looked at herself in the full length mirror of the wardrobe. In the high black heeled shoes she stood an impressive five foot ten. With such naturally long dark eyelashes, and broad dark eyebrows, she needed only a little make-up on the lids and they and her lips were a glossy silver lilac. The neckline of the shimmering silver and black top was only low enough to show the beginning of cleavage and the bra she had chosen gave her a more pointed look. Under the black leather knee-length skirt was black lace, and suspenders held stockings that had a two-tone effect of shiny charcoal or silver in different lights. She examined the nail varnish which matched her make-up, and the single silver ring on either hand and the wristwatch and earrings. 'Classy' she thought, and she wondered if the girl in the mirror would be recognized by Mick O'Looney as the one who had worn a blue tracksuit on the footpath by the river only a few hours before.

She thought she would go downstairs and fix herself another drink. She put the black leather shoulder bag on the kitchen table by her glass, then put some ice in the glass and let a large Gordon's pour slowly over the cubes, followed by the pleasantly fizzing tonic water. She took a half-read paperback from the mantelpiece over the old iron fireplace and took it and the drink with her to sit in the cool air from the open back door.

She became immersed in the book and it seemed as if no time at all had passed before a sound distinct from the crepuscular sounds of the garden and its surroundings caused her to look up. A long white convertible with its roof down had halted gently with just a slight crunch of the stones in the lane at the end of the garden. The small driver was apparently alone in the car. He did not sound the horn or get out, glancing only briefly at the cottage and then lighting a cigarette.

Coral put a green leather bookmark in the paperback and replaced it on the shelf. She drank the now melted ice from the glass, slipped the strap of the bag over her shoulder and locked the back door behind her as she went out into the garden. As she crossed the garden on the stepping stones, the still air was heavy with the evening smell of flowers and as she reached the wicket gate, the driver got out of the car and opened the rear door for her. He exhaled smoke and coughed. "Good evening, Miss. Mr O'Looney's car."

"Good evening." Coral slid on to the Bentley's white hide upholstery and swung her legs in, noticing the little man's obvious interest. "A wonderful evening isn't it … um?"

"Yes, Miss. It's Duggie, Miss."

Coral smiled to herself. So this was Duggie. He of the energetic ride in the caravan. He closed the door, then slid back in behind the wheel and closed his own. He stubbed out his cigarette and looked at her fantastic reflection in the mirror. That's some horn manure you're wearing, miss, he felt like saying. Instead he started the engine.

"Mr O'Looney said I was to take you straight to the new house, Miss. It's about ten minutes' drive."

"Oh," Coral said, "the party hasn't been called off, has it?" She immediately flinched after saying it, wondering how much Duggie knew about her, if anything.

"Oh no, the party's still on all right," he said. "No worries there. But it won't get started before the pubs chuck out. It won't be high water till then anyway, and with all the grub and booze I've been taking aboard, she'll need that to get afloat!"

"She?" Coral asked, not wishing to show any prior knowledge. "Yeah, the 'Pachydermatous'. The guvnor's boat. What a boat though, a floating palace, that's what she is. No other word for it. The guvnor and me have been living aboard while the new house has been got ready. You've never been on board, have you, Miss? Aren't you new around here?"

"That's right," she said quickly. He watched her in the mirror, waiting for more. When nothing came he shrugged his shoulders and grinned.

"Well," he said, "nothing like living near your work, is there?"

She didn't like the insinuation and didn't answer. Duggie pressed the accelerator gently and eased the big car along the narrow lane. Coral felt relieved as the movement of the car with the roof down would discourage him from further conversation. She settled back to watch the passing countryside.

The car turned north at the end of the lane and after about a mile on that road they were on the by-pass. The fields they passed were heavily green and here and there was a startlingly yellow strip of rape on the higher ground of the Downs.

Coral's thoughts turned to the evening's work ahead of her. He's a terribly big, heavy man that Mr O'Looney, she thought. And Miss Steine had alluded that he had some rather unusual preferences. Still, he couldn't be any weirder than some of those old boys in the city; and she had become well used to their little kinks and fetishes. Any other deviations were hardly likely to shock her. She enjoyed the country again for a while and presently she felt the car lose speed as Duggie turned left into a lane as narrow as the one at the rear of her garden. The hedgerows were barely two feet from either side of the Bentley.

"Not far now, Miss," Duggie told her. "Mr O'Looney's Merc broke down just here this morning and he had to have it towed in. We've got this monster from the garage while it's being sorted. They use it for weddings. At weekends mostly. One thing's for sure, though, it's a bit on the large side for these lanes, eh?" Coral nodded her agreement. "Anyway, we turn off here," he added.

Duggie slowed the enormous motor and turned slowly right into the entrance to the track leading up to the house. "The guvnor's already here," he said. "I dropped him off earlier. Some place, eh?"

Coral nodded again at the impressive front of the house, then looked back at the swirling mist of white chalk dust that they were leaving in the car's wake as it crunched its way up the track past the stacks of turfs.

Duggie half circled the huge shape of the future flower bed and stopped the car with Coral's door a few feet from the stone front porch of the farmhouse. He got out of the car and opened her door for her, watching those wonderful legs again as they swung out. The air was different here above the seemingly unmoving summer heat down by the river. She breathed deeply as she looked back, down over the distant town like a model village by the flat, silvery sea.

Duggie had left the car engine running and had already opened the front door of the house. "Mr O'Looney will be in his den, Miss. Off the lounge. First door on your right."

Coral hesitated, still taking in the wonderful sweeping vista of the land falling away to the Channel shore.

"He said you could go straight in, Miss." Duggie grinned from the porch. He was holding the door open for her and as she stepped into the hall she had to brush past him. She could feel his eyes all over her. She heard the door close faintly but heavily behind her and then the sound of the car door and the muffled sound of the tyres for a moment. She stood there alone in the hall. It was very still and quiet but it had the feel of a new building and the smell of new paint and polish, allaying what would have been a spooky atmosphere for her in an older house.

She knocked with clenched knuckles on the red-brown door on her right. No answer came so she gripped the brass door handle and eased the door open. What she saw was a large lounge with a big bay window at the front, expensively carpeted and furnished. There was already some soft lighting from a table lamp and some wall lights which gently emphasized some gilt framed paintings. There was a big brick-built fireplace with an iron basket and silver barked logs ready for autumn evenings, and at the far end of the room a door stood ajar. Coral went to the door and pushed it slowly open.

O'Looney was dressed in a red paisley silk dressing gown but all she could see of him was his vast round behind as he was bent tinkering with a large television set.

"Mr O'Looney?" There was a loud click as Coral closed the door behind her.

"Hallo there," the huge red roundness said without looking round. "Pour yourself a drink. I'll be with you in a tick. I'm just trying to get this thing set up right."

He carried on fiddling while she went over to a brash glass and chromium bar in a corner. The den had a thick brown carpet and brown walls and ceiling. All dark brown. The only apparent illumination was the bar itself, which was lit up in a garish electric blue. It was chock full of bottles and its chrome legs looked as if their curvature might have been caused by the weight. Coral poured a large splash from a bottle of Gordon's and topped it up with tonic over the ice she had scooped from a cut glass bucket that had a double skin, like a thermos flask.

"Shall I get something for you?" she asked, then added: "and should I go on calling you Mr O'Looney?"

"Just a beer this early," he said, still preoccupied with the video machine below the TV set. "You'll find some cold ones in that chilled cabinet there. Oh, and Mick'll do."

Coral opened the glass door of the cabinet and found it was full of dark brown bottles of Steam Bitter. She took the top off one and poured its contents into a tall pint glass, carefully tilting it to ensure that it had a half inch of creamy white head. She held it out towards the still bent figure.

"I think I'd like to go on calling you Mr O'Looney anyway," she smiled. "Far more business-like, don't you think?"

"That's it," O'Looney said. Satisfied that he had mastered the infernal machine, he patted the TV and turned towards her. "Call me what you like, dear, just don't call me early!" He cracked as he turned. "And don't I know that lovely voice of yours from somewhere?"

He took the glass from her and looked her over, eyes wide in admiration.

He smiled hugely and his mouth dropped open for a moment. "My God, it's you," he murmured.

"Coral."

"Yourself. My God, you're looking beautiful." "Thank you."

"So you're one of Miss Steine's little packages, eh? She's

never disappointed me yet. I can hardly believe me eyes!" He took a long draught from the glass, downing most of the beer and leaving a white arc of froth on his upper lip. The glass looked tiny in his big pink paw. He was barefoot and she saw that the legs below the vast red dressing gown had a covering of thick red hair that glistened in the strange light from the bar. He finished the beer and handed her the empty glass.

"Will yer come along to me little party later, Coral? You'll have a great time, I can promise you. It's going to be a real hoot of a do, they always are. I know you told me you had a previous engagement this morning, but now it seems that I am it so to speak and once we've got the little matter of the business over, you could come along with me to me boat, couldn't you now?"

"Couldn't it get rather awkward? I mean, it would really, wouldn't it? Your driver knows our relationship now and that I live locally. Even WHERE I live, I mean."

"Duggie, d'ye mean!" O'Looney guffawed. "Sure Duggie's as safe as houses. Sound as a pound, so he is. He'd never be cracking on about it to a living soul. Isn't it part of his job to be blind, deaf and dumb. And you could always arrive at the boat on yer own; didn't I invite you along to the party this morning meself!"

Coral put her glass down with his on the bar top. She smiled at him and moved towards him without taking her eyes from his. Mick swallowed hard as she pressed against his massive belly and slipped her hands inside the silk gown. He was naked beneath the red paisley covering.

"Oh Jayzuss" ... he murmured and his eyes rolled up to the ceiling as she slowly untied the sash from his waist and let the dressing gown fall open. She slid her right hand down and found that he was already hard.

O'Looney's red eyelashes fluttered as she gently held him.

"Is there anything particular that you'd like?" she whispered.

O'Looney mumbled incoherently, his eyes now closed with their lids twitching. Coral nuzzled her nose and mouth into his neck.

"What was that you said, Mr O'Looney?" she whispered again but more huskily as she worked her hand slowly.

Bloody hell, O'Looney thought. That Miss Steine has done it again sure enough! He started mumbling again, then with a great effort checked himself and spoke very slowly and measuredly, his eyes still closed.

"Yes," he swallowed. "I did have something in mind for this evening. It's one of my favourites. If you'd like to get undressed here, I'll fetch the things." He waved towards some fitted wardrobes. "They're in there. I keep all the things in there."

Coral released him and stepped back. He opened his eyes.

"Don't you want me to wear anything?" she asked him. "I've brought some things with me, I mean."

"No," he said. "That'll not be necessary. I've got all the gear we'll need in there. All except balloons, that is. But then you'll be carrying a supply of those yourself, I expect?"

Coral sat down on a big white leather sofa where she had put her shoulder bag. She opened the bag and took out a small packet and held it up."

"Balloons," she said. "Great."

She dropped the packet back in the bag. She had already slipped one shoe off and began slowly slipping off the other with her stockinged foot. Then without taking her eyes off him she began to unbutton the front of her silver and black top.

"I … I'll just get the gear!" Mick blurted out and as he turned away in his hurry, he cracked a shin on a coffee table covered with magazines. He limped to the wardrobes, rubbing the shin with one hand and muttering obscenities.

Coral stood up and removed the rest of her clothes. She went over to the bar and fixed herself another drink. As she sipped it she noticed for the first time that the room had no window. She studied the painting on the wall over the bar. It was a Jean Beraud Paris street scene. O'Looney was still rummaging about in the dark interior of the wardrobes. When he emerged into the weird light he was stark naked, but for a huge grin, and he had over each arm what appeared to be huge brown fur coats. He stopped and looked her nakedness over.

"Marvellous," he said. "Bloody exquisite. Now sit yourself down there on the sofa with your drink. I'll just get meself another beer and then I'll switch the telly on."

Coral watched him throw the furs over the end of the sofa and wondered what role they were going to play in the proceedings as he poured the contents of another dark bottle into his glass. He took a long swallow from it and then switched on the TV before sitting down next to her on the cool leather. Their bare thighs were touching and he raised his glass to clink against hers.

"There now, this is nice and cosy, eh?"

"Very nice," Coral said, somewhat bemused. "What are we going to watch, by the way?"

O'Looney leaned forward with one hand around his glass and the other between her thighs.

"It's a nature programme. Wildlife I mean, not silly bloody nudists. I tape a lot of wildlife."

"Oh," was all Coral could manage just then. I've met some funny ones in my time, she thought.

"Ah, here it comes now," he said excitedly. "This is it now, this is it!" His hand squeezed the inside of her thigh a little harder.

Christ, she thought, he's getting all worked up like a little
boy at the Saturday morning pictures!

The screen suddenly filled with bright colours, A sweeping
panoramic view of beautiful mountains and green wooded
slopes and valleys. Amongst the trees, deer were browsing
in the lush grass, occasionally raising their heads to sniff the
breeze and look around.

"Dammit," O'Looney struggled to his feet. "There's no
bloody sound. You've got to have the sound to appreciate the
stag."

He turned up the volume just as a large stag with a great
spread of antlers came into picture. He too sniffed at the
breeze, then made the sound of the rut. A great moan of
sound like a fog-horn, with his white breath left hanging in
the mountain air.

The well known narrator's voice was saying that it was
the time of the rut, and that the stag was extremely aroused.
With some forty females to service, he was moving amongst
them until one would make it known that she was willing to
be the first to receive him.

"There! Did you ever hear the like o'that?" O'Looney
was bouncing up and down on the white leather. "The lucky
bastard! Imagine, forty of the little beauties and all yours!"

He knocked back the rest of his pint and put the glass
down amongst the magazines on the table. He was gripping
his own knees with both hands now, his eyes bulging with
excitement as he watched the stag sniffing around the rear end
of a female. He started fidgeting excitedly as the stag mounted
the female and began his hurried thrustings. "That's it, that's
it. Jaze I can't wait any longer." He leapt to his feet with a
bright pink erection.

"What are you doing?"

"I'm stopping the tape and we'll run it again from the

start." He picked up the smaller of the two fur coats and handed it to her. "Put this on will you, while I get me head-gear?"

Coral slipped the knee-length fur on while he plunged into the wardrobes again. When he reappeared he had to come out sideways. He was wearing a real stag's head mask, complete with antlers. Only the lower jaw was missing. Coral clapped a hand to her mouth but failed to suppress her laughter.

"That good," Mick said. "Glad to see you're entering into the spirit of things!"

He heaved his own fur on and switched the TV on again, his right antler catching the frame of the painting as he stooped and tearing it from its wall fixing.

"Never mind that," he said hurriedly, ignoring the crash as it bounced off the bar. "Get one of your balloons from the bag!"

Coral took the packet from her bag and removed one of its sachets. She peeled off the wrapper and while O'Looney held his coat open, she fitted him with his sheath.

"That's it, that's it!" The huge comic figure was panting heavily. "Now brace yourself against the back of the sofa there."

Coral did as he said, going round behind the sofa and placing her hands wide apart on the top of its back. As she spread her feet apart O'Looney got round behind her. She felt the coat being lifted up over her bare rump and she could hear him sniffing around there.

"Sod it," he complained. "I can't get in properly with these antlers on. It's always the same. They keep hitting against the sofa."

As he stood up she felt his big hands come up inside the coat from behind to close gently on her breasts and she felt his huge belly against the base of her spine.

"That's better. Look at that now," he said over her shoulder as the stag mounted again.

As they watched the stag's erratic jerkings Mick began his own movement, blowing a beery fog-horn blast not unlike the rutting animal's.

"D'ye know," he said seriously, "I'll have to get that one about the fruit bats. Would you believe they do it hanging upside down in trees!"

20

B each Green Guest House. First Floor Front. Room with Sea View.

The jarring metallic rattle of the alarm clock jigging across the scratched bedside table woke Duncan at nine. On returning from the pub at six thirty he had discovered to his glee, that his landlady, a particularly mistrustful type called Mrs Collins, was out of the house. Her husband Les, for whom Duncan sympathized with a passion, kept out of the place as much as possible, so Duncan availed himself of the unguarded kitchen. He carefully constructed a pile of doorstep style ham and salad sandwiches and retired upstairs to his room.

He had been dozing since seven o'clock. As the alarm clock rattled against the empty plate on the table he reached out with a numb hand and fumblingly pressed the button. He had been lying on that arm and it had lost most of its feeling. The small room was half lit by a nearby street lamp. As he squinted in the gloom he could see the dark shape that was his uniform hanging on the back of the door and his helmet like a fat dark owl on top of the wardrobe. He felt a sudden horror at the thought of going on duty, then with a flush of relief remembered that his old recurring back trouble had given him a few days' respite. Duncan eased himself up and sat on the edge of the bed, rubbing the cold arm to get the circulation going. He was tempted to crash out again until morning, but the need for more beer prevailed over everything. He got up and gingerly hoisted the straps of his dangling braces up over his shoulders, then went over to the washbasin and switched on the little strip light over it by pulling its tacky, soiled string. Even now his belch brought back memories of the morning's kippers. He stuck out his tongue and examined it in the speckled shaving mirror. It looked like the remains of an old yellow face flannel. He was aware of the reek of his own breath; he brushed his teeth, using a green, super plaque-shifting, power-whitener of a bacteria killer and then splashed cold water on his face. He had opened the window to freshen the stuffy room when he had come in earlier; he turned off the tap and drew back the flimsy curtain.

He breathed deeply of the warm evening air. It was almost still, with a barely discernible movement bringing the sea smell from the beach across the green on the other side of the road. A concrete path ran across the green and then ran parallel with the beach past the Dolphin Beach Café. Duncan could make out its name in big white letters on its red tiled roof. An extension had been built on to the café to house space age children's amusements. He could see the dark shapes of the players against the flashing lights of the machines and he was thankful that the place was inaudible from his room. Next to the extension was an area of beach used by local fishermen. The boats drawn up on the pebbles and their winch- boxes and stacks of crab pots and nets seemed to be glowing in the green and white from the long fluorescent strip lights outside the building. The boats and gear were in a very vulnerable location, but strangely there had never been any report of theft or damage.

Outside the café several large motorcycles were stood gleaming and unattended on the footpath. Duncan had something else to be thankful for;if he had seen them whilst on duty he would have had to get their owners out of there and move them on. The bikes didn't look like local ones and it might easily have caused more trouble than it was worth.

His brain felt sluggish from the afternoon's drinking, as if someone had inserted a funnel in his ear whilst he dozed and poured heavy gear oil in. He shook his head and sat down on the bed again; it was going to take some effort if he was going to get himself moving and make it to that party. Again he was tempted to fall back on the bed and stay there till Mrs Collins rang the bell for the early breakfast sitting.

He told himself that a shower and change would make all the difference. That would do the trick. He stood up and shook himself all over, then undressed and wrapped a towel around his middle. He left the room and padded barefoot along the cracked linoleum of the landing to the bathroom.

The plastic shower curtain was torn and hung from only three of its original rings as if having miraculously survived a great storm, and the shower itself was an ancient contraption with an enormous down-turned head on a bent copper pipe clipped to the cracked wall tiles. It always looked to Duncan like a top-heavy sunflower. He knew from experience that the thing would only work occasionally, but the presence of a globule of water hanging from the lowest of its perforations filled him with hope. He watched it for a while, expecting it to become a drip, but it refused to budge even when he blew on it coaxingly.

Duncan turned its corroded tap and waited, but other than a sound like a death rattle from the pipe, followed by a loud clonk from somewhere above, nothing happened. He grabbed the pipe and shook it, and at last the single tear-drop moved from side to side and then fell, but not a bead more would it shed, despite a slap from the palm of his hand that left it vibrating and making a buzzing sound as he stormed out.

"Sod the thing!" He would make a slight detour in his

route and take a shower at the police station.

Back in his room he pondered whether or not to wear the dreaded corset to the party as insurance. He decided against it as he knew he would be able to shower and dress at the station without being watched, and after the injuries that had been sustained earlier the local arm of the law was unlikely to be represented at the party by anyone other than himself.

After dressing hurriedly, he brushed his teeth again before leaving the guest house. Outside the warm breeze had shifted slightly and the sea smell had been drowned by that of hot dogs and onions from the café. Its green and white exterior lights were brighter in the gathering darkness and out on the black sea the deck lights of a freighter at anchor off the harbour came on suddenly, illuminating her white superstructure. Duncan sniffed the hot food smell, happily as he envisaged the sumptuous spread of booze and eats that Mick O'Looney was sure to be laying on. The vision made him feel much better and he smiled broadly in anticipation.

It was with little interest therefore that he noticed the number of motorcycles outside the café had increased since he had looked from his window; tonight they were to be someone else's problem. It was only five minutes' walk to the station and little more from there to the pub. All he needed in between was that shower.

Beneath his newly cleaned and pressed suit and new white shirt he felt hot and sticky. The thought of standing under the shower, like his hunger and thirst was eager to be redressed, but the knowledge that all three were soon to be sated was exquisitely enjoyable in itself.

In the churchyard, some newly installed white stone surrounds like small tombs, held floodlights that illuminated the flints and stone blocks of the building and the reflected light on the surrounding gravestones showed them eerily bright against the darkness surrounding the yew trees and bushes.

Duncan was enjoying his sticky body's yearning for the freshening water of the shower. When he turned the corner at the churchyard gate he could see the police station and the brightly lit railway crossing beyond. The sight of the station reminded him of when young Morris had first come to them from training school. Duncan had come across the lad asleep in one of the cells when he should have been out on his beat checking that shops and things were properly locked for the night. It was past midnight after a hot sunny day and the streets outside were as empty as a gold rush town after the claims had been milked dry. You could have fired a cannon load of grape-shot up the High Street and not hit a living thing. There had been no rain for over a month, but he roused the youngster hastily and told him it was pissing down in horse troughs outside and that Sarge Chopin had come in and was asking for him at the desk. The Young Morris, with a look of sheer terror in his eyes, donned his helmet and dived under the shower in full uniform. When suitably doused by the artificial rainwater he hurried back along the corridor to the desk, saluting frantically and blurting on about wasn't it a filthy night outside with the unexpected rain, and how he had just come in off his beat to use the toilet.

The Sarge let him finish and then explained that he had come in for a glass of orange squash as it was such a hot and arid night outside. He never did admonish the lad; he didn't have to. The expression of horrific realization on the youngster's wet shiny face was sufficient evidence for the Sarge to know that he would not forget that night for as long as he lived.

Through the glass of the front door Duncan could see the same Young Morris alone behind the desk reading one of his magazines. Pushing the door open gently, Duncan went in. The stillness in the high-ceilinged room was enhanced by the regular tick-tock of the big round-faced clock on the wall. Its Roman numerals said it was still only nine thirty. In between the tick and the tock you could have heard a gnat fart. Duncan summoned up a belch and the Young Morris looked up with a start.

"Koi carp?" Duncan nodded at the magazine.

"Yes. I can't afford the really good ones, but it's nice to look at them though."

"Maybe we'll catch the bugger who's been netting them from gardens at night, eh? We could confiscate a few for you!"

The young constable looked at him suspiciously, unsure if it were a joke or not.

"You been here all day, then?" Duncan asked.

"I volunteered for some overtime. We're short of men after that trouble this morning."

"Ah, yes." Duncan lifted the flap. "I'm just going through to the back for a shower."

He watched for Young Morris's reaction. Young Morris winced at the painful memory. "Yes of course," he said with his face reddening.

Duncan went through smiling. There was a cell door on either side of the corridor leading to the shower room and the toilets. H stopped and squinted through the tiny observation hole in the door on his right. The room was empty, save for its narrow bed and a chair with a bucket under it. He put his eyeball to the hole in the other door. The giant Hughie was stretched out on the bed with his eyes closed and his hands behind his dark shaggy head. He was still wearing his filthy string vest and shorts and his huge booted feet projected more than a foot beyond the end of the bed's metal frame. On the chair was a plastic plate with a plastic knife and fork and a tea mug.

Duncan's gentle pressure on the door told him that it wasn't locked. The silly young sod must have forgotten to lock it after taking Hughie's supper into him. He shrugged his off-duty shoulders as he made for the shower room. It wasn't his problem and the mild mannered colossus wasn't likely to try the door anyway.

He stripped and stood under the shower, admiring its modern streamlined head as much as he had loathed the antique sunflower back in the guest house. He wanted to savour this yearning of his before turning on the tap. When he did let the water come the sensation was initially ecstatic, but like all good things it quickly paled, like that first clean taste of a cold beer. He soon tired of it and the desire to get to the pub prevailed. He reached from behind the curtain for the nice clean white towel that should have been on the rail there on the wall. It wasn't.

He stuck his head out and shouted. "Oi Morris, fetch us a towel, will you?"

His bellow volleyed around the tiled room and out through the open doorway and down the corridor. Young Morris's came back ricocheting off the walls. "Righto!"

The sudden commotion roused Hughie from wherever his reverie had transported him. He heard footsteps in the corridor and thinking that they might be bringing in a drunk that he would probably know, he got up and opened the door to have a look.

Young Morris had taken a clean towel from the stores and gone into the shower room with it. Hughie closed the cell door behind him and sauntered off down the corridor and out through the open gap. By the time the lad got back to his Koi carp The Tree was out in the street. He sniffed the briny air and it occurred to him that it would be nice to spend the night on the beach. He would enjoy a moonlight dip and then sleep under one of the overturned boats the way they used to back home. Taking great deep breaths of the night, and with long leisurely strides, he set off for the footbridge and the seashore beyond.

21

Duncan got to The Smack at a little after ten. The bar was almost full to capacity and he could feel the rise in temperature as he entered. There was at least sufficient room to get to the bar, as a few drinkers had gone out into the pub's garden which could be reached by going round the corner of the museum next door and along the side street to a gate in the wall. Drinks were served to the garden patrons through a hatch from the kitchen, and the door from the bar to the kitchen was open, as was the front door and the door leading to the toilets at the rear, allowing some passage of air through the bar. Despite the open doors and extractor fans going at both ends of the room, between the beams of the low ceiling and around the heads of the standing clientele there hung a blue, canopy-like layer of smoke which despite the considerable body heat was thickening and lowering itself to shoulder level.

Duncan could feel the heat coming from the bodies that he squeezed between in his quest for service at the bar.

Frank was standing there at the corner of its L-shaped counter between Arthur and a fantastic looking blonde. She was almost as tall as Duncan even though she was wearing low heels, and the pastel pink creation she was wearing was accentuating her golden tan and leaving little to work on for the imagination. She had her arm locked around Frank's and Doreen was looking very sharp daggers at her from her stool at the end of the bar.

Frank and Arthur made room between them.

"Hallo, Duncan." Frank said. "How's the old back?"
"Bloody awful." Duncan economized with the truth.

Norman was being assisted behind the bar by the pint-
sized Dot. He passed Duncan's pint over her head to Frank
who passed it on. "There, you'll feel better with that inside
you. Oh, this is Monika. Monika, Duncan."

She smiled wonderfully and held out newly painted red
talons. Duncan held her hand gently for a moment. It felt
strangely cool, considering. He was getting hotter by the
second and wishing he'd left his jacket in the wardrobe.
"Bloody warm, isn't it," Arthur observed. He had changed
for the evening and was now wearing a red beret and smock,
his Gauloise helping considerably with the build up of fug.

"Sure is." Duncan took a long swallow from the stinging
cold draught lager. He thought it had never tasted so good.

But then he always felt that way about the first one of a
session.

"Frank's new friend," Arthur mouthed secretively when
he was sure only Duncan would hear. He raised his eyebrows
and cast a quick, wide eyed glance in Monika's direction.

"Ah," Duncan said. He detected a hint of green in the
painter's blue eyes.

"Seen all those bikes outside the beach cafe?" Arthur
asked more loudly.

"Yes. Not my problem tonight though, I'm glad to say.
Off duty." "Oh yes. The back." Arthur caught Doreen's
malevolent glare and averted his gaze. "They don't know what
to install next in that place, do they? Have you seen that fluffy
red parrot thing in a cage outside now? The thing sits there
not saying a word till someone passes, then in one of those
hideous robot voices it says "Hallo. Come here and talk to

me!" I mean, how the hell does it know someone's there, eh? Body heat or something?"

"Search me," Duncan shrugged. "Remember that big laughing policeman they had in there? They got so fed up with the drunks pissing up against it they got rid of it after a month."

"Didn't you have to arrest somebody over that once?"

"Some day-tripper from south London somewhere. God knows how he found his way along here. He'd been to the races with a coach load of his mates. They all went into Brighton in the evening and somehow he got separated and ended up here. Pissed as a newt, he was. He went into the amusements and pissed all over the policeman's legs. Then it started its laughing and he started punching hell out of it. By the time I got there he'd dragged it out onto the concrete path outside and he was kicking seven colours of shit out of it. He was yelling something like 'Laugh at me now, you fat bastard!' and jumping up and down on its head."

"Did it still manage to raise a laugh, then?" "No, he'd ripped its wiring out of the wall." "What did he get then?"

"Just a night in a cell and a fine."

"They didn't press more serious charges, then?"

"No. It's funny really, there wasn't a mark on the policeman but they got rid of it soon after that."

Duncan looked rather disappointed with the taste of his second gulp of lager. Arthur resumed his scrutiny of Frank's mysterious and fabulous new friend. He was also feeling a bit miffed about the heavenly twins not turning up yet. When Weldon and Ladybird had returned about half an hour before, they had said that the girls would be along later and how they wouldn't miss the party for anything. Arthur had visions of them being picked up by some young disco dancers and deciding to stick to their own age group. The fact that Frank was enjoying some success rankled, and the fact that Monika was so damned gorgeous only added to his discomfort.

The conversations and laughter around them had become an unintelligible hubbub. Duncan cast his eyes around the faces that he could see amongst the throng.

Fishy Phil had resurfaced and was to all outward appearances as sober as when he had come into the pub more than eight hours before. Fred the Fence, who had followed him in not long after ten that morning, was sitting in a corner with an aloof look on his face and a large Glenmorangie in his hand. Kowloon Moon had returned weeping with joy from the races with every pocket stuffed with paper money and was now attempting to spend it as quickly as possible with the expert assistance of The Plunger and Ernie Rudd. Albert Hoskins had Peter cornered nicely by the fireplace and Eric had Weldon pinned against the oak post at the bar, whilst Ladybird had joined Doreen on the stool next to her and they were enjoying a morose conversation which concerned their respective husbands.

Duncan had had enough of people watching. He was feeling extremely uncomfortable and thought he would get out into the garden. The manoeuvre meant squeezing out through the press and round the side street. He finished his rapidly warming lager and made for the open doorway and the sweet evening air. He saw Eric wink knowingly at him and press yet closer to Weldon as he eased apologetically past them.

Eric had brightened considerably since his last visit to the toilet and had been farting frequently yet inaudibly with a happy confidence, secure in the knowledge that once he had this settled feeling he would have no further trouble from his bowels until early morning. Unfortunately for Weldon, with that confidence came the need that some inebriates have of holding one-sided conversations. He belched some sickly sweet breath into the American's face and took another sip of beer before going on to the next subject.

Weldon steeled himself for the forthcoming ear bashing. He was more than a little concerned that it might go all over his shirt front.

"Did I ever tell you, Weldon, about when I worked in the power station after the war?" Eric belched again. "No? It's funny how many old matelots ended up as stokers in power stations and boiler houses, innit? I was on a minesweeper, y'know, a converted trawler she was..." He took another sip from his glass. "...the old Norbury 'B' station, I worked at. I had that place running like a dream, I did. Sweet as a nut. Ninety eight per cent perfect, it was. Only two per cent shit went out of them chimneys. Electro-static precipitators they were. Six hundred cubic yards of dust and ash per day."

"Really." Weldon tried to catch Norman's eye, in the hope that in ordering some more drinks he might be able to slip from Eric's clutches. Nothing doing.

Eric, on the other hand, truly believed that he had a fascinated listener. "Oh yes," he slurred on. "Not much call for them these days o'course. You should have seen the wrapping gear, though. A bloody great cog goes round and it shakes the precipitators, see? Then the particles are charged plus and minus and the dust drops down and gets drawn off by vacuum..."

"You don't say. I wonder what happened to Ladybird and the girls..."

"Your good lady wife is just behind you. Behind the post with Doreen." Eric waved his glass around, slopping beer on the carpet. "Do you know what they used all that dust for?"

"No, I ..."

"Blocks. They used it to make lightweight building blocks.

They made 'em in the brickworks, they did."

"Really."

"Oh yes. It's called P. F. dust. Stands for pulverized fuel that does." "Really ..."

"Oh, yes." Eric leaned forward as if about to impart some vital tit-bit of classified information. "D'you know what," he breathed in Weldon's ear. "It was ninety six feet down. That's from the top door down to the ash pit!"

"Is that a fact!"

"Yeah, they were great days all right." Eric stared gloomily at his beer for a moment but perked up quickly at some more old memories. "I had me old motorbike in them days, Trigger I called her. I used to go to Lingfield races of an evening with my lady friend up on the pillion and we'd stop at every pub on the left on the way there, and then every pub on the right on the way back."

"Er, pardon me but surely they're the same thing, aren't they?" Weldon asked. He was glad to be away from the power station at last.

Eric thought for a moment. "Same thing? How can they be the same? One lot's on the left hand side of the road and the other lot's on the right. I should know, shouldn't I'?"

Weldon sensed the imminent drunk's sudden switch from affable camaraderie to belligerence. "Oh, I get what you mean now," he said quickly. "You mean every pub on the left going out to the track, and then each one on the left coming back. Whey would have been on the right going out."

"Of course," Eric said happily. "Isn't that what I said before then? I'm sure it was."

"Yes, I think that's what you said."

"I thought so. Anyway, that's what we used to do, and when we got back we'd have a drink in the pub by Streatham Common. After we'd been in the woods there for a knee trembler, that is. She liked to have it up against one particular tree, she did. It must have held special memories for her."

"Very likely," Weldon said. And this damn post will have them for me, he thought.

"One morning after, when I woke up I couldn't remember where I'd been or who I was with, or where I left the bike or anything, we were that pissed. Anyway, when I went back to the pub, there she was, right where I'd left her!"

"Your … er …lady friend?"

"No, the ruddy bike, old Trigger! Bloody marvellous eh, you couldn't do that these days, could you, eh? Find her still there next morning!"

Weldon's bladder was by now feeling fit to burst. "No, I guess you couldn't," he grimaced. He tried to wriggle free from the pressure of the post on his back, but Eric grabbed him by the arm with his free hand while his glass waved around in the other. The glass was almost empty as most of its contents had ended on the floor. Eric was not so far gone that he failed to make sure that it was seen to be empty before continuing with his reminiscences; he quaffed the remainder and waved the empty glass around under Weldon's nose before putting it down.

"I didn't tell you about this bloke who was at the old Norbury 'B'," he said as he tightened his grip. "He was a proper caution, I can tell you. There was a few of us on a shift, see, and when we finished we all took showers together, being covered in shitty soot and dust, like. Well, this bloke Bill, he had a great big beer gut he did, and he used to get his John Thomas erected and then stroll up and down in front of us in the changing room. It wasn't what anyone would call really big or anything, but a handy sort of size like, and he'd offer to slip anyone a length who fancied it. I don't recall that he ever got any takers but then you never know, do you? He used

to recite a bloody good poem too, that Bill. Hang on while
I remember how the thing went. I know it, I know it! It had
a bloody good old rhythm to it, like that one about the little
idol to the north of whatsname. Just give me a minute and
I'll get it."

Weldon was more than happy to give him as long as he
wanted. The longer the better. As Eric released his hold in
order to scratch his forehead in an effort to revive some dying,
if not long dead brain cells, he managed to push him back far
enough to get away from the post. With his bladder feeling like
it was the size of an over inflated party balloon, he made for
the toilets, pushing the door open while unzipping the front
of his trousers with the other hand. As he pissed against the
shiny white urinal, he watched as the pressure of the frothing,
hot liquid stream began to dislodge some cigarette ends from
around the trough's outlet, and with a loud gurgle, it emptied.

The door opened behind him, and the swarthy, swaying
figure, of José Mackay crashed against the wall next to him.
The fetor of his hot garlic breath, mixed with the reek from
the dark axillas that lurked inside José's Rioja-marinated
jersey, rose to assail Weldon's nostrils. It even overpowered
the strong, moth-ball like smell that had wafted up from the
freshly exposed blue cubes in the trough at their feet.

"Lookathat," José nodded sleepily down at his tool, which
was deflating in his hand as his bladder ernptied. "Jussa
pissaproud, he was!" He leaned forward against the wall.

"I know the feeling," Weldon sympathized through gritted
teeth; as he tucked his tool back into his boxer shorts he saw
that the fisherman's wavering aim was spraying over his
handmade shoes and trousers. "This place sure is lively," he
said. "Surely you guys don't keep up the drinking like this
every day, do you?"

José had almost gone back to sleep standing up, but the

question jerked him back to a hazy, muddled consciousness. He knew that his local bar in Gibraltar didn't have such a hygienic looking pisshole and he was trying to recall where the hell he was. Suddenly it came to him.

"No-no, issanorralikeathissaeverydai. Every fridayissa likeathis. Everybody pissaoutahissabrains." He swayed back and then forward again, stopping with his face pressed to the cool white tiles of the wall. "Tonight issabiga party …" His voice trailed off as he began to lose consciousness again and slid to his right with his nose and lips bent and flattened, leaving a smear in the moisture on the tiles.

Weldon caught him before he collapsed into the trough which had begun to fill again. "Say, I'd better get you back in there and get you seated," he said remembering that there is no such thing as 'a little garlic' as José unleashed a long asphyxiating sigh full in his face. He got an arm round and by lifting under an armpit tried to lug him to the door. José, with boots dragging on the wet quarry tiles, was fumbling with both hands somewhere near where he thought his tool should be. He knew it was still out but couldn't find it.

"C'mon, José, for Chrissakes!"

"Jussaminute, I gotta find … ah! Hereaheis!" He had found his limp tool with one hand and the tab of his zip with the other. With his eyes closed and his head under Weldon's chin he tucked the soft penis in and hoisted the zip at what was unfortunately the same time. The tiny metal teeth of the zip seized as savagely as any piranha on the tender pink flesh.

"Aaaaaaaaiaaaiy!" José's agonized shriek must have been heard back home on the Rock. He flung both arms around Weldon's neck and hung there with his boots six inches off the floor, his teeth clenched and with tears pouring down his darkly stubbled cheeks. The excruciating pain had rendered him incapable of speech. Only a pathetic animal whine came from between his locked jaws.

Jesus, Weldon thought. What to do with him? He felt more than a little dubious about hauling his all but unconscious burden back into the bar. Negotiating the heavy, spring loaded door would be difficult enough, never mind how he would explain how he came to be locked in the embrace of a drunken Gibraltarian fisherman in a toilet, and how he had come to get caught up in his zip!

Get him seated in the crapper, that was it! That way he could get help without causing uproar in the bar. Just a quiet word with one of the others, that was it.

The fisherman's blackly matted arms were still clasped around his neck and his old rubber wellies stood tip-toed on Weldon's expensive leather shoes. Weldon began a slow, strange, backward moving dance with his comatose partner towards the crapper cubicle, sliding his feet along under José's boots on the red tiled floor. The movement must have aggravated the stocky dark man's pincered wound, but he did not cry out; his fetid breath still came in that terrible whining and his brimful eyes opened and rolled upwards, xanthic and crazed with pain and terror.

A few sliding steps and Weldon had got him into the cubicle. He stooped and lowered the other's backside onto the seat. José had begun mumbling incoherently in Spanish, still maintaining a strong hold around Weldon's neck while his head rolled from side to side in his agony.

Weldon gripped his wrists and managed to release the arms from around his neck. "You poor bastard," he muttered. "Now don't try to move from there. Stay right where you are, I'm going to get some help."

José said something unintelligible through foaming lips and Weldon patted him comfortingly on the shoulder and went back into the noise of the bar. After a struggle he got to the counter, but he was only able to get close enough to one person that he knew. Eric, still with an empty glass.

"Oh, there you are, Weldon," he brightened considerably. "You were a bloody long time in there, weren't you? I remember how that poem goes now, you know, the one that Bill used to recite in the showers at the power station."

"Oh, great."

"I knew you'd be pleased. I thought you were never coming back. Here." Eric leaned closer, ever ready to listen to a fellow sufferer's plight. "You haven't got a touch of the William Pitts like I had earlier, have you?"

"William Pitts, what the hell are they? Oh, I see what you're getting at! Hell, no. Listen there's been a slight accident in the john; that little Spanish guy, or whatever he is…"

"You mean José." "That's him."

"José Mackay. He's Gibraltarian."

"Whatever. How the hell did he get a name like Mackay?"

"His father was a Smelly Sock."

"A what? Hey, what is it with you guys? William Pitts and Smelly Socks, is that all part of that rhyming slang I heard about? I thought that was only cockneys!"

Eric looked from Weldon's face to his empty glass and back again. "Frank and Arthur and myself are … well, Londoners anyway. I don't think you have to have been born within earshot of Bow bells anymore. We've got a black boxer from Crawley who's called a cockney by the media!"

"You don't say," Weldon said seriously. "Hey, where's my little Ladybird? I gotta tell her we're drinking not only with descendants of the men who were at Hastings but some real live cockneys, too!"

"The crowd's moved around a bit while you were away," Eric told him. "She's in that alcove by the fireplace with your grand-daughters: They're quite excited; Mick O'Looney looked in and made your invitation official."

Weldon had caught his wife's attention somehow through the smoke enshrouded heads. "Hey, Ladybird! Ladybird!"

"Whaaaat?" Her voice whined like a starting air raid siren. "This guy Eric is a cockney, and some of the others too!" "Whaaaat?"

"I said, some of these guys are cockneys!" "Whaaaat?" The twins had started too.

"Jesus!" Weldon raised his voice some more and exaggerated each word with slow and purposeful mouth shapes. "I said. … these … guys… here … are …Goddam … cockneys!"

"Whaaaat?"

"The mothers are goddarn fucking cockneys for Chrissakes!" he bawled to no avail. "Aw, shit! Just forget it, will ya, Honey!"

"Whaaaat?"

"Awww …" Weldon needed a drink. Much to Eric's delight he caught Norman's eye and two pints were coming up. As he put his hand in his pocket Weldon felt a firm hot grip on his arm. José was standing behind him, grinning from ear to ear and offering to buy the drinks, with a five pound note.

"Jesus, José. You poor bastard, I didn't mean to forget you in there! How the hell did you get free?"

José patted his fly, which was securely fastened. "Issallaright," he beamed as he took a clasp knife from his pocket and opened it. He made a sawing motion with the razor-sharp blade. "Jussa like the time the anchor snag and I can'tagetahimup. Thatta time I saw athrough the rope. This time mucha more easy; I jussaw athrough a little bit askin!"

"But you must have lost some blood, surely?"

José was looking at the clock. "Iss nothing," he said in what had suddenly become sober, almost perfect English. He slapped the fiver down on the bar and shook Weldon's hand, solemnly. "It's a near the time of last orders," he told the amazed visitor. "If I am to attend a Mr O'Looney's then I have to return to boat to a change."

He nodded to them both and disappeared into the crowd.

"Gee, what an amazing guy." Weldon marvelled. "He seems to be quite sober now."

"He is," Eric said. "He'll make it to the party all right, he always does. Wouldn't miss a free piss up. Remarkable how they can do it, though. I won't be going."

"You won't?"

"No, the old liver's had it. And the kidneys. Insides are all shot to pieces. I've had my quota for the night, if I have any more I'll be ill tomorrow; and the day after too probably."

"I'm very sorry to hear that, Eric," Weldon said as he saw Norman glance at his watch. Others along the bar had seen it too and they began drinking up hurriedly and clamouring for more. There were orders being shouted through the hatch from the garden as well and Doreen tottered into the kitchen to serve there for the last ten minutes.

Eric picked up his glass and sent the pint down to his clapped out liver in two gulps. He looked at the five pound note on the bar.

"Are you sure I can't get you one more before you go?" Weldon asked.

"Well … all right then," Eric said after some mock deliberation. "You're a good bloke, Weldon, Now I can give dear old José his fiver back in the morning, it's more than likely all the silly sod's got!"

22

The incoming tide had filled the river and it was high above the green weed on the legs of the footbridge. By midnight it would be one of the highest tides of the year.

Only when a very high tide occurred at a time when a great amount of rainwater was being forced down river to meet it would the level have been any higher.

Across the river from the town, a bright silver moon hung above the rooftops of the bungalows in the dark, starry speckled night. There was no flow on the river now and there was no breeze to move the boats floating so serenely at their moorings on the town side. The boats nearest the green by the footbridge shone in the orange glow from the street lights, and the occasional night flying seagull coming out of the darkness was lightened yellow as it passed overhead. There was very little passing traffic in the High Street, and anyone who found himself standing there on the pavement above the green, with his elbows on the rail in the quiet of the warm summer night might have imagined he were lounging on a promenade by one of the Italian lakes or anywhere else that he might fancy or have dreamed of.

The pubs closed at eleven, and by about ten minutes past the first few of the procession of people coming from all six pubs in the High Street, and from the three by the railway station could be seen crossing the footbridge. A few more who were leaving the Lady Caroline on the other side had a far shorter journey to the common destination and were already on the footpath leading to the houseboats. Most of the dark hulls were unlit, and the bright moon cast dark shadows on the footpath and on the water.

Other than the cargo vessels that plied to and from the harbour, the Pachydermatous was the biggest craft on the river. The thirty metres long Dutch steel barge had been decorated with red, white and blue light bulbs and bunting around her entire length overhead, whilst on her slightly raised foredeck, O'Looney had installed a five piece jazz band. They were dressed in straw boaters and striped jackets and had already started belting out a few numbers after spending a couple of hours in the riverside bar of the Lady Caroline. Behind them was a crane which could be used for the loading or unloading of a small car for use on long cruises; from this hung three huge lanterns which bathed the musicians in red, white and blue light.

O'Looney was very pleased with the band. He had listened to their opening number, which although it could be heard clearly from the railway station, had not a listener on deck, from below. With all the portholes, windows and hatches open, their rendition of 'Stranger on the Shore' had come through very nicely to the main saloon where Duggie was putting the final touches to the layout of plates and bowls of cold meats and salads.

Duggie had worked hard on the provisioning and the spread with the help of The Moon Garden's chief cook who was on hire for the night. Mick Tong was now in the galley wearing his personal head-set, and listening to the Elvis sound and look-alike as he worked over the hot stove. The wonderful smells from the cooking wafted tantalizingly out through the various openings and into the warm night air to meet the nostrils of the arriving guests.

Standing at the top of the wooden gangway in the glare from a massive searchlight mounted on the wheelhouse roof, Mick O'Looney shone like a monstrously bloated kingfisher in his new bottle green velvet jacket, open necked orange shirt with a yellow cravat, and blue trousers that seemed to be giving off a luminous glow.

He had positioned himself there to welcome his guests aboard as they ascended from the riverside path to the main deck. As the band blared happily away from their little stage, the party-goers came on board in varying styles of dress. Some were smartly casual, some were just casual, and there were the inevitable Henley Regattas and even a few Royal Ascots.

O'Looney was loving it. For all his blustery outward appearance, he was a sensitive observer, and his delight in seeing people enjoying themselves was being heightened by the fact that many of the arrivals were making heavier going of the incline than a few others had, due to having already been quite well refreshed as indeed he himself had been.

All were welcomed heartily and told that they could use any part of the vessel. In fact that wasn't quite true, as he had locked the master cabin and only he and one of the guests had a key.

That guest was now using the cabin before O'Looney literally pushed the boat out. Coral was sitting on the king-size bed attending to her lipstick after yet another shower, having arrived on her own from the farmhouse by taxi.

It wasn't long before there were more than fifty people on board. On the stroke of midnight, when there was no sign of a straggler on the footbridge, O'Looney gave Duggie the order to cast off and joined the guys 'n' dolls in the rather confined wheelhouse.

After accepting a large gin and tonic, he stood at the wheel and pressed the starter button. From somewhere down below the big diesel engine growled at starting, and the band took the opportunity to stop playing as one man and grab their pint jugs from the table beside them and get a few much needed gulps down their throats.

Through the colourful array on deck, O'Looney watched as Duggie cast off the ropes fore and aft. As there was no flow to contend with he took a sip from his glass, and then a longer swig, sucking on an ice cube before he eased the long hull of the Pachydermatous away from the river bank and out onto the almost brimful, moonlit river.

The sudden, but gentle movement brought cheers up from the deck and the band started up again as they passed under the footbridge.

Captain O'Looney held a steady straight course down the middle of the river between the moored boats on either side. Past the now dark Yacht Club and the boatyards and the fish market, past the derelict site where he would make a fat killing if the Marina ever got the go-ahead from those bastards on the council; four of whom were at his party with their good lady wives.

The wake of the Pachydermatous bubbled like silver coins at her stern and her wash rocked the sleeping boats along the way to the harbour, where they passed the high sided grey ships and the huge stacks of great timbers that had come thousands of miles from vanishing forests to be unloaded in this little port.

Soon they passed the big corrugated building that housed the car auctions and then the ramp from the lifeboat shed and the old stone lighthouse.

O'Looney spread his feet a little wider apart and adopted a severe, masterly look as he turned the bows to what he called 'the right'.

Ahead now was the harbour mouth and the flat, silver-smooth sea.

23

"Oh, the Duchess she was dressing, a-dressing for the ball, when she spied a bloody greet trooper pissing up against a wall.

With his bloody great kidney wiper, he stood there six foot three, and there was half a yard to the foreskin hanging down below his knee.

The Duchess sent a note to him, and in it she did say "I would rather be fucked by a trooper than my old man any day."

So he mounted on his charger, yes he mounted it astride, with his prick slung over his shoulder and his bollocks by his side. He rode into the mansion house, he rode into the ball, and a doorman cried 'God help us, he has come to fuck us all!'"

Eric was reciting the poem aloud to himself as he sat in total darkness in the little brick-built toilet at the bottom of the rear garden of his beach road bungalow.

He had been summoned there at two o'clock in the morning by the return of his searingly hot stomach pains, and had only just made it in time to the pan, down the cracked path, barefoot in his pyjamas.

He was sitting in the dark because the tiny building had no electricity. Actually, the darkness suited his mood. He had been unable to sleep in the clammy heat of his untidy, dusty bedroom, and now he reflected gloomily that he would probably never get another chance to let Weldon hear the poem from his old power station days. He heaved a sigh of resignation.

He didn't fancy going back to the musty smelling sheets in his airless room. He thought he would get his deck chair from the garden shed and sit in the comparative cool of the night under the stars. As he hitched up his pyjama trousers, he heard the rumble of powerful motorcycles on the beach road. It was unusual to hear any traffic at all along there so late at night and Eric listened intently in the darkness, with his ear pressed to the diamond shaped ventilation hole in the wooden door. From the sounds he could tell that there were several machines and that they had stopped on the road nearby. For a few seconds the motors ticked over and then there was silence.

Eric waited with his ear straining at the hole. A slight breeze had come from the west, and he could feel his ear cooling. The breeze brought voices on it, subdued voices that carried a conspiratorial air. He heard one voice raised suddenly above the others, as if a leader were encouraging some act to begin, and then he caught a brief whiff of petrol before the smoke.

The bike engines roared into life again and then their exhaust sounds died slowly as they went off round the bend by the tiny church on the beach.

Through the hole in the door he could see a brightening glow coming from the beach; there was a gap of about thirty feet between his home and the next bungalow and the two buildings were silhouetted dark against the strengthening light. Eric pulled the chain to flush the clanking iron cistern.

Once he was outside he could hear the crackling of fire and he could feel increasing heat being brought towards him.

He hurried up the path and into the bungalow, through his smelly, uncared for kitchen into the front living room.

From its front bay window he could see that one of the string of beach huts to the west was well and truly ablaze.

His drink-fuddled mind cleared enough to make him grab the phone to call the fire brigade; there was a gap of only two to three feet between the painted wooden huts and he knew that the breeze would spread the fire from one to the next in no time. In the glow he could see that the felt covered roof of the next hut was already smouldering and sparks were being carried further along the line. It was only as he dialled the third nine that he remembered that the phone had been disconnected because of non-payment a week earlier.

Eric slammed the receiver down and his thoughts were a panicking confusion. He raced into the kitchen and looked at the rear of the bungalow next door. All was dark except for a faint light coming from the bedside lamp of the widowed Mrs Colquhoun.

Mrs Colquhoun was in her seventies, and although she was always in her bed before eleven, she claimed that she never slept during the hours of darkness, preferring to take a nap during the afternoons and spending her nights reading tales of the supernatural or listening to the massive radio which had been the pride and joy of her late husband.

Mr Colquhoun had been a builder of organs who upon his retirement had dedicated himself to getting his name on a little brass plaque on one of the benches in the town's churchyard. Although an irregular church- goer, he had done a great deal of work in his time on the organ there, and in due time he got his name put on one of the new benches. It had taken him a little more than two years to drink himself to death, but then he had been in training for it for at least fifty before that.

Eric pounded on her back door for a full minute before the light came on in the kitchen. Wearing a pink dressing gown and what looked like a matching tea-cosy on her head, she was holding a small, rolled umbrella before her like an erect truncheon.

"It's only me, Mrs Colquhoun." Eric pressed his face against the glass to show her. She gave a little shriek and jumped backwards, fumbling with the button on the umbrella handle.

It suddenly sprung open like a parachute. Eric waited until her little wrinkled face peered from behind it.

"It's only me," he repeated through the glass. "It's Eric. We must phone the fire brigade. The beach huts are on fire."

A look of recognition dawned on Mrs Colquhoun's creviced features. For a while she struggled with the umbrella, eventually getting it shut and laying it on the kitchen table. She came over and drew back the bolts on the door and turned the key.

"I do hope it will be all right," she said as Eric came in.

"Quick …The phone," he said breathlessly.

"In the front room," said Mrs Colquhoun. "Oh, I do hope it'll be all right."

She followed him into the front room, shaking her head so that the tea- cosy slipped from side to side. "I do hope it'll be all right," she said again.

"If they're quick enough they'll be able to stop it spreading too far, anyway," Eric said as he dialled.

Mrs Colquhoun sank into one of her deep armchairs.

"It can bring such bad luck, opening an umbrella indoors, you see," she sighed.

Eric got through to the fire station and explained the circumstances. He put down the receiver and looked out at the crackling blaze across the road. A second hut was alight now and the next was beginning to smoulder. Mrs Colquhoun had come over and was standing next to him, tiny and frail.

They had not switched on the light in the room and the glow from the fire made shadows jump around them. A yellow flame flickered in each of her eyes as she looked up at him. "What did the man at the fire station say we should do?"

Eric knew all the men at the station. "It was Dennis," he shrugged his shoulders. "He said 'keep it going till we get there'."

24

Here and there on the black arms of the harbour mouth shone the lamps of the anglers who came to fish from the walls during the hour before and the hour after high tide.

Their faces were small glowing dots in the darkness as they watched the brilliant, noisy passing of the Pachydermatous from the harbour to the open sea. With hands thrust into pockets, they watched her go until her stern was just a haloed black spot on the moonlit silver sea and they could no longer hear the music; then without speaking they went back to watching for a tugging movement of their rod tips.

Once clear of the harbour, O'Looney had let George take over from him at the wheel. George was the neighbour of Liz and Frank and Arthur, and he had been voted in recently as Commodore of the dinghy racing section of the Graywacke Yacht Club. He had been standing behind O'Looney and watching his every move like a driving test examiner ever since their departure from the river bank.

On his way home from the City that afternoon, George had had his usual couple of gin and tonics in the buffet car on the train before going home to change before going to the pub.

Gone now was the immaculate suit and bowler. For George the weekends started at four o'clock on a Friday afternoon when he stepped aboard that return train.

He now wore a blue T shirt, white trousers and blue canvas shoes. He took over the responsibility of the wheel with a serious pride. With a jutting jaw and a steely look in his eye, he scanned the horizon as the old Portuguese explorers must have done as they left the safety of Sagres to sail off over the edge of the world.

O'Looney had gone down to the main saloon to mingle and to raid the spread of mouth-watering delights that were laid out there. Before he left the wheelhouse, he told George to proceed along the coast at their present leisurely rate until past the pier, and then to return in a wide sweeping arc taking them out about five miles, which would bring them back while there was still enough water in the river for them to get up as far as the yacht club. There they would tie up and continue with the festivities.

And so they cruised pleasantly westward, leaving behind them the tall white chimneys of the power station bright in the moonlight, and behind those the sparkle of lights along the coast below the dark mound of the racecourse hill. Streetlights formed a twinkling orange necklace along the coast road and occasionally there was the bright speck of a fisherman's lamp somewhere along the dark strip that was the pebble beach.

The band played on as people ate and drank and danced while their laughter and chatter and the music mingled and wafted away over the stern as the coast slowly passed them by. It was possible to make out the buildings along the coast road, but further inland, on the dark chain of humps that were the Downs few lights showed, and they seemed so far away that they might have been lonely stars.

George watched the flash of the timed red light on the buoy that marked the end of the outlet pipe. They passed well outside the buoy, but close enough for their lights to show its rusty red. Until they had reached it, the buoy sat motionless on the sea. George was by no means the only person on board whose thoughts were of it in very different weather, when it disappeared from sight in the troughs, and if you were sailing close enough you could see the lank green weed on its bottom as it pitched and rolled.

Two miles further on they passed the end of the pier. It had been closed for the night two hours before, and the windows of the theatre and the amusements and the shelters were dark, but all its outside lights were blazing and more than a few on the boat felt it was a shame that there were no promenaders at its rails to wave to. Fred and Phil and José Mackay, who sitting on a table by the band, waved and called 'halloos' anyway.

Two hundred yards past the pier George began the long sweep to port. As he took them all further out to sea, a little something occurred to him that would never have occurred to the boat's owner. With her garlands of brightly coloured lights, the huge lantern hanging above the band and the blazing searchlight on the roof, the Pachydermatous was a potentially lethal danger to shipping. And to George.

George took a large swig from his G & T. Being so close to the port, they would soon be in the lanes of the cargo carriers. H took another slug and swung the bows round further. Only two miles out he could see the riding lights of vessels waiting their turn to enter harbour; he thought he would keep them at that distance. They passed the end of the pier and then the buoy again, this time from half a mile further off, but that was far enough for George. He would take them back past the harbour mouth and then cruise in circles until it was time to go in. He was gazing ahead at the mound of lights that were London-by-the Sea when Fishy Phil and José Mackay lurched into the wheelhouse, arm in arm.

"Hallo, George!" Phil sank onto the swivel chair next to him and waved a Bushmills bottle in the air. "Have a drink why don't you!"

George indicated that he had already got one. Phil put the

bottle down on the wheelhouse floor and raised his glass. "To the good ship Pachy... what's he call her?"

"Pachydermatous," George said. José looked baffled.

"That's the one!" Phil tried to swallow a mouthful, and because he was already full to the gills, some whiskey ran down from the corners of his mouth. Although George didn't know it, not a single person on board had thrown up yet, probably due to the calm conditions. It was still a remarkable fact though, because by now several of them would have done even if the party had been on dry land. Anyway, he thought Phil was about to lay his kit out there and then and turned his head away to look at the coast. To his surprise he heard only a great gulp and then a belch.

"That shifted the bastard!" Phil said appreciatively. Then after pondering awhile: "Do you know what," he said. "I am pissed out of my tiny mind."

His eyelids drooped and his head nodded. José, realizing with horror that he was about to spill his drink, steadied his friend's hand.

"Wharrayouneed issafood," he advised. "Come on, lessa gerra below to the foodsadeck."

Phil seemed to have taken in the logic of the advice. He shook his head vigorously and stood up. He swayed a little but refused José's offer of a supportive hand. They both knocked back their drinks and put the glasses on a shelf over the chart table. Phil picked up the bottle, and lovingly placed it with them, using both hands.

"We'll be back," he told George. "I am trusting you, dear friend, to guard this bottle with your very life."

They left the wheelhouse in search of the victuals that were necessary to sustain them sufficiently for the task ahead of them. They had no idea what time it was, but simply because it was still dark they could spend some time eating happily in the knowledge that there was plenty of drinking time still to come.

It was a much relieved George who took a little drink, but his respite was to be a short one. Ernie Rudd fell into the wheelhouse and grabbed for the nearest means of support. It was the chart table. He gripped its edges with his eyes closed. When he opened them the first thing he saw was the Bushmills bottle. He grabbed it and drank hastily from its neck.

"Pow!" He wiped his sleeve across his lips. "Irish, that's better!"

He surveyed the green-lit array of dials on the console before seeming to notice that George was there at the wheel.

"Oh, sorry!" he apologized and saluted. "Good evening to you, commodore. Just thought I'd check that all's well on the bridge."

"Yes, fine," George said wearily.

They both watched the passing coast for a while without speaking. Then Ernie said, "Ere, what's that?"

"What's what?"

"I seen something." Ernie screwed up his face as he leaned forward and concentrated on something along the beach. "I seen a light," he murmured.

"Seen the Light, Ernie? Now that really would be something!" "No, A light, I mean. One that shouldn't be there."

George chuckled. "You're always seeing things."

Ernie was growing more excited. "There you are, it's getting bigger!"

George was watching someone throwing up over the side. He couldn't make out who it was. "What are you on about?" he said tiredly.

"There," Ernie pointed a wavering finger. "It's getting brighter. There at the top of the beach, just this side of the beach church. See it now, do yer?"

George looked along the dark line of the beach until he located the little spire of the church silhouetted against a block of flats that glowed orange in the light from the streetlamps. A little to the left of the church was a small bright flame that grew dim and then flickered and grew brighter again.

"Yes, I see it now all right. It looks like something's burning."

"It could just be a beach party," Ernie suggested. "They're always lighting fires and having barbecues and things. Just an excuse for a shag on the beach, if you ask me."

"We could put in closer and have a look."

Ernie pictured himself on the roof, operating the powerful searchlight's beam to play on writhing naked couples. "Yes, I suppose we could …" he mused. "How much water have we got under us?"

George glanced at the echo sounder screen. "Plenty out here and we can get in a good way yet," he said. "Here, have a dekko through these."

Capting Rudd took the binoculars from him and focused them on the coast as George swung the bows to port. Using binocs at night can create an eerie sensation in the eye of the beholder. Ernie didn't like it and he lowered them quickly. "It's one of the huts," he said sadly. "Some bugger's set fire to one of the huts."

"Let's see how close we can get," George said.

"Go ahead till you're past the church before you go in or we'll be on the Church Rocks," Ernie told him. "There's a lot of nets and crab pots around them too. Mine, some of 'em. I'm surprised you haven't run any down yet, anyway, the way you're running around without a lookout. I'll get up on the roof with the searchlight. Go wide of the church and we'll have room to spare. I'll stamp on the roof if there's anything ahead. Remember, dead slow."

The Capting took a slug from the whiskey bottle before swinging himself out and up onto the wheelhouse roof.

It was true about the nets, George thought. They were all over the place along here. It was easy enough to spot their black flags when you were scudding along in a sailing dinghy in broad daylight, but you'd never know they were there in the dark. He felt a little hollow chill in his gut as he wondered if he had already mown a path through some of them, ripping them apart with the big bronze teeth of the propeller.

The change of light and colours on the scene before him brought him out of his reverie and he was glad to put those unsettling thoughts behind him. He watched the brilliant glare from the searchlight leave the crowded dancers and the band. They were left in the pleasant soft half-light from the coloured bulbs while the intense beam from above swung dizzily around until Ernie got it concentrated in a greenish pool on the surface about thirty yards in front of the bows.

George followed the eerie looking pool of light towards the beach; it was like an illuminated stagnant garden pond glowing there whilst the band and the dancers were on a patio and he was looking down from an upstairs window. He watched the echo sounder as it showed the depth of water below the barge gradually decreasing. Down there on the sandy sea bed, dozing flat-fish were startled by the sudden green light and crabs scurried to either side as the huge, black whale-like shape on the surface came after it, giving off its own lesser light and the passing discord of music, voices and the cushioned thump of its iron heartbeat.

They were less than a hundred yards from the beach when Ernie s boot began stamping vigorously on the roof. George knew they were well clear of any natural obstacles and for a moment the ghastly thought of the nets flashed back to him. Suddenly the horrific sight of Ernie's upside- down face appeared before his eyes and George felt his heart leap like a hammer blow to his chest.

"Cut the motor!" the Capting shouted through the glass screen. "Something in the water. Looks like it could be a body."

George cut the engine and let her tick over in neutral. The Pachydermatous swung sideways on the tidal stream to lay parallel with the beach. The deck was too crowded for any mass movement, but those nearest the rails were leaning and pointing at something alongside in the water.

The terrible apparition had gone from the screen. Ernie was back at his post, turning the searchlight downwards to bring the pool of light alongside the boat. George stuck his head out of the wheelhouse. About twenty yards away between the boat and the beach he could see a long white floating figure. Its large, dark head was up out of the water and it floated on its back in the crucifix position, with its two sets of toes visible at the other extremity. Although somewhat distracted, the band played on as more and more necks were being craned to get a look at the strange sea creature. Ernie came down from the roof, using one of George's shoulders as a half way step.

"Thanks," Ernie said as he landed on deck beside him. They both looked down into the dazzling light on the water. The creature from the deep had modestly adopted the vertical position, showing only its wet, shiny dark head of hair.

O'Looney came blustering out onto the deck. He was not in the best of moods, having only just returned to Coral in the master cabin when he had heard the engine die. He had come back from the saloon with a whole salmon on a plate of cucumber slices, some oysters on crushed blue ice and a raging hard on; now he had to put his appetence on hold for a while until he had sorted out whatever the problem was.

"What the fock's going on?" He bawled at the wheelhouse which was invisible beneath the brilliance of the light.

"Down there, Guv," Ernie shouted, "take a look for yourself."

Mick pushed a few guests aside and leaned with his fists on the rail. "What the hell are you doing out here?" he demanded, but with a certain gentleness as if he knew who the swimmer was.

The swimmer's face turned up to the light and there were a few gasps from the few others there who recognized it.

Hughie the Tree's face was a ghastly white in the glare and when he forced a twisted, embarrassed smile there were more shocked gasps.

"It feels like oi've been in the water half the night," he said and his voice tremored with the cold of it. "But, what the hell are you doing in the water?"

Hughie raised a long white arm and pointed towards the beach. There were two small figures there leaving the water's edge, holding hands to help each other over the pebbles. It was only then that O'Looney saw the burning beach hut.

"Jesus Christ." He gripped the rail. "How the fock did that get started?"

"Oi've been waiting for them two little witches to leave the beach," Hughie explained. "Oi left me shorts and me boots on the beach there while oi came in for a dip. Then they turned up out of nowhere and came in for a swim an'all. Oi couldn't get out to me togs without going right past 'em and at their age oi thought the sight of me in the nuddy might have been a bit much. So here oi've been, stuck here waiting for 'em to go!"

Hettie and Lettie often took a nocturnal swim in summer. The two little sisters had climbed the beach and could be seen warming themselves in the glow from the fire.

It was then that Mick O'Looney felt the weight of what is called Greatness being thrust upon him. Actually, the feeling was inspired by the sudden realization that he had no insurance cover on the huts which he owned and rented out, and those huts were just down-wind of the fire along the chain. H threw a rolled up towel at Hughie which the giant caught above his head. "Go on, get yourself ashore," he bawled at him, and then at the wheelhouse:

"Commodore, get that light trained on the beach and take this thing in.

We're going to put that bastard blaze out!"

George looked at Ernie, who shrugged his shoulders and clambered out onto the roof. George took the wheel with a resigned expression and slowly increased the revs to take her in.

25

R oger woke up feeling hot and stiff and somewhat dazed. It was very dark, and it took him a while to gather his thoughts and remember where he was and what he was doing there on the back seat of his company car.

He recoiled momentarily from the black, bat-like figure which seemed to be hovering at the nearside window, but which was in fact his suit jacket on its hanger. He swung his feet down from the seat and sat up. He felt terrible.

It was stifling in the car, but when he wound the window down it only seemed to draw in hotter air from the night outside. He yawned from his foul, tacky mouth and rubbed his eyes with the backs of his fists. Leaning over the back of the driving seat he could see the green glow of the car's clock. Its green hands told him it was almost two fifteen.

Roger had been sleeping on the back seat of his car because when he had come out of the Crab Apple at closing time, he had been too drunk to walk the two miles to his home on the caravan park by the river.

Not too drunk to drive, just too drunk to walk. When he had found that he couldn't reach the steering wheel he had abandoned the idea and had curled up where he was and gone quickly to sleep.

Now he was awake, and with a terrible pain in the back of his neck. He'd be buggered if he was going to spend the rest of the night there. He got out of the car and leaned unsteadily against its side while he took some deep breaths and looked around.

The pub car park was otherwise deserted and the houses across the road were all devoid of lights. Roger closed the car door gently, and urinated against the rear wheel as he gazed at the amazing array of bright stars in the blackness overhead. Beyond the uncountable, more obvious sparklers, he could even make out milky clusters which were so far off that they played tricks with his eyesight as they faded and then appeared again over and over as he tried to focus on them.

When the trickling of his water stopped, he couldn't hear a thing. Then he heard a faint snuffling sound, like someone with a running nose cold. It seemed to be coming from the ground near his feet.

When Roger looked down, he saw the darkly glistening shape of a wet hedgehog. He'd just given the little chap the proverbial golden shower. He imagined that now that it was cooling, it was probably glad of it on a night like this.

He watched the hedgehog cross the car park with a surprising turn of speed before disappearing below the dark bushes at its edge. Roger got into the car in the driver's seat. He wound down the window and with his head tilted back, he thought about the reason for his recent heavy drinking.

He was thirty-four and he had been involved with a local girl for the past two years, seeing her at weekends when he stayed at her step-father's pub. She would be at work there most of the time, but on Saturday nights they would go out for a meal and on Sundays they would spend some time walking or lazing on the beach.

She had always insisted that she couldn't possibly leave the coast for the dirty bustle of the city, so he had gone about making the move from London.

He had found himself a good position as surveyor with a

construction company on the coast and after selling his south London flat had bought the luxury caravan and moved down. Loisa's mother and her stepfather were now comfortably retired in a cul-de-sac of little bungalows, and his great hope was that she would soon be leaving them to move in with him.

Only a fortnight after his move all his hopes had been dashed.

Loisa suddenly informed him that she had started seeing an old flame again. That she had met up with him by a complete coincidence in Hove while he was over on a catering course, and that over a salad and dry white wine he had asked her to return to Alderney with him where they would run a quaint little quayside cafe together.

The little darling went away for a few days, supposedly alone, to 'Think my life out,' and she had returned to tell good old Roger that she would be flying out at the end of that week to be with the jumped-up dish washer.

Roger had always been a daily drinker, but all this had driven him over the top. He had neglected his work and for the past week had been travelling not so much between office and the various building sites as between office and as many pubs as he could fit into the day.

This Friday had been heavier still, finishing with a three-hour session here in The Crab Apple.

He stared morosely through the windscreen at the black night and contemplated the walk home. He felt very tired but as he vaguely recalled telling himself earlier, he would have a shower and his own bed and not that back seat. "Sod that bitch and sod the walk," he said aloud.

He turned the ignition key and switched on the car's headlights. Once out of the car park it was one long road to the junction where he would turn left along the lane which passed the entrance to the caravan park. He thought he would be able to manage that all right.

The long road was lit only by the moon and stars and he clipped four parked cars before reaching the junction. He glanced off their sides and swerved violently across the road each time, leaving dents and gouges behind and lengths of chrome strips and shattered orange and red indicators on the road. Roger was getting the dreaded double vision of the drunken driver as he cradled the wheel in his arms and squinted into the dazzling beams from his own headlights.

He managed the left turn all right, but didn't straighten up. He had passed out with his face resting sideways on the wheel.

His continuing turn took the Ford up and over the grass verge, where it straightened itself and careered up the slope of the Fire Station's forecourt.

Dennis Nails was seated at his desk at an upstairs window where he had just taken Eric's telephone call from the beach road bungalow. He watched in sudden, open-mouthed terror as the car roared up the forecourt and smashed headlong into the big wooden doors below his office.

When Dennis went downstairs, his colleagues, whose game of darts in a back room had been rudely interrupted by the smash, had already arrived to investigate.

Roger had come to and was sitting there in the car with an imbecilic grin on his face below a bloody split nose.

His car had almost demolished the doors, but had somehow contrived to leave them hanging there, sufficiently smashed and twisted in their frame to render the shiny red vehicles inside temporarily useless.

There was nothing else for it. Dennis and his merry men began unloading some wrecking tools.

26

M rs Colquhoun had named their black cat 'stop' before
her husband's death, in honour of his noble profession
and not because of the old boy's drinking problem.

Stop had jumped up from his usual place on the settee
to sit on the window ledge , pawing at the glass and mewing
to let them know that he wanted to get out and take a closer
look at the fire.

A second hut was alight now, sending up showers of
fascinating sparks to drift next door on the light breeze and
the third was shimmering in a steam-like haze like a cooking
meat pudding.

Mrs Colquhoun opened the window and the cat miaowed
in appreciation as he jumped down to the front lawn and shot
across the garden to cross the beach road.

Eric and Mrs Colquhoun watched him go.

"I do hope he doesn't get too close," she said concernedly.

"Oh, they've got more sense than that," Eric assured her.
"I wonder where that fire engine's got to!"

Mrs Colquhoun took the pink tea-cosy from her head and
wrung it in her bony hands as if it were a wet cloth.

"They are a long time, aren't they?" she tut-tutted. "Shall
I put the kettle on?"

She watched the cosy regain its shape. Eric was staring
across the road at the fire.

"That's a good idea," he said. "In the meantime, I really

ought to be doing something, I suppose. I've got a garden hose
in the garage, but I don't think it would reach across there."

"Oh, mine would!" Mrs Colquhoun exclaimed. "What a
good idea. Yes, I'm sure it would reach easily. Just a tick and
I'll fetch you the key to the shed."

She hurried into the kitchen and came back with a padlock
key on a loop of string. "There you are."

Eric looked at the key and then studied the fire again.

It was looking bigger all the time and he thought the hose-
pipe idea might make him look a little foolish out there. Mrs.
Colquhoun made his mind up for him.

"Well, go on then. Off you go."

He took the key from her and went to the front door. "You
might as well make a big pot," he called back to her. "The
firemen should be here soon."

She went back to the kitchen to put the kettle on and Eric
went round to the little shed at the side of the bungalow. When
he had released the padlock and opened the door he found
the light switch on the wall. The hose was already connected
to the outside tap and was coiled neatly on the concrete floor.
It occurred to him that he had never seen Mrs Colquhoun
using it since her husband had died. It must have been lying
there coiled like that ever since. At least it looked long enough,
anyway.

Eric took hold of the end of the hose and turned on the
tap. A pool of water spread slowly on the floor from beneath
the pile of coils. He could see a little fountain spraying from
a hole somewhere in the red rubber.

"Sod it," he muttered, "must be perished to hell. About as
much use as a double bed for the Pope."

Above his head was a wooden shelf with old paint tins,
packets of weed and slug killers, brushes and the sundry other
items common to your common-a-garden shed. Eric looked

along it until he found what remained of a roll of sticky, greased repair tape, wrapped in a plastic bag. He peeled the gooey tape from its cardboard roll and plastered it around the leak.

When he increased the water pressure it seemed to hold, and a fairly powerful jet shot from the end of the pipe into one of the pair of green wellies that he had spotted on his way in and was going to put on his bare feet.

He turned the water off and emptied the boot. Then after putting them on and tucking in the legs of his candy-striped pyjamas, he crossed the front garden, pulling the hose along behind him.

Mrs Colquhoun was standing silhouetted against the light in the front porch.

Eric noticed that she didn't have the tea cosy with her. When he got to the front gate he called back to her.

"You can turn on now, please Mrs C."

She scampered nimbly round to the shed, and as he crossed the road Eric felt the kick of life in the rubber hose.

It reached the fire with a few feet to spare. Although the light breeze was taking the smoke away from him, the heat stopped him at a safe distance. The fire had also shifted a colony of rats from beneath one of the huts and he saw one dash squealing across the pebbles, closely pursued by a wild eyed Stop. "He must have known, that mog," Eric thought. 'Oh well, it's an ill wind, I suppose…"

He raised his hand above shoulder height to let the water play on the roof of the third hut along from the first one to burn.

Raising the pipe had the effect of lessening the power of its jet. Eric looked back along the pipeline and he saw several small pools joining to form one where it crossed the road.

He lowered his arm and let the slightly increased flow run

down the steaming wall of the hut. Trying to repair the rotted pipe would be a waste of time, but he might be able to keep this flank cool enough to save it until the fire brigade arrived.

Eric wondered where they could have got to. Surely they couldn't have got lost; there's only one way to the sea after all. Still anything's possible, I s'pose. Take the case of the Fookarwe tribe of pygmies in the Congo. They've been living there for thousands of years, but the poor little sods still spend all their time wandering around in the tall grass, jumping up and down and shouting: "Where the fook are we?"

Above the crackle of the fire, Eric heard the sound of a racing engine, and he looked towards the bend by the church expecting to see a flashing blue light. No such luck; it was a white van accelerating fast out of the bend.

The van screeched to a halt after running over the hose-pipe end administering the coup-de-grace. The stream of hope from Eric's hand ceased abruptly and he watched the dark pool spreading across the concrete road.

The occupants of the van were Pam the flower seller and her son Gabriel.

Gabe leapt from the vehicle and raced across the twenty yards of shingle, followed far more slowly by his tottering mum, who was to put it mildly, more than a little Franz Liszt.

Gabriel started jumping up and down and waving his fists around his greasy head.

"Who started it? What dirty bastard started it!" he raved.

"That was our one, wasn't it?" Pam asked bemusedly as she pointed to the black heap that was the remains of the first hut to go.

"'Course it was," Gabe bawled. "I had a load of good gear in there!" "It won't be much good now," Eric observed.

"That's fairly bleedin' obvious, innit!" Gabe wailed. "Have you phoned the fire brigade, then?"

"I have, yes."

"I should bleedin' think so an'all," Gabe vented his frustration. "Your bleedin' 'ose-pipe's not much good, is it? I mean, just look at it, Mum. I could do better pissing on it!"

"So could I," his mum agreed. She felt like doing it in fact, and staggered off to squat down between two huts a few yards up-wind of the fire.

"Buckets. We've got to get some buckets," Gabe said with more control. "I've got some more gear in a hut down the line there. I can't start taking it out to the van, cos the Old Bill'll turn up any minute with the firemen. Where can we get some buckets?"

"I've got two or three in my garage," Eric offered, "and I saw some in Mrs Colquhoun's shed. My garage isn't locked, there's nothing much in it."

"Brilliant!" Gabe ran across the road into Eric's front garden as Mrs Colquhoun called from her front porch.

"Youhoo, the tea's ready!"

Eric dropped the end of the hose and went across to her. He was joined by Pam, who as looking relieved but rather uncertain of her footing.

"Do you take sugar?" Mrs C asked of her. "I know you do, Eric."

"I'd rather have something more invigorating," Pam told her as she leaned against the porch.

"Oh," the old lady shook her head. "I'm afraid I've only got a little brandy left from Christmas, and some sherry for when the vicar calls."

"They'll do," Pam assured her.

Mrs C went inside, then returned with a tray on which were the two bottles and one glass, and a cup of milky looking tea. She put the tray down on the window sill.

"There you are," she said sweetly as she handed the cup

to Eric on its saucer.

"Thanks," he said, and a pang of alcoholic envy shook him from head to foot as he watched Pam grab the quarter bottle of brandy and almost fill her tumbler.

He watched her take a long swig from it and then looked down at his own insipid beverage.

"Do you think I might have a tiny drop of that in my tea?" he asked with an affected tone of innocence. "It must be the shock and excitement. I feel quite faint, you know."

He saw Pam's satirical grin and tried not to smile at her. "Just a little drop would help."

"Of course, of course." Mrs Colquhoun commiserated.

She unscrewed the bottle top and poured what would have been no more than half a pub measure into Eric's tea. "There you are." She smiled up at him. "We mustn't overdo it."

"Thanks," he said flatly as Pam turned her face away with a smirk.

Eric knocked the lukewarm tea back in one and then they saw Gabriel emerge from the side of the bungalow.

He had been filling buckets from the tap in Mrs C's shed.

They watched him trying to hurry up the path with two of them. Eric gave the brandy bottle a rueful look.

"I suppose I'd better give him a hand," he sighed.

"That's the spirit." Pam drained her glass. "I'm with you. Once more into the … um …"

"Beach?" Eric said.

They went round the side to the shed, where they found four more large buckets which Gabriel had left brimful. They took two each and struggled waddling up the path with water slopping over the rims and down their legs.

Eric managed the trip quite well, but by the time she had crossed the road and traversed the shifting shingle, Pam's buckets were only half full. Gabriel had passed them without speaking on his return journey.

Eric threw the contents of each bucket in turn on the fourth hut, which steamed nicely immediately. He was about to start back when Pam let out a squeal that would have filled the pants of a body snatcher. It was perhaps a good thing for Eric that he had spent half the past twenty-four hours on various toilets. But he did drop his buckets and almost left the green wellies standing.

"Oh my God, what are they?" Pam croaked.

Two yellow, glowing figures like pixies, with tight-fitting rubber headwear were creeping out of the darkness, hand-in-hand around the fire towards them. They seemed to be performing some strange dance, as if the pebbles were hot coals beneath their tiny feet.

"Christ, it's only Hettie and Lettie," Eric said with a dry throat. "They must have been swimming again."

As the elfin-like figures came around the arc of heat, a much larger figure suddenly appeared from the blackness behind them. It was the brilliantly attired form of Mick O'Looney, his jacket and trousers shining in the firelight as if lit from within like some loud stage comedian's. He had just come charging up the beach from the Pachydermatous, whose flat bottom was now resting on the still submerged sand at its foot.

He marched round to the others' side of the fire, very much out of breath from his exertions, and it was a while before he was able to get his voice out with something approaching its usual blaring power.

"I see you've got some buckets!" he blasted. "That's good, that is. Sound as a pound!"

Gabriel appeared and threw the water from two more on to the steaming hut.

"Good lad," O'Looney praised him. "Sound as a pound.

Now keep them coming. We've formed a double line up and down the beach. I've got Duncan the copper organizing things back there. We've got buckets and bowls and saucepans and things from the boat. Where's the focking fire brigade anyhow?"

"No idea," Eric told him. "I phoned them some time ago."

"Typical. Bloody typical. Hallo, who's this? Oh, it's only Norman."

The publican was sauntering casually across the road carrying a long beach-casting rod and a tackle bag.

Eric thought there was a good chance of there being a bottle or few cans in it.

"Hallo Norman," he said cheerily, "been fishing then?"

"No, bear hunting," Norman answered. He put down the bag and held the rod vertically, with its butt on the ground. "What's occurring, then?"

"We saw them start the fire you know," Hettie said. "We were in the water."

"A gang of motor-bike boys," her sister added.

Gabriel threw down his empty buckets in despair. "So that's it. They must have found out about those dodgy gearboxes, the bastards!"

"Where were you fishing then?" Eric asked chummily of Norman. "I didn't see your lamp."

"Two groynes along. I had to get out tonight or go mad. Doreen's been in a right mood. And you know we've got that mother of hers there as well."

O'Looney stood back, aghast at this trivial banter that was going on in the midst of his potentially disastrous financial tragedy.

"Don't you use the old Tilley lamp now then?" Eric continued.

"Don't have to now," Norman told him. "I've got one of

those little bite indicators that you clip on your rod tip. They light up. You can see a bite easily in the dark. You only need a torch for baiting up. Bloody marvellous little things, they are. They run on a tiny hearing aid battery. Lasts for ages."

"Well I'll be," Eric said, still looking at the bag and licking his lips. "Did you catch anything, by the …"

O'Looney's motor was reaching boiling point. Suddenly his head gasket blew.

"Never mind the bloody fishing," he ranted through foaming lips. "Get on with saving my bloody huts!"

As Gabriel snatched up his empties and ran across the road there was a terrific bang which was followed by the whistling sound of some missile passing close by the cowering forms that they had instantaneously adopted.

O'Looney was the first to straighten up.

"Jesus suffering Christ, that was a gas bottle!" he raved. "The bastards use 'em for brewing a cup of tea. The weekenders. The bastards know they're not supposed to leave 'em in the huts!"

He decided that a tactical withdrawal down the beach would be his most prudent course and crunched away down the pebbly slope.

The scene on the beach looked like a night shift during the Great Fire of London.

The Pachydermatous was resting with her bows against the shingle, and a collapsible aluminium stairway had been lowered to the beach from her fore-deck, where the jazz band was still playing merrily with Fishy Phil acting as conductor, standing on a drinks table and waving a Glenmorangie bottle around like a baton.

Duncan had got the fire crew wonderfully organized. It was only about thirty yards up the beach from the boat to the huts, and he had strung out two columns of guests to pass the buckets and bowls and saucepans from hand to sweaty hand. One line bringing the water from the great inexhaustible reservoir behind them to the fire, and the other returning the empty vessels to the well.

There were a few obsolete revellers leaning with their drinks on the rails, watching the task force, and incredibly even a few who were still dancing.

Over the whole, crazy shifting scene on the beach, from the wheelhouse roof Capting Rudd swept the searchlight brilliant beam back and forth, whilst Dave Death marched up and down the lines shouting: "Heave! Heave, you bastards heave!" and followed by Duggie, who was filming the whole adventure on O'Looney's video camera.

From beneath an overturned row-boat, Big Hughie, who had been joined in his temporary home by the lad Snakebite and his dog, watched the whole thing in wide eyed disbelief. People paid good money to see shows that were nothing on this.

What they were watching, was like a magic lantern show being flashed upon the dark screen of the night; a mad kaleidoscope, an oasis of glare in the middle of a black desert under a black sky. It did not last long, however.

A great deal of water can be moved by the organized chain method, and in ten minutes or so it was all over. The crackling blaze was dead, the beam from the searchlight was aimed at the moon, and only the cabin lights and the coloured bulbs and lanterns showed along the beach.

As the last few gallons were being emptied over the reeking dark heaps of ashes and charred timber, the fire engine went past with blue lights and siren going. It hurtled on and then stopped at the end of Beach Road, having missed the scene of the fire in the dark. Garbled, unintelligible conversation could be heard coming from its radio, and then it slowly reversed back to the smouldering ruins.

"Typical, that is." O'Looney repeated: "Bloody typical."

He threw up his arms in exasperation as the police car arrived, just as Gabriel had predicted, and had to brake hard with the driver sounding his horn to prevent the fire engine from reversing into it.

O'Looney took off his jacket and trudged down the beach again.

He climbed the aluminium steps to the deck and went to the wheelhouse, where George had remained at his post throughout the entire proceedings. Mick threw his new jacket carelessly over the wheel and took a megaphone from beneath the chart table. He took it with him to the foredeck, flapping a hand at the band, who gradually slowed then stopped playing. They grabbed their drinks while he raised the red cone to his mouth. A few of the guests were ascending the steps but most were milling about the useless fire engine with their empty receptacles, wondering what to do next.

"All party guests on the beach," Mick bawled through the funnel. "Oh, and any other intrepid fire fighters! The Pachydermatous, as you know, is aground. The tide is only about halfway down, so it will be about ten in the morning before there's enough water to get her off again. Rest assured, however, that the merrymaking will continue on board throughout the night. We have more than enough of everything, and those of you who stay long enough will even be served breakfast! Those of you who think the night has been long enough already, can of course make your way home. Otherwise, get yourselves up here so's we can pull up the ladder and get stuck into the crack!"

He tossed the megaphone into the wheelhouse and told George that as he would have no further duties for a few hours, he might as well leave his bottle and join him for a drink in the saloon. When they got there they found it was quickly filling again.

Albert Hoskins and José Mackay had been there all along, having dodged the working party and taking the opportunity to fill a couple of carrier bags with chicken drumsticks and other delicacies, and secreting them behind the sofa to be retrieved when they got back to port. Somehow they were still vertical, and they were sampling a bottle of Schiedam and wolfing down prawns and brown bread and butter.

Liz was slumped on the sofa with a large gin. She was slipping into her melancholy phase and getting an earhole bashing from Kowloon Moon. He was telling her about his day at the races and showing her wads of notes, watched over all the time by the Plunger.

Liz wasn't listening to him. She was reliving that sensation of having the serose stubble on Duggie's chin rasping like glass-paper on the sensitive flesh of her inner thighs.

Frank was smooching with Monika in a corner to the slow number the band had just started up and Arthur was attempting to dance with both heavenly twins at once.

Mick steered George over to the bar and fixed him a large Gordon's. Peter and his large friend were standing there chatting and a terrified Eddie was out on deck where he was avoiding contact with them, having recognized Ted's rear elevation. It had brought back alarming memories of the casino toilets.

Coral suddenly appeared at O'Looney's side with two bottles of shampoo in an ice bucket. He put his arm round her waist.

"I can't believe so much has happened in one day," she told him. "I mean, I'd heard that Graywacke's Fridays were rather special, but surely they're not all so eventful as this!"

"Oh they're usually a great crack," Mick said. "There's

usually something turns up to enliven proceedings!"

He held her close and she whispered something in his hot, red ear.

"Tut-tut, my girl." He chortled. "And weren't you telling me only this morning that meat never passes your lips!"

"Let's go back to the cabin," she said softly as she moved away from him. As she swung the ice bucket, she moved her hips deliberately and delightfully.

There was a narrow passage with cabins and other doors to showers and toilets or cupboards on either side. As they made for it, Liz lurched across the saloon from the sofa to get in front of them.

"Where's Duggie?" she demanded with that imperious tone of the haughty drunk. "I haven't seen him for ages, and I want him. Need to see him, I mean."

"I'm afraid I haven't seen the little fella meself, Liz," O'Looney told her. "But if I do, then I'll be sure to tell him you want to see him."

He and Coral squeezed past her into the passage and he grasped hold of the brass door knob of the master cabin.

"You go in first," he said to Coral. "I'm roasting in this gear. I must have a nice quick shower. You go in and I'll be along as quick as I can."

When she had closed the cabin door behind her, he tapped with his knuckles on the next door. The tapping was in a sequence known only to himself and one other person.

The bolt clicked inside and he pushed the door open.

Duggie was standing there fully clothed in the shower tray with the video camera held in position.

O'Looney held a finger to his lips. "Don't be using that thing on us anymore, Duggie," he whispered. "And I'm going to destroy that fillum that you shot of us up at the house this evening. I'm really becoming so very fond of this girl. It wouldn't feel right with her anymore. Not like it was with all the others."

"Whatever you say, Guv." Duggie slipped the camera back into the bag that hung from his shoulder. "I can get back to the goodies then, eh? That sure beats making movies. Even our sort, I mean!"

"That's the way now, Duggie bruv." His boss smiled. "You get along and enjoy yourself. In fact, there's a lady in the saloon rought now waiting for youse. That Liz. Rather to. In fact, I reckon she's got a terrible need for youse altogether!"

Duggie rubbed his palms together. "Oh boy. Do you know, I can feel the old one eyed trouser snake on the move already!"

"The bald headed traveller himself, d'you mean?"

"That's the bloke, Guv. The old pyjama python! Another good Friday, eh?"

O'Looney clapped the little man on the shoulder as he let him pass. "Good man yourself, Duggie bruv. Another very good Friday!"

A few of the guests had wandered off homewards, but most had returned on board the Pachydermatous. For them it was still Friday night, but for Young Snakebite and Big Hughie it was Saturday morning, and the dawn would come only too quickly.

For the runaway lad it would bring another day's search for food and shelter. For the giant it would mean ambling back to the police station to give himself up. He knew that he could hardly melt into Graywacke's daytime crowd. Not even a Wembley FA Cup one. He had found his shorts and boots on the beach and he would get something to eat on the barge before going back. Might even get a second breakfast in his little cell.

Snakebite could hear the muffled sound of the band,

although through tiring eyes he could only make out a faint glow from the barge's light bulbs and lanterns above the dark ridge of the beach.

He rolled onto his back and rested his head, using his warm sleeping dog as a pillow. He could feel the rise and fall of the dog's breathing and he listened as Hughie's deep snoring filled the pitch-blackness under the curvature of the wooden row-boat's clinker hull.

Oh well, there's always next Friday …

THE END

Printed in Great Britain
by Amazon

46253505R00161